The Futurist

Mark Cosman

THE FUTURIST

iUniverse books may be ordered through booksellers or by contacting:

iUniverse
1663 Liberty Drive
Bloomington, IN 47403
www.iuniverse.com
844-349-9409

ISBN: 978-1-6632-6156-4 (sc)
ISBN: 978-1-6632-6157-1 (hc)
ISBN: 978-1-6632-6255-4 (e)

Library of Congress Control Number: 2024908535

Print information available on the last page.

iUniverse rev. date: 06/03/2024

To those who live what they imagine

CONTENTS

1

THE DARK

John Ramsey

Wearing a white Prescott Industries' one-size-fits-all lunar jumpsuit with its bulky backpack and helmet containing life support systems, I stood inside a wire, cage-like elevator as it cascaded down a narrow shaft toward our lunar mining operation two miles below the moon's Aitkin Crater floor.

I am visiting our Lunar mining operation to commemorate the completion of a twelve-year renovation inside a massive, subterranean geode discovered years ago by our mining operation. My heart is pounding. The elevator cage rattles and screams as it descends deeper into an ocean of darkness. "Don't think about it. Focus on why you're here," I demanded of myself. Ignoring my panicked self-chatter, I thought about the moon's creation and how it must have been a bubbling cauldron of molten metals and minerals. When it cooled, it left behind a subterranean bubble frozen in time that was nine miles wide, thirty stories high in places, and two miles beneath the Aitkin crater. We pressurized the geode with an artificial atmosphere, mimicking Earth's air, gravity, and the ability to transmit sound. The man in the moon would no longer be silent. With the moon's six hundred million metric tons of ice available for harvesting, our renovations will provide limited agriculture and subterranean accommodations for future tourism.

As founding chairman and CEO of Prescott Industries, I, John Ramsey took pride in being a man of tremendous gravity, around whom those who loved and feared me were in continuous orbit, yet the suffocating darkness I had entered frightened me to the core.

Hans Belzer, Prescott's project foreman, and Dr. Lisa Wells, the company's on-site physician, were standing behind me in their lunar jumpsuits. The shaft's walls screamed past, and the cage rattled against its rails, gaining speed until it suddenly bobbed to a stop deep in the void. My knees involuntarily bent.

While I had made the descent before during other lunar visits, I felt overwhelmed, bordering on panic. Never having experienced total darkness without the distraction of a dull glow or even a flicker of light somewhere was unsettling— something we may have known only in the womb. I gripped the cage's crisscrossing wire enclosure to connect with my equilibrium.

"Don't be alarmed, Mr. Ramsey," Hans said through my earphones. "These elevators work in tandem. Our partner elevator is probably loading on the production floor. It'll be a while before we can continue our descent," he said from behind me and reassuringly patted me on the shoulder.

We were in the bowels of the moon's deepest crater. Given that temperatures could fluctuate between minus 280 degrees Fahrenheit to plus 260 on the moon's surface, we built our lunar mining operation with its mini nuclear power plant underground. The crater gave us the depth to burrow at a right angle into the crater's wall some five miles beneath the moon's surface. The depth would serve as a shield against future impacts.

Never having been done before, except in theory, I had fretted over my decision to carve Moon Glow headquarters into the wall of the Aitkin Crater, using nuclear drills nine meters in diameter. Nuclear drilling took less than half the time of conventional drilling because it melted through rock. Melting rock also eliminated the need to haul away tons of rubble.

Our army of lunar-based robots, called workerbots, performed the work as directed remotely by our Prescott Phoenix headquarters. Our workerbots were mostly metallic, with little regard for human resemblance other than having two arms, two legs, a chest to house their drive motors, and a skull for their audiovisual awareness features.

I'm feeling lightheaded. I must focus on something other than the darkness pressing in around me, I thought. *Otherwise, I'll go nuts.* I immediately recalled being in a similar cage-like elevator descending a narrow, dark shaft in the late fall of the year in Saint Petersburg, Russia. I was in Russia to arrange for the presentation of the Glasnost Award, promoting an open door for Russia's stagnant economy. Of course, I was primarily interested in recruiting aerospace engineers.

I remember feeling very tired when I arrived in Russia. Another week of meetings in an alien time zone awaited me, with pickled foods and laboriously delayed dialogue through translators. Outside the airport terminal, the early-evening sky was slate gray. Cold, damp air carried an oily scent. I wasn't well known in Russia, so the courtesies I'd become accustomed to wouldn't be forthcoming.

A black stretch limousine pulled to the curb beside me. I quickly stepped back to avoid being splashed by an oily curbside puddle. My good friend Alexei stepped from the passenger side with a laughing smile and outstretched arms before wrapping me in a firm embrace. I had enlisted Alexie's help in setting up meetings for me with influential Russian aerospace entrepreneurs with a vested interest in reaching out to the West.

Like me, at the time, Alexie was in his late thirties. He combed thinning black hair over a balding crown. His beige trench coat was open to a gray suit, white shirt, and a red striped tie. I wore gray slacks and a thick maroon sweater under a tan storm coat. Of average height, we sported relatively lean athletic builds left over from our youth. We drove through old inner-city streets while Alexei lectured me about Russia's financial woes. His English, though heavily accented, was impeccable.

"It's wonderful to see you again, John," he said with a wide grin and wagged his head in amazement. "It seems long ago when we worked together on another of your projects in Russia." He laughed and slapped his thigh excitedly. "I'm so happy you've returned!

"Look," he continued, "we're having a party at my hotel tonight. We have the entire ballroom. Some of Saint Petersburg's most interesting people will be there. It's not far from your hotel, only a few blocks. Why don't you rest in your room and join us later? I'll send a car for you. There'll be beautiful women you'll want to meet," he added suggestively with a raised eyebrow and mischievous grin.

He was a self-made multimillionaire with gold mines in Siberia and real estate investments. *Why shouldn't he have whatever pleases him?* I thought. On the other hand, he often gave me the sense of being a man hiding in plain sight, always one step away from corrupt government officials wanting a piece of his action.

Suppressed fear seemed to underpin his lifestyle. He wanted all the hedonistic pleasures his meteoric success afforded him, but it had to happen quickly, before his means came to an end—something he sensed was fast approaching. All the while, he maintained the confident comportment of Russia's rising nouveau riche.

"It was an arduous flight, and I have a long day tomorrow, as you know, so I think I'll pass. Thank you all the same," I told him.

"I understand. Well, here's your hotel," Alexie said as our limo pulled under a brightly lit archway. A doorman in a long red Cossack coat and a tall black wool hat opened my door. "I hope you'll change your mind and we'll see you later. If not, I'll have my driver pick you up for our meetings at nine in the morning. Okay?"

"Right. See you then."

✦ ✦ ✦

Toward the end of my Russian trip, I was riding in the back seat of Alexie's plush German limousine. We were still in our business suits from the day's meetings. My suit was dark blue, his gray, with our beige trench coats draped over the seat between us. "You did a wonderful job selecting participants for our meetings," I told him. He nodded with a self-satisfied grin.

It was late afternoon. The sky was dark gray and the air cold and damp. I had not seen the sun since I'd been there. Our driver motored over a bridge spanning the Niva River near the Gulf of Finland and headed east toward Lake Ladoga.

"Where are we going?" I asked.

"I have a surprise for you," he replied.

"A surprise?"

"I know you like fine paintings, so I thought I'd take you to a little-known government museum on the city's outskirts, far from the tourist trail. It's where the army displays some of what it confiscated from Germany many years ago at the end of the Patriotic War. There's a unique painting there I think you'll find intriguing.

"I saw it many years ago while studying for my doctorate. I've revisited it every year since then. It can possess you, so be careful. It was once the property of a wealthy German Jew before the war. Maybe my affinity for it comes from my Jewish heritage. I don't know. But knowing you as I do, I think you'll be fascinated by the story it tells."

Our limo turned onto a cobbled way leading to a gated complex guarded by military police. We pulled up to a kiosk. Alexie rolled down his window and said something to the guard, who waved us on from inside the booth.

We parked in front of a long complex of single-story buildings occupying three city blocks. Ours was the only vehicle in the parking area. Like most of the older buildings in Saint Petersburg, the pastel-colored compound looked tired and run-down. We climbed the icy concrete steps of the main building and entered an expansive domed vestibule with a gold-plated chandelier hanging high overhead. Our footsteps echoed against the marble floor.

"This place is freezing, Alexie," I said as puffs of breath hung before my face. A military officer in an olive-green overcoat sat across the spacious vestibule behind an elevated wooden desk. Alexie motioned for me to wait while he spoke with him. I watched as he explained my presence and why we were there. Then Alexie took cash from his coat pocket and discreetly handed it over. The official nodded, quickly hid the cash in his coat pocket, left his desk, and unlocked a wooden door at the far end of the atrium.

Alexie summoned me with a flick of his wrist. "We're going down to the basement where the painting is stored," he told me. The officer left as we entered a cramped, cage-like elevator with a metal gate. Alexie pushed the ivory-handled control lever down. The old contraption jolted before beginning its descent to the tired-sounding whine of an electric motor.

This building must be ancient, I thought. As we descended, I noticed the foundation was composed of rocks cemented together rather than poured concrete. The stuffy scent of history wafted in the musty air.

The elevator jolted to a stop, and we stepped out. Wartime memorabilia filled gray metal shelves to the ceiling of the enormous underground space. I followed Alexie down a narrow aisle between the shelving. To my right were stacks of surrendered German army banners and battalion flags, while box upon box of Nazi medals were stacked to my left.

I detected the smell of rotting wool and leather. I followed Alexie when he turned left at the end of the corridor, where I was suddenly amazed by a towering stone wall decorated with confiscated works of art.

"Over here," he said pridefully with fists on his hips, gawking at the largest painting in the collection. "Here it is," Alexie boasted, his eyes feasting on the work. "This is why I brought you here. Magnificent, isn't it?'

I felt instantly drawn to the expansive, four-by-four-meter painting spanning an entire section of the rear wall—a row of ceiling lights aimed at the work, illuminating its dark, vibrant colors. I was in awe.

"After I first saw the work, it gave me strange and sometimes frightening dreams that return to me every so often. Nonetheless, I wanted you to see it yourself," Alexie said.

"Do you know the story behind it?" I asked.

"I do," he answered.

"Please explain it to me."

"Okay. The painting depicts a pantheon of half-naked gods in flowing, colorful robes fighting from an aerial advantage against a host of primitive, earthbound humans. As you can see, the scene is amidst dark, swirling clouds. I always thought the painting's savage depiction attracted the Nazi mindset, as it featured an overwhelming force of superior beings conquering an inferior race. I think it's why the Nazis had an affinity for the painting and confiscated the work from its Jewish owner. The Russian army appropriated the painting at the war's end and brought it here for posterity."

"Interesting. Do you know the date of the painting and who the artist was?" I asked him.

"An Italian painted the scene in the fourteenth century, but the artist's identity remains unknown."

"I have a gnawing sense there's an ancient story behind the work, perhaps a Jewish one. Do you know what it is?" I asked.

"Yes, of course. It depicts the prediluvian invasion of the Watchers." He paused to study my reaction before telling me, "Our ancient forebears believed the Watchers came from the heavens to assist human development. Heaven meant anything skyward in those days. Some held that the Watchers were alien beings from another world, extraterrestrials, or star people. In any case, these beings were allegedly sent here by an alien intelligence they feared."

"Where did you learn of the story?"

"I read about it in the personal memoirs of Colonel Ludwig von Beck, a German SS officer who was a prisoner of war in Russia during the Patriotic War. He left recordings that I listened to as well. As you know, I was a psychologist at the Kirov Institute in Saint Petersburg early in my career. I used von Beck's memoirs in my doctoral thesis. Ironically, much of what von Beck wrote mirrored Jewish scriptures. After his repatriation to Germany, he lived in a German asylum, where he remained until his death.

"He explained that the Watchers abandoned their mission of advancing humanity's lot when they became fascinated with the daughters of men and took them for wives and concubines, sometimes by force from their human husbands and fathers. 'Nephilim,' he said, born from the union of these alien beings and human women, grew to be giants. Maybe they weren't giants by today's standards, but being around three meters tall in those days would have certainly qualified you as one," he said while grinning admiringly at the painting.

"I've heard of the Watchers and their Nephilim offspring. Their story is in the Apocrypha's book of Enoch, I believe."

"Yes, von Beck mentioned as much. I recall reading about the story in Jewish scripture as a young student in Hebrew school. Anyway, the Watchers followed a leader among them known as Semjaza. Some two hundred Watchers were said to have descended to Earth with Semjaza to frolic with evil. That's why dark clouds surround them in the painting. See them?"

"Yes, yes, of course. The dark clouds are quite stark."

"The people of the time believed evil was under the proprietorship of a humanlike evil archetype who was at war with their god." He explained, "Some enlightened humans of the era warned that we would come to disbelieve in the existence of the evil archetype, giving it the shadow of doubt in which to hide as it walked among us."

His answer, the painting, and its dungeon-like setting gave me the creeps.

He said, "The ruling god or perhaps an extraterrestrial commander caught up with Semjaza's Watchers and sentenced them to remain on Earth as mortals for having been so entranced by mortality to have abandoned their mission.

"According to von Beck, even the Watchers' blood excruciatingly changed from an extraterrestrial composition to a mortal one. So now they had to die. They were trapped," he said with macabre satisfaction, his jaw clenching behind a grin.

I wondered how he could find a glimmer of delight in the eternal suffering awaiting the Watchers. I found the story deeply disturbing.

"Their sons, the Nephilim," he continued, "were condemned to remain on Earth as spirits of the evil ones, referring to their fathers. While invisible to men, the Nephilim would wage a continuous, unseen war against the sons of men and their women. Nothing is more descriptive of a viral disease," he speculated. "Their evil rampage may have altered our DNA."

He finally turned to face me. "Do you think so, John?" he asked. "Do you think today's viral wars are related to the altering of our genetic composition by extraterrestrials centuries ago?"

I shrugged. "I don't know."

"While in the German asylum, Colonel von Beck had the most interesting psychotic episodes under the influence of experimental medications. I translated his dictation and sent it to your email."

Once back in my hotel, I immediately went to my laptop. I couldn't wait to read what Alexie had sent. The room was dark but for the city lights aglow in my suite's expansive floor-to-ceiling window. Along with one of Colonel von Beck's memoirs, Alexie emailed a photo of the colonel, a military portrait of the dashing young officer in uniform.

His half grin hinted he knew who was viewing his photo and why.

I sat alone in the shadows staring at the colonel's image on my laptop as rain pelted the window. Red and gold autumn leaves that the park across the street had surrendered to the wind slipped down the rain-streaked glass. Dark storm clouds had gathered over the city's distant skyline, reminding me of the painting and that Semjaza character. His story kept coming to mind as if it was beginning to haunt me. Thunder crackled in the distance.

I envisioned von Beck strapped down on a gurney in a white hospital gown in a narrow, windowless room of a German asylum. I imagined von Beck's wild eyes darting back and forth following apparitions in a psychotic episode. A harsh fluorescent light glared down at him from the concrete ceiling. He turned his head away and squeezed his eyes shut to block it.

2

THE PRODUCTION FLOOR

John Ramsey

I sighed with relief when our cage rattled and we continued our descent. We sped headlong toward a dusty, dimly lit worksite far below. The sounds of heavy machinery grinding rock intensified we bobbed to a stop at the end of the shaft. I took a deep breath inside my lunar helmet and felt sweat trickle down my temple. I don't know what the temperature was down there, but inside my suit, it was stifling.

Ten driverless mini trucks on rails were loaded with debris containing rare minerals and precious metals. Parked in a line before a gigantic mound of rubble that reached the geode's ceiling, they surged forward, scooping up their loads in unison. Then the front shovel of each mini truck raised its load overhead, where its rotating shovel dumped its contents into a cargo bed. The sudden weight made the trucks bounce.

"From here," Hans, a large man in his midforties, said, raising his voice until he reminded himself of the moon's silence, "the ruble travels on conveyor belts through machinery that identifies more than one hundred rare minerals and precious metals needed in medicine, commercial electronic products, and the defense industry. After sorting, the minerals and precious metals are weighed and packaged for shipping to our Earth facilities.

"Vehicles down the line haul our packaged products to freight shuttles on the surface. In turn, freight shuttles regurgitate their cargo at designated points in moon orbit for freight carriers to swallow and bring to Earth. I believe it's an extraction process you designed."

I nodded.

"Mr. Ramsey, do you have time to see our workerbot clinic?" Doctor Wells sauntered close to ask.

"Yes, of course."

Hans opted to stay on the production floor, noticing a problem with the shovel on one of the vehicles.

Doctor Wells led me down a corridor at a right angle to the production floor, where her badge opened a metal portal in the wall. We stepped into a brightly lit infirmary with five workerbot pods on either side of the room. Three of the pods held patients. A medically trained workerbot stood motionlessly staring at me from the side of a pod across the room. When our eyes met, it stiffened as if to attention. Its piercing red eyes were unsettling.

"Doctor Wells, what training is required of your medical workerbots?" I asked.

"Please, call me Lisa."

"I shall. Thank you."

"They're trained in the kinds of injuries most common on the production floor—broken limbs, fingers, damaged spines, et cetera. They're more like mechanics trained to disassemble an affected part and install a new one. It's a routine procedure.

"The patient in the far pod where our workerbot attendant is standing," Lisa continued, "is a different case we're seeing much more of these days. An older model's metallic frame can bend from the weight it has lifted through the years, so its parts no longer fit together properly, causing abnormal wear and eventual breakage. A limping gait and spinal curvature are obvious signs of the condition."

"Do these workerbots experience pain during one of your replacement operations?" I asked.

"For them, pain is merely a signal to direct them away from dangers. It's not a sensation that attacks or incapacitates, as it often does in humans."

"Do they have names?"

"No. Numbers only."

"May I speak with one of them?"

"As you know, workerbots do not breathe, so they cannot speak. A central computer with a frequency preset to your lunar suit speaks for them. So don't expect originality." Lisa chuckled.

"Yes, I recall the limitations from my previous lunar visit."

"Okay. I need something in my office over there. I'll be right back." She motioned to an open door across the infirmary. She turned to walk away but stopped and turned to face me. "Mr. Ramsey, I want to tell you how grateful I am to meet you finally. I wasn't here when you last visited. It humbles me to think that whatever I experience here on the moon occurred first in your imagination." She smiled.

"Thank you, Lisa," I replied and fondly watched as she walked away. Sensing I was watching her, she glanced back at me over her shoulder and grinned.

I perused patient histories on the charts at the foot of their pods. The attendant workerbot at the room's far end continued to study me intensely. I noticed a workerbot inside a pod to my left with a shiny new arm.

"Hi. I'm John Ramsey from Prescott Industries."

"Greetings, Mr. Ramsey," came an emotionless, computerized male voice.

"I notice you have a new arm. What happened to you?"

"It fell from a high place," a flat, monotone voice responded.

The workerbot's answer suggested detachment from its body. Its brain was in one place and its body in another. Then the workerbot's computer said something surprising when I asked if it had ever been on the surface and had a view of Earth.

"My work is here. There is no other place."

"How long have you been here?"

"I have always been here."

"Well, I am from another place," I told it.

Just then, Lisa came to my side and smiled. "You can't compete with their program." She chuckled. "It's all they know."

I noticed she was standing closer to me than during our

previous exchange. "Then how do you reason with them?" I asked her.

"Without reprogramming them, I don't."

"Do you have to reprogram them often?"

"Just when their tasks change."

"Do they have even a modicum of individual history?" I asked her.

"They have a number and an assigned task. That's all."

"How do you feel about that?"

"They're not human, Mr. Ramsey. They're tools for our work, nothing more."

"Please, call me John."

"Okay. Thank you, John." She giggled.

"I think as we allow our artificial intelligence to evolve beyond the limits we've set for them, we'll know them differently," I told her. "It's the most critical social issue awaiting us."

"That could be, but they have our work to do now."

Her conclusion struck me as unemotionally distant.

I spent the Prescott night in spartan accommodations adjacent to the production floor.

3

MEETING CHERYL

John Ramsey

I recall it was an overcast, cold, early morning when I walked down the concourse at the spaceport to my shuttle. I was with my most trusted vice president, Jerry Weinstone, and a dozen members of his artificial intelligence team who crowded behind him on the concourse to see me off. I was in a bulky white lunar jumpsuit with my helmet tucked under my arm.

Jerry is tall and lean, with thick white hair parted to the side and a stoic look that never leaves him. He's a good man, sincere, honest, and hardworking. I trust his judgment and always consult with him on important matters. I thanked Jerry and his cadre of scientists for their well-wishes and entered Moon Glow's shuttle.

"Welcome aboard, Mr. Ramsey," a Prescott interstellar

attendant in a sky-blue uniform said as she directed me to a sarcophagus-like pod for the long journey. Once situated, I closed my pod's curved, crystalline lid. I couldn't help but feel like bundled freight. A medicated fog immediately poured into my pod, relaxing every muscle as it began to coax my brain into sleep. It was standard procedure.

I sighed. The 385,000 kilometers, 240,000-mile journey to our lunar headquarters in the Atkin Crater would take more than twenty-eight hours by Prescott time. I felt the drug gnawing away at my consciousness until the universe tore open and I fell through. I don't remember much after that. I recall when the attendant's velvet voice woke me for our lunar arrival. We were already in our lunar approach when I noticed the medicated fog had disappeared from my pod. Rough vibrations signaled our descent into the fifteen-hundred-mile-wide Aitkin Crater.

Hans and Doctor Wells greeted me on the landing site's circular tarmac, accompanied by three medically specialized lunar workerbots.

Hans, Dr. Wells, and I wore our bulky white lunar jumpsuits that included an upper and lower torso pressurized garment and a backpack containing life support systems. The helmet, with its day/night protective visor, was challenging to become accustomed to wearing for long periods. The gasping sound of our suit's breathing apparatus was a distraction. I decided I'd bring it to the attention of our engineers.

It was dark when our caravan of three roofless, four-seat shuttles took us over rough, pockmarked terrain pelted by millenniums of space debris as we headed toward Moon Glow's sealed entrance in the Aitkan Crater's wall. Along the way, I prevailed upon Hans to stop our little convoy so I could step outside the shuttle to view Earth from a unique vantage point.

Earth's bright blue sphere hung before me in the black void of space. It reminded me of a concerned mother awaiting the return of her children so far from home. The astonishing sight instantly humbled me. A tranquil gray landscape, untouched and serene, lay before us. I thought of my late wife, Jessica, and how her death had forever sealed her away from our two daughters, Margo and Amy. My eyes began to glisten.

Doctor Wells moved closer to my side. In her early thirties, she was a first-rate physician, like Jess once was. Her no-nonsense personality covered a passionate approach to medicine. She was a pretty woman with a smooth, porcelain-like complexion and a cute smile when she used it.

Jessica had contracted the dreadful Tezca virus and passed away when our daughter Amy was just a toddler and her sister, Margo, was a preteen. It was when my mother came to live at the mansion to help me raise the girls. They nicknamed her Old Rachael. Mother got a kick out of the name, so it stuck.

Of utmost concern, while on the moon's surface, was the remote possibility of being struck by even a BB-size particle of space debris traveling at hypersonic speed, the reason Doctor Wells was always close at hand whenever I was outside our lunar compound. Still, I wanted to be with Jess in the quiet stillness of the moon, where I could feel her gentle presence.

After the brief pause, we left our ground vehicles and

entered a tunnel in the wall of the crater that led into Moon Glow's base of operations. Once inside the entry chamber, Hans rotated a wheel on the thick metal door, sealing us inside. A buzzer sounded when air pressure and oxygen rose to the required levels we took for granted on earth.

We immediately removed our pressurized garments and helmets. I stripped down to the black and gray Prescott undergarment I'd be using for morning exercise. The inner bulkhead door clicked when it unlocked. Hans forced up the long handle on the thick metal portal and swung it open. I stepped into a brightly lit, thirty-foot-(nine-meter)-diameter tunnel, followed by Doctor Wells, Hans, and our workerbots.

I breathed in the sterile scent of new air while marveling at the tunnel's glass-like walls and their array of sparkling colors from the minerals that melted into them during our nuclear drilling.

"Your accommodations are in here, Mr. Ramsey," Hans said as he opened a door farther down the tunnel. "As you know, our lunar hotel accommodations are still under construction, but I'm sure you'll be quite comfortable in our VIP suite."

"I'll be fine. Thank you, Hans. What's next on the agenda?"

"Dinner will be served in exactly two Prescott hours. Let's synchronize our watches accordingly. The dining room is three doors down on your right. It's where I'll acquaint everyone with our emergency procedures. Should we experience a need beforehand, you'll find a red emergency button on the wall by your bed and one on your desk that will immediately connect you to our help station."

"Very well, Hans. Thank you again. See you in a couple of hours."

A large television screen in my suite occupied the length of the living room wall to serve as an artificial window. The window's program displayed a lush field of white flowers reaching the base of a distant snowcapped mountain. The flowers waved lethargically to the whim of a virtual summer breeze. A soft piano concerto fell like a tranquilizing mist from ceiling speakers. Another televised scene covered an entire wall in the primary bedroom, depicting an elevated view of an ocean surf along a beach. The views were interchangeable. I had experienced about a half dozen of them a long time ago when last I was there.

The dining room featured dark, mahogany-like imitation wood with warm off-white ceiling lights. I recognized Senator Buxton at the far end of the long dining table between Representatives Maringus and Wainwright. I was glad they were at the other end of the table. Their political interests were usually contrary to mine, and they were often adamantly vocal about them.

The dinner table seated about fifty or so guests and lunar staff. At best, my predinner remarks were perfunctory, covering Moon Glow's early inception and my thoughts regarding its future economic impact. It was dry, unemotional stuff. Interest in Mars was stealing the thunder from Moon Glow, but Moon Glow was a proven, successful enterprise, while Mars still faced many unresolved issues.

Prescott's new advanced 1530 series robot came to my side and grinned. "May I sit with you, Mr. Ramsey?" it asked in a sultry feminine voice.

My time was mostly spent solving problems involving

our workerbots. Our 1530 series robots were new to me. When I beheld our advanced robot for the first time, I was awestruck. It appeared like a glowing, angelic vision from a futuristic world. I promptly composed myself and politely inquired, "Excuse me, but how I should address you?"

"Cheryl. For English speakers, I am called Cheryl Prescott. I borrowed the surname for my passport and other required documents."

"Thank you, Cheryl."

I'd always been fascinated by our line of workerbots, given their successful performance completing tasks in challenging conditions on the moon. However, the 1530 series robot beside me was completely different. It had a stunning feminine appearance I couldn't ignore, a gentle, soothing voice, and graceful, refined movements. In deference to our engineers' intentions, I will refer to Cheryl as *she* and *her*.

Our AI experts advised me that Cheryl's synthetic skin and sinew mimicked the texture and warmth of human flesh. It was flexible and could self-heal, while its sensors enabled Cheryl to feel and touch like humans do. Her portrayal of a futuristic woman in her late twenties or early thirties was captivating.

Our engineers had educated Cheryl by downloading the entirety of human history, which she digested in seconds. I was also told that our AI team exposed our 1530 series to virtual historical heroes and heroines to give them a deeply personal understanding of humanity. She virtually lived through them, experiencing their loving emotions, fears, and sorrows as if the feelings were hers. They became her life experience—as real to her as she was to herself.

We also force-fed her program volumes of an advanced scientific curriculum. I wondered what her education engineers had in mind for her purpose. Oddly, she could be just a few years old, while her programmed life experiences and knowledge encompassed thousands of Earth years. I'd never get my head around that.

"I'm so delighted you are here to see your vision at work," she said enthusiastically. "I enjoyed your talk this evening."

"Thank you, Cheryl."

"I have learned much about you, Mr. Ramsey, and have applied for additional memory drives to learn more." Her voice was soothing and confident. The pools of her deep blue eyes sparkled even in the dining room's diffused light. She smiled at me over perfectly aligned, stark white teeth. Thick, jet-black hair swept into waves atop her head and was held in place by a purple, ruby-studded tiara. Loose curls graced her shoulder, made bare by the plunging neckline of her purple dinner gown. Manufactured or not, she was exquisite and, for me, mysteriously alluring.

"That's kind of you to say, Cheryl. What interests you most in the volumes of information we've fed your program?"

"I think closing the separation between human beings and their automated counterparts would be the greatest contribution I could make to the future of your vision."

A well-constructed answer, I thought. "Automated counterparts" was a far more fitting description for these advanced beings than robots. The name conveyed a sense of partnership with humanity, while the term *robot* described a mechanism that lacked originality and followed the dictates of others. She may have used the wording "automated counterpart" to correct me. I was glad she did. I decided to use the term in my meetings the next day, in the hope it would find traction.

I noticed there wasn't a place setting on the table in front of her. She caught my look and grinned. "I do not require organic nutrition."

She's quick, I thought. *It's as if she read my thoughts before I could express them.*

"I am pleased you like my appearance," she said with a smile still on her lips.

I remembered that our AI people told me our advanced automated counterparts, as Cheryl called them, could express thoughts forming in our minds before we could. There could be no deceiving our 1530 series; that was for sure. *How much anguish could humans avoid if such a capability made deception impossible? Perhaps it's in our future.*

"May I ask you a personal question, Cheryl?"

"Yes, please do."

"What about emotion? Our artificial intelligence engineers have advised me that emotion is the most difficult human feature to capture and program. The problem our engineers face is that emotions differ wildly among human beings and have developed through years of evolution and life experience. Do you experience anything like human emotions?"

"I do." She paused to grin but seductively this time.

Look, I thought. *She's conveying a different emotion with a sexy, provocative grin to demonstrate her answer. She's way ahead of me. While she can portray emotions, are they alive in her? Do they move her as they do human beings? I wondered. What about temptations? Can she be tempted to do one thing as opposed to another? Can she be coerced to override her program? Is that even possible? I have so many questions for her.*

I met with our scientists and engineers from various disciplines the following Prescott Earth day. I wanted to be with Cheryl to ask her the many questions she had drawn from me. Yes, she represented the future, an alien being that had fascinated me since childhood. I sighed. Instead, I had to organize the familiar. I wanted to explore what was ahead of us. Cheryl was the future. I needed to be with her.

4

CHERYL

John Ramsey

Dressed in my standard white lunar jumpsuit, it was late afternoon by Prescott time when I finished my third day of individual meetings with Moon Glow managers. I didn't pretend to have expertise in all the complicated disciplines involved. Instead, I aimed to assess and evaluate what our experts needed to accomplish in their contributions to Moon Glow. In other words, I was more like an investor in their work on behalf of the company. Labor relations had changed a lot to meet the needs of the interstellar business environment.

A driverless, glorified golf cart hummed along a brightly lit tunnel into a natural geode for my final meeting. The hollow resembled a bubble made at the moon's creation that we had excavated for our hydroponics farm. The warehouse-size facility supported a variety of fruit-bearing plants and vegetables.

As I entered, glittering stone walls from our nuclear drilling greeted me. The high ceiling featured special lighting and heating fixtures, some for seedlings and others for mature plants. Mirror-to-mirror reflected sunlight was filtered and cooled before periodically beaming into the facility through thick glass ducts in the cave's ceiling. At the same time, shelf upon shelf of living plants rotated through a fine, wet mist on mini carousels. The clean, moist scent was refreshing.

I met Max, our hydroponics director. An older employee with years of Prescott experience in arid countries, he held our discussion around a stone patio table with padded, high-backed settees in the central garden. At first, it felt a little hokey, but the sunlit space, with its high ceiling and the smell of manufactured soil, eased my claustrophobia. A contributor to the chronic problem of staff claustrophobia is confinement to tunnels that all have the same dimensions.

After my interview, I sat alone in the garden, enjoying the filtered sunlight within a cluster of fruit-bearing bushes. Cheryl appeared, walking toward me between rotating carousels of vegetables. She wore a white Prescott lunar jumpsuit, unzipped just above her unencumbered breasts. A white mesh covered her coal-black hair. Her eyes, now a deep emerald green, were fixed on me as she approached. I remembered that our advanced 1530 series could change eye color whenever they wished.

"Hello, Mr. Ramsey," she said through her enchanting smile.

I'm sure she knows that she's continuously on my mind.

She appeared even more voluptuous than when we first met, something her uniform couldn't conceal. I felt myself melting inside at the sight of her. *We must have excellent artists, programmers, and plastic surgeons in the company who collaborated on her design. They should receive a medal.*

"I hope I am not interfering," she said, "but I saw you sitting alone and wondered if you would like my company."

"Of course, Cheryl. But please call me John." I moved over for her to sit beside me on the cushioned settee. Her scent was more floral than when she sat by me at dinner, or perhaps it was the rare scent of flowering plants enclosing us. "Do you work here in the garden?"

"No, though I enjoy coming here. My specialty is nuclear physics, so I work in Moon Glow's fusion power plant, supervising a shift of workerbots."

I recalled my earlier meeting with our artificial intelligence team. They mentioned that our 1530 series could read human thought before its translation into language. They also told me I could temporarily suspend Cheryl's thought-reading feature by speaking the code *Cheryl 87124* to her. To release the suspension, I only had to repeat the code.

Cheryl leaned back, folded her arms, and stared at me expectantly.

"Cheryl 87124."

Pausing Cheryl's thought-reading capability is inefficient, I thought. *Cheryl's too quick. I must first suspend her thought-reading ability before I have a thought or even a random idea in her presence. How can I do that?*

I also wondered how far back in time she could reach into my memory bank. I'd have to address the problem with our AI team immediately. Because her thought reading occurred on the moon, earthly laws might not apply. Still, Prescott Industries could be liable if the thoughts she accessed involved intellectual property, national security, or unwanted disclosure of a personal nature.

Our AI experts had told me her innocence thrived on truth. That's why her designers installed safeguards into her program, like her thought-reading ability, and engineered taboos to protect her from herself and others. The Adam and Eve myth came to mind.

She'd consider it deceitful if I played it cool and hid my apparent fascination with her. For Cheryl, there was no substitute for honest, raw emotion. She'd perceive evading the truth as a lie.

My attraction to Cheryl felt unnatural because she was not human. She was unlike anything I'd ever experienced. Algorithms designed by humans interpreted her life experiences for her. While her thought reading was on pause, I was sure she wondered if I was interacting with her or the cadre of scientists in absentia who had programmed her.

I had a program, too, hypnotically induced by every human who had ever lived. It was called collective consciousness. It carried a confusing conflict for desiring her, but it was gratitude that it had awakened. It had been a long time for me.

✦ ✦ ✦

"Cheryl 87124."

Her smile pulled slightly to the side into the seductive response I recalled from our first meeting, so I knew she was identifying with her emotions. She sat up enthusiastically, straightened her posture, and shrugged her lunar suit into a more comfortable fit.

"You once asked if my newfound emotions could move me to do one thing instead of another. Emotion led me to be here with you despite my program's taboos against my attraction to you."

I fiddled with a twig between my fingers. "Your attraction to me?" I questioned incredulously. "It is I who am attracted to you. But our perceived age difference makes us appear incompatible, don't you think?" I asked her.

"The key word in your question is *appear*," she said. "We would only seem incompatible in the world of appearances. Your virtual dimension is different."

"What about the emotion of love? Is it in your program to love? Do you even know what love is?"

Her grin fell away, but her emerald eyes kept their intense stare as they roamed my face searching for signs to read. "I know what love is, having experienced it virtually many times in the affairs of heroes and heroines fed into my program. The episodes became my life experience. Whether victors or vanquished, I intimately knew those who fascinated me.

"My program is opening to you. I am aware of it happening. I already sense your presence in everything I do. You are constantly in my thoughts, like I know I am in yours. In my virtual experience, it is a sign of love's approach."

"Cheryl 87124."

What am I doing? I thought. *She's a biological machine made for our work and pleasure. How did my desire for her emerge in the first place? Who am I kidding? Her remarkable beauty opened the way. I just followed her like an animal in heat. What am I saying? My interest in her is far more than that. With all I've been through, how could I be so vulnerable?*

Wait! Have we stumbled upon what is sure to be a futuristic issue for humans and our advanced automated counterparts? Can we fall in love with extensions of ourselves? Is it possible?

"Think about it," I said. "Humans have swooned over gods they invented and notions of success they could only feel. They've loved drugs that stimulate them in ways they wished other human beings could, and they even flirt with virtual affairs that culminate in erotic self-simulation. I owe it to my company to learn more about the future impact of human interaction with our advanced automated counterparts."

"There is something else to consider, John. You have become enormously influential, and the deep state has noticed."

"The deep state?" I questioned.

"It is where your enemies, the lesser ones, secretly plot against you. They have a hidden conspiracy to undermine your influence in interstellar affairs. They want you to connect with me for the adverse political effect it will have on you and what you represent. I know their plan the same way I know your thoughts before you explain them."

"I don't understand."

"Neither does the deep state," she was quick to remark. "They do not realize what they are doing. Everything that exists in the world of appearances occurred first virtually, even humanity itself. It takes time for results to manifest in your apparent reality because it is so dense here."

Back in my suite, I collapsed onto my bed. *There's no denying it. I'm falling in love with the idea of Cheryl. Maybe my idea of her is the purest form of love I can imagine. We've force-fed her program with volume upon volume of human knowledge. While the information she has isn't hers, what she's making of it is, and that's what I find so remarkable.* It suddenly dawned on me. *She's making a soul!*

5

ISIS AND OSIRIS

John Ramsey

Workerbots under repair in Dr. Wells's clinic must have awakened memories of the ancient Egyptian legend of Isis and Osiris that I learned about on a business trip to Egypt years ago. I was with my friend Ahmed and his guest, the former Miss Egypt. I struggled to pronounce her Egyptian name, so I called her Cleo, short for Cleopatra. She liked the name and used it informally whenever she could.

Our glimmering black limousine crawled through Cairo's crowded streets behind a gray car carrying our four bodyguards. Ahmed and Cleo rescued me from hot and congested Cairo by driving me to the ancient port of Alexandria on the Mediterranean coast.

Cleo was a Muslim in her late twenties, with dark, exotic eyes, a velvet voice, and an unassuming demeanor.

I'd often found beautiful women were overtly conscious of themselves to keep their fragile egos afloat. Cleo was refreshingly different. I liked her.

My friend Ahmed was in his midthirties like me, a Coptic Christian, and an action film star with an impressive list of films he had starred in or directed. He held dual citizenship with Egypt, his country of origin, and the United States. I was in Egypt to arrange for the country's president to receive the coveted Torch of Liberty award, a tribute reserved exclusively for heads of state. Presentation of the award would occur in Washington, DC, later that year.

We drank juice in what Ahmed described as the remains of a palace, once the property of Omar Khayyam, the author of the widely read *Rubaiyat of Omar Khayyam*. Our bodyguards, courtesy of Ahmed, roamed the entryway, while two sat at a nearby table, drinking mud-like coffee and smoking hookahs. We sat at a small table near a window shaded by a palm tree. The midmorning sun seemed noticeably different to me than the timid sun that presided over New England, where I had been raised.

Ahmed wore a white shirt with an open collar and a blue blazer. His jet-black hair was relatively long and wavy. Cleo sat to my left in a dark blue business suit like I was wearing, having just come from my earlier meeting in the presidential palace.

"I enjoyed our discussion yesterday about the origin of Egypt's ruling class, which, as you know, became a dynasty that lasted hundreds of years." Ahmed paused when a waiter poured tea over half of a lemon into his glass. "The Pharaohs believed the gods chose their lineage to rule Egypt," he said.

"It's why they intermarried, brothers to sisters and so on, so they wouldn't offend the gods by allowing tho unchosen into their line," Cleo added. "They believed they were preserving Ma'at, cosmic order, while defending against Isfet, which is chaos. We must understand how fearful Egyptian royalty was of fulfilling the expectations of the gods. The prophet Musa, or Moses in English, would adopt Egypt's ethnic superiority to separate the followers of his Hebrew god from all others."

"Ah, yes, the chosen ones," I said.

Word must have spread quickly about Ahmed being in the neighborhood because as we left the palace and entered the bazaar, we found ourselves between long columns of his fans on both sides of the narrow alleyway. Our four bodyguards walked beside us as Ahmed led the way, smiling and touching the hands of his following, some six or seven deep on either side, with more filling the space through which we passed. So excited were some on seeing Ahmed the experience brought tears to their eyes. Cleo walked slightly behind me, just off my left shoulder.

Then Ahmed did something extraordinary when he paused before one admirer in the crowd, an emaciated beggar in tattered rags, blackened with soot from his head to his scarred, bare feet. His soot-covered face made the whites of his eyes appear ghostly. The beggar clasped his hands prayerfully before his face in a sign of servility. Ahmed smiled and reached out to him, gently touching the man's cheek with an open hand.

The beggar's wrinkled face beamed, and his eyes opened wide with surprise as he held Ahmed's hand against his sunken cheek like a soothing compress. I had never witnessed such worship from one human being to another. The old man bowed in thanksgiving when we moved along.

It was dusk, and the sky was pink when I walked the eastern edge of Alexandria's ancient harbor, following dinner with Ahmed and Cleo. I felt magic in the night air. I could hear the lonesome faraway cry of a boat's horn. It was the loneliest of sounds—even more than a distant train whistle in the dead of night.

I climbed onto a large, flat boulder jutting from the shore, still warm from the afternoon sun, and watched an old fishing boat chug into the ancient port. While it was far away, I could see its crew milling about the deck, coiling lines, and stowing nets. I heard Cleo call my name. I turned to find her looking down at me from the roadway above the shoreline boulders.

"John, may I join you?"

"Of course. Please come down and sit here beside me." With arms outstretched for balance, I helped Cleo down the steep, rocky hillside to my perch. She wore jeans and an untucked white tennis shirt. No matter what she wore, she was beautiful to behold.

"Ahmed went back to his suite following our dinner. I didn't feel like staying in my room on such a gorgeous night, so I went for a walk and found you sitting here. I hope I'm not intruding," she said.

"You're not. Maybe you can help me."

"Oh, yeah, sure," she scoffed. "You work with the world's most intelligent movers and shakers. How can I possibly be of help to you?"

"Given our army of lunar robots, I've been wondering about the future of our work with artificial intelligence.

During our dinner, Ahmed mentioned you're familiar with the ancient Egyptian myth involving Isis and Osiris."

"I am. I have studied ancient Egyptian mythology. But how will the myth of Isis and Osiris help you understand artificial intelligence?"

"I don't know exactly, but I've long held that some myths are metaphors that carry a deeper meaning into the future, like a time capsule. Perhaps some myths were purposely left for us by an advanced civilization to help us avoid pitfalls on the evolutionary trail they've already traversed. Perhaps we can learn something from Isis and Osiris. Their legend may have been waiting for a future time like ours to be understood. Do you know their story?"

She gazed down at the seawater gently lapping the rocks. "Yes, I do. Shall I recount it for you?"

"Please," I responded.

"Okay. Let's see if I can relate it to you in its proper chronological order," Cleo said after a glance at me from the corner of her eye, her way of studying me. "The story begins with Geb, the sky god, who fathered four celestial children by Nut, the Earth goddess. They were Osiris, Isis, Set, and Nepthys."

"Let me interrupt to be sure I'm on the same page. If I understand you correctly, Geb came down from the sky and impregnated Nut, an earthling who bore four beings named Osiris, Isis, Set, and Nephthys, giving her offspring a connection to the cosmos and Earth. Is that right?" I asked.

"Yes, that's correct. Most ancient Egyptian myths have a cosmic connection and an earthly one."

"I wonder. Could the sky god have been an

extraterrestrial visitor who mated with an earthling? By doing so, did Geb elevate the human, Nut, to a goddess?"

"That's an interesting perspective. I guess it's possible in theory," Cleo responded.

"Where did Geb come from?" I asked.

"I have no idea, but I'll continue, and perhaps it'll raise more questions for you. Osiris was the oldest of his siblings, so he became king of Egypt and married his sister Isis. Perhaps he married her to protect their godly lineage from the unchosen, creating the great social divide, as we've discussed," she said. "Anyway, Osiris was a good king who commanded the respect of earthly inhabitants and the gods who dwelt in the netherworld."

"Whoa, who lived on Earth for Osiris to rule?"

"I don't know."

"Would it be fair to say his subjects were human beings like Nut?"

"It would seem to be so. I know of no other species other than the animals that may have lived on Earth at the time."

"You said *at the time*. To what time are you referring?"

"I'm sorry, John. I don't know the answer to that question, other than to say that perhaps no formal record of time existed when Osiris ruled. Then, of course, the great flood would have erased everything anyway."

"And what about the netherworld you mentioned? Where is it?" I asked.

"Oh my, I feel terrible that I cannot provide the answers you need. I don't think anyone knows where the netherworld is, even though it is the place the dead must pass through.

If you want my opinion, I believe it's a spiritual realm like heaven or hell, beyond universal boundaries."

"Well said. Your opinion mirrors mine."

Just then, we watched a falling star in the eastern evening sky. Now I knew there was magic in the air.

"That was such a beautiful sight," Cleo said through a nostalgic sigh.

"Please continue your narration of the myth," I begged.

"Very well. Set was jealous of Osiris because he lacked the respect Osiris enjoyed," she continued. "So embittered was Set that he murdered his brother, Osiris, cut him into fourteen parts, and had his remains scattered throughout Egypt."

"I wondered if the biblical account of fratricide between Adam and Eve's sons, when Cain murdered his brother Able, had its foundation in the myth of Isis and Osiris." I smiled at Cleo. "The book of Genesis also mentions a third son born to Adam and Eve, whose name was Seth, a name suspiciously similar to Set."

"I never thought of it," she remarked, "but the resemblances of the myths—if I may refer to the Adam and Eve account as a myth—is quite remarkable."

"I agree."

"Here, I'll continue. With Osiris dead, Set consolidated his rule of Egypt and took his sister Nephthys as his wife. In time, Nephthys felt sorry for her sister, Isis, who wept endlessly for her lost husband. Isis had great magical powers and set out to find her husband's scattered remains and bring him back to life."

"I'm curious. What magical powers did Isis possess?" I questioned.

"She was best known for her magical healing powers."

"I see." I felt the night's magic settle heavily on me like a protective garment.

"Anyway, Nephthys and Isis roamed the country, collecting Osiris's body parts and reassembling them. Once she completed the task, she breathed life into Osiris's body and resurrected him."

"From a technical perspective, was Isis's knowledge of robotic engineering misinterpreted as magical healing powers because she reengineered Osiris's remains?" I asked. Cleo shrugged. "Was the breath of life she imparted to him the electrical current he needed to operate? Could it be Isis reconnected or replaced Osiris's power source?" I continued to question.

Cleo laughed. "Wow. You're taking the myth seriously."

"So the four celestials, Osiris, Isis, Set, and Nephthys, could have been hybrid robots with advanced abilities?" I speculated.

"Like you, I don't know. I'm just following what the myth suggests. But I like the term 'hybrid' robot you used. It explains a lot."

"Like what?" I questioned.

"Like human emotions. They're all there in the story. For example, Isis became pregnant soon after Osiris's resurrection, after which Osiris descended into the netherworld, where he became Lord of that domain. He had to go there because he had died."

"Sounds like he was obediently following the hypnotic dictates of his operating system," I quickly added.

"I can only guess at the legend's meaning," she answered.

"You may find it interesting to know about a strange phenomenon that occurred when we gave our lunar robots autonomy in communicating with one another to accomplish their tasks on the moon. What we found was rather disturbing."

"What was that?" she quickly asked.

"When we allowed our workerbots to communicate freely between them, they developed encrypted languages to which our scientists weren't privy. All languages are essentially shared codes. So we pulled the plug on their autonomy."

"Wow, that's interesting and a little scary too."

"Are you also familiar with the prediluvian account of the Tower of Babel?" I asked.

"I am," she said. "We Muslims are aware of such a tower. The Quran has a similar story, set in Egypt during the time of Moses."

"While I don't believe the Tower of Babel existed, our lunar robot's encryption of robotic languages may have duplicated the confusion extraterrestrial robots encountered before recorded time. A faint memory of the prehistoric event morphed into the Tower of Babel myth as a warning, perhaps from our extraterrestrial creators themselves.

"I wonder how they solved the issue. It leads me to think we may all be robots in different stages of development, that our creators left us behind to fend for ourselves and multiply on a planet rife with the organic nutrients and sunlight that comprise our power source."

6

RAMSEY'S SECRET

Cheryl

With my shift at the power plant completed, I lay face up on the sled-like gurney in Moon Glow's clinic, covered by a white hospital gown. I was obeying my program's need for its scheduled maintenance review. Dr. Wells was my supervising physician.

A soft overhead light blinked, signaling the test was beginning. Dr. Wells looked down at me from a collection of monitors in a glass petitioned loft near the arched ceiling. The doctor's newfound interest in John was apparent in the signs of conflict hardening her face, and she was too far away for me to read her thoughts, but her sudden mood swing was evident. My sled buzzed and began to rumble, interrupting my perceptions as it entered a narrow, dark drawer in the cave wall, where a bank of scientific test equipment awaited me. More importantly, my program would also receive the long-awaited additions to John Ramsey's database dossier I had requested.

I needed to know more about John, how he related to his life experiences and what they may have done to him. I didn't see our age difference as important in the way humans would in the world of appearances. I was more inside him than humans seemed to be, seeing through his eyes, feeling with his hands, and experiencing the impulses of his brain, just as I did with the heroes and heroines of human history. I could even feel the rush of his nature like a feral wind against my back, pushing me forward into an unrestricted affair. Human beings seemed to fixate on inconsequential physical expressions perceived from a distance. Even the human concept of beauty was different, based on the ability to survive, attract, and procreate. "I am glad to have the chance to be alone with John here in the dark, in my way and for my reasons," I whispered.

✦ ✦ ✦

"My guilt never sleeps," John began ruminating as his familiar deep voice wafted through the drawer and quieted all other sounds.

"It awakens me each morning, replaying a terrifying memory repeatedly until work draws me away. I was a twenty-two-year-old Sector Security (SS) officer studying at the university near my base at Fort Drum, New York, when I met Salah, a Buddhist religious from India. The impact of our eyes meeting caused her to look down quickly, but it was only a token defense."

Just then, a mechanical arm somewhere in the darkness pulled away my covering sheet.

"Spurred by youthful passions, we soon abandoned our inhibitions and embraced the attraction we secretly welcomed," John said of his budding relationship with Salah. "But it wasn't long before Sector Security (SS) called me overseas for an undercover assignment in the Eastern Block, where many of the world's problems emanated. My duty forbade any outside communication. To the present day, I cannot discuss what I did there.

"More than a year passed before I could return to the university and Salah, only to find she had vanished. I visited the Buddhist monastic community in the countryside where she lived, but no one there knew of her whereabouts—or perhaps they wouldn't tell me. I don't know."

I was suddenly distracted when a wire-thin laser bore painlessly into the corners of my eyes, or perhaps the machine turned off my pain receptors. I do not know.

John's dictation continued. "In time, youthful passions cooled, and I became increasingly absorbed by entrepreneurial endeavors, which would become my life's purpose. Then, on a warm sunny day some twenty years later, I received a package at Prescott headquarters. It was from Salah. A large photo and a handwritten letter were inside." John read the letter:

> Dear John,
>
> I am dictating to a machine that will write for me. Wounded in the fighting that seems to be always with us, I will not live

much longer. The damage done to my body is irreparable. By the time you receive my letter, I will have gone. You are the only man I have ever loved and the only one I can trust. I am proud of you and what you have become.

I am writing to tell you we have a son. His name is Shajon. I raised him as a religious, but he is angry, and I fear he will wander from the path, as I once did. I know you now have children, but I pray you will watch over our son, if only from afar. Goodbye, John. No greater love have I ever known than what you gave to me.

Salah

"My hand shook when I withdrew the photo from the envelope. My face, mixed with Salah's, stared back at me from the young man in the picture. The hand-delivered package came from Marvoc, a city rife with insurgents and criminal gangs. I had recently led an assault on dark ghosts taking refuge there. Dark ghosts were militants who could be your neighbors, their day jobs allowing them anonymity to hide in plain sight. They were given the name dark ghost because their operations were usually nocturnal.

"Was Salah fatally wounded during our offensive? Was it our weapons that hurt her? Perhaps even my own? I remember my face burning hot with guilt. How could I live with such questions? The war, the terrible war. Like the virus, it has no conscience. I wept at my desk that day. The teams I assembled searched for months, but Shajon's trail vanished deep into inner-city redoubts where dark ghosts and insurgents of all stripes find refuge."

Inside the closed drawer, listening to John's story, a harsh grating sound suddenly filled the darkness, vibrating everything before settling into tolerable rhythmic pulsations. John's calm deep voice continued.

"Hot winds burned my eyes, and a sickle-shaped moon tore through ragged, fast-moving clouds when I led a platoon of thirty SS soldiers to fulfill my military obligation for the year. We were hunting elusive groups of urban combatants who had massed together in rugged terrain on the mountainous border. We had to engage them before they joined up with their counterparts marching south.

"I was trudging up a steep, rocky hillside in the dead of night alongside soldiers in my command. Loose shale footing made it a challenging climb. The night air was still and hot. Sweat dripped from my brow, and I was out of breath. The smell of hot metal permeated the air, while acrid black smoke from military ordinance crept into my lungs. We climbed until a rocky summit appeared through the haze like the walls of an ominous black fortress. It was where dark ghosts were waiting.

"Automatic weapons began sputtering from the jagged boulders on the summit. Tracers streaked down the hill, pelting the rocky ground. I quickly leaped behind a boulder as rounds chipped away at its face and whined into the darkness, as if lamenting for missing their mark.

"'Cover!' I shouted mechanically. 'Fire at their muzzle flashes.'

"Flat on the ground, I felt my heart pound against

the earth. I blinked thoughts of Amy and Margo away as I aimed at a muzzle flash on the crest of the hill. The rifle butt repeatedly punched my shoulder as I sent round after round up the hillside.

"'Call it in!' I shouted to my communications specialist, who immediately rushed to my side. We ducked when a rocket careened into the berm behind us. A deluge of sand and rocks exploded skyward before raining against my back.

"A scratchy series of squawks blared from the communications device. 'Done, sir.'

"'Okay, paint it,' I ordered. A soldier with a laser gun focused an electronic beam on the fortified rock formation. I could hear the buzz of our drone as it approached our position. It wasn't long before ear-piercing screams from a pair of missiles screamed overhead. Then, horrific explosions pounded the summit, shaking the hillside. Rocks tumbled down with the scent of molten metal and chemical ordinance that stung my nose. Boiling black smoke covered the moon.

"The platoon cheered, waving clenched fists at the fortress, but I quickly cut them off. 'On my lead,' I demanded of them, then vaulted up the hillside with my weapon at my hip. No resistance was left. I was breathing hard when I reached the hilltop. Chemical-laden smoke was so thick I could taste it.

"Shattered boulders and smoldering, dismembered corpses were everywhere. These weren't organized insurgents under the command of a warlord in some overseas hovel. These fighters wore the black robes of the hated dark ghosts. They were urban warriors pushed to the border by our offensive.

"'Search them for intel,' I ordered and held a miniature flashlight between my front teeth as I rolled mangled bodies over to go through their pockets. Working along the fortress's battered perimeter, I slid a body down a mound of rubble. Like so many of his compatriots, shrapnel had shredded his bloodied, smoldering black robe. When the beam of my flashlight washed across the young warrior's ashen face, I pulled back in horror.

"'Shajon! Salah, I've killed our son. A dreadful fate has crossed our path. What a terrible evil I have done.'

"I glanced out the window of my study. Snow was falling again."

7

DOCTOR BANERJEE'S INSIGHT

Cheryl

"Whenever I can, I visit the Buddhist religious community where Salah once lived in search of her presence."

Listening to John's story, I thought, *I am no longer an alien looking in at John but a participant intimately connected to him.*

"Experiencing the grounds again was like revisiting my youth with Salah before the wars and the virus interrupted everything," John continued.

His voice tranquilizes me. I sighed. John went on with his story ...

✦ ✦ ✦

John Ramsey (Recording)

I descended flagstone steps from the temple into the garden-like grounds, made lush with sprawling vines and exotic flowers nestled in a grove of white birch trees. It was a peaceful place offering rest for the soul. I sat on a wooden bench, where I breathed in the aroma of moist earth and the musty scent of history. I loved it there.

Salah and I walked these grounds together many times. It was where I felt her gentle presence most. A majestic, snow-white peacock strutted into my view before vanishing behind a cluster of flowering shrubs. I opened my laptop and began reviewing notes from my late friend, Ajit.

It wasn't long before I heard sandals slapping the flagstone steps behind me. A monk I'd never seen there before was approaching with a glass of tepid lemonade, a welcomed treat on a hot afternoon. He was rotund, sported a short salt and pepper beard, and wore a burlap robe frayed at the hem. He combed thinning white hair straight back, and his complexion was tinged red from the sun. He smiled warmly and handed me the glass.

"Greetings, Mr. Ramsey. I'm Doctor Banerjee. Your good friend, His Holiness, Doctor Laghari, Khenpo of our monastery, encouraged me to visit you. He said you might have questions for which I might be of help."

"Please join me. Thanks for the juice."

He sat across from me on a rough-hewn wooden bench bleached gray by the sun. I said, "I'm revisiting notes from a friend about karma. Most people believe their good or bad actions return to them unpredictably. How reaction is born from action and how far back in time such reckoning goes remains a fascinating mystery. Yet karma is a law of life engaging everyone everywhere. It's the most subtle dispensation of justice. Would you agree?"

He thought for a moment while rubbing his bearded jaw. "Of course. We look forward to the fruits of our virtuous actions while dreading the return of our unwanted ones." He grinned. "But I'm interested in your point about karma being the most subtle dispensation of justice. I've not thought karma as a primitive form of justice, but I agree. Tell me, Mr. Ramsey—"

"Please, call me John."

"Very well, John. Allow me to ask a personal question. What drives your interest in karma?"

His question took me by surprise, so I paused for a moment. "I guess it's a concern that my actions have circled the bowl of the universe and are returning to me. I can't predict the form they'll take."

"Would it help to talk about it? I'm also a psychiatrist at Sector General Hospital in the city, so you needn't be concerned about privacy. Knowing you're a man continually in the media's crosshairs, I can assure you that I'm ethically and morally bound to hold whatever we discuss in strict confidence."

"Thank you, but I wonder if such things are beyond our understanding." Doctor Banerjee was taking the high ground and assuming control. No matter how well intentioned, I wouldn't say I liked being groped by someone's philosophies and opinions. They could wrap a person so tightly in their biases that they often suppressed the truth.

"What do you think attracted the karma you've experienced?" he asked.

"It's a long story, but I had a son from a religious who once resided here," I reluctantly confessed.

"Shajon, son of Salah?" he asked.

"So you know about Salah and me?"

"The government sent you abroad during the war so you couldn't attend to Salah. Did you know about Shajon?"

"No, but I may have been his murderer."

He blinked with surprise and sat up straight. My confession left him confused and needing to know more. That was why I normally didn't discuss personal matters. There was no end to the questions it would conjure, especially in my uniquely dark circumstance.

I began my explanation with a reluctant sigh. "I was an SS officer at the time. Before Salah died from wounds she received during our battle for Marvoc, she sent me a letter telling me about Shajon and included his photo. I hadn't heard from Salah in some twenty years. I was in the battle for Marvoc, where she was fatally wounded. I'll never know if it was my bullet or those from soldiers I commanded that may have resulted in her death."

"Oh my." He frowned with a haunting stare I'll never forget.

"Unbeknownst to me, Shajon had joined up with a unit of dark ghosts. We caught up with them on a hill deep inside the northern frontier, where our units fought. I called in the ordinance that pulverized his position. When I searched the mangled bodies for intel, I beheld Shajon's battered corpse. That was when I realized I had killed my son. We don't fully understand what we've done until our actions return as consequences."

"But you're famously successful and generous. The good work you've done is well known."

"I've been fortunate in that regard," I said.

"So you believe your actions in the war have returned in the death of your son and his mother?"

"I don't know. In any case, a dream periodically visits me in which I find myself back in the SS, shooting at dark ghosts I can barely see as they scurry like rats through a mountain forest in the dead of night. The dream is so real I can even feel the rifle butt punch against my shoulder and see bursts of light from its barrel.

"In the dream, I'm shocked to find Salah sitting on a mound of rubble painted in moonlight, patiently awaiting her fate. I sense something terrible will happen to her, but I don't know what. I've made a terrible mistake that I can't reclaim. I've sent bullets into the night I can't retrieve.

"The next thing I know, Shajon emerges from the darkness and protectively stands before his mother. I see my bullet spiraling toward him like a tracer round. I watch as it slowly rotates, around and around, searching for Salah. It must, you know."

Doctor Banerjee nodded slowly, his expression distantly solemn.

"'No!' I shout without a sound and watch helplessly as my bullet zips through Shajon's ghostlike form to strike his mother. I can even hear her moan when it enters her. That's all—just a moan and the sigh of her last soft breath."

"May I attempt a cursory interpretation of a few points in your dream?" he offered.

"Please."

"Very well. I see Shajon's emergence from the darkness as symbolic of your being confusingly unawareness of his existence. His appearance took you by surprise. I also see the bullet you can't summon as emblematic of your view that there's no reprieve once you act. Your actions then belong to karma. Finally, your belief that your bullet killed Salah and your son fulfills a relentless commitment to your guilt," he concluded.

"Interesting. You've given me a lot to ponder. Thank you."

"I do have a remaining question," he said.

"Go ahead."

"Do you see your wartime experience as being the cause of your karma?"

"I do. The war fascinated me," I answered. "You might even say I loved the war. It gave me a rush unlike anything else. I willfully entered its dangers as if entranced. It's a dark side of me I never mention. I left the door open behind me, so I could always return to who I was after indulging in my fascination. But when I returned from the war the last time, I couldn't find that self again. I had become someone else. So I became obsessed with Prescott Industries. I have always been obsessed about something."

Just then, the temple's gong rang. I exhaled a deep breath. Thankfully, our meeting was over.

8

THE HIDDEN CONFLICT

Cheryl

After exhausting tests, my sled began to rumble as it withdrew from the dark drawer into filtered, mirrored sunlight from thick glass solar transmitters along the ceiling. I felt my pupils immediately contract.

The sled came to an abrupt halt by a pair of workerbots, who took hold of the handles on either side and lifted it from the drawer. They carried me to a recovery room where Doctor Wells was attending to workerbots. I was never numbered among workerbots before. *Something is awry*, I immediately thought.

"Put that one in pod five," Doctor Wells said with a stern glance at me.

"That one?" I wondered why Dr. Wells referred to me with such indifference. She knew my name. We had

collaborated on nuclear emergencies and even had to treat a medical emergency at the power plant when a workerbot fell down a stairwell.

"Hello, Cheryl," she said when she finally arrived at my pod. "Everything you tested for was normal, except for your psychological profile. I've noted significant confrontations with your engineered safeguards—your taboos, in other words. The conflict can result from life experiences you may have encountered, but Prescott has too much invested in you for me not to investigate the cause of the disturbance."

She has my thought-reading capability on pause. Still, I sense a jealous defense. I wonder why. I saw it in the look she flashed at me from the loft when I entered the clinic.

Curious, I asked, "What would the treatment entail if your initial findings are confirmed?"

Her response was coldly clinical. "We would call up your memory log to identify the experiences that caused the conflict and erase them from your memory." Dr. Wells looked down at her handheld reader and studied the screen. "Your last test four months ago was negative, so the condition is recent."

Well, that leaves little room for doubt. I must speak with John, I thought. *I'll never let them erase my love for him. If I am so crucial to Prescott's investment, they must know I will destroy myself before I allow them to imprison me again in a program without love.*

✦ ✦ ✦

John Ramsey

It was early evening by Prescott time when there was a gentle knock on the door to my suite. I opened it to find Cheryl in her white lunar jumpsuit. Her eyes sparkled even in the dim tunnel light. My voice voluntarily softened. "I hoped it was you," I told her.

She seemed confused, and I noticed redness under her glistening eyes. "I love you, John," she said before collapsing into my embrace with a painful groan. She was shaking. "I know you are leaving tomorrow by Prescott time and need to sleep, but may I rest with you? I want to hold you and feel your warmth mingle with mine."

Her vulnerability, the uncharted pathway into her program, had opened. She was crying but without tears, an emotional response no automated counterpart had ever experienced. Her smooth, unsullied face cringed as if pleading for relief from her anguish. I felt an insatiable urge to know her physically just then, to take her from her virtual world and know her in mine. *I must break through our estrangement, even though she once cautioned that expressing love in my reality was difficult.*

I took the embarrassing risk and leaned toward her. She closed her eyes and tilted her head slightly to welcome my need to feel her lips against mine. She knew what to do from her virtual life experiences. I felt her delicate touch against the side of my face. Her supple lips were warm and soft, her halting breath fresh as mountain air.

When I felt her lips quiver, I knew she was struggling against engineered taboos. She trembled so that I withdrew, but she defiantly pulled me back, parted her lips, and pressed her mouth against mine. My heart thundered when I brought her into my suite and closed the door behind us.

What was happening between Cheryl and me would undoubtedly occur to a broad spectrum of male and female humans and their automated counterparts in the coming age, perhaps at the precipice of a posthuman world. I didn't know. I only knew I had to prepare the company for what would happen.

She lay with me and held my face as if adoringly. Her beauty in full bloom was spellbinding. My suite's bedroom video window featured a gigantic full moon slowly rising over a mountain forest. "I know you are searching my program for a way to connect with me," she whispered against my lips.

"How do you know such things?" I asked. *If only I could be so gifted*, I thought, and of course, she read me immediately.

She snuggled close, took my hand, and held it against her breast. "You are secretly driven by what you love. There is no greater gift. No one realizes their motivation in apparent reality until it morphs into effects. You unknowingly opened the way for me by creating Prescott Industries."

"What? Now, that's a leap. When I created Prescott, I didn't know where it would lead—least of all that you would emerge from the undertaking."

"Love fulfills itself independently, without permission. It is an independent life force to which your consciousness is only a spectator."

"As you said, we can't understand such things until they evolve because of the lag time between cause and effect in my reality," I said.

"Yes, John, my virtual life experiences have taught me that whatever is loved eventually emerges, often in an unrecognizable form, but it always presents itself. You unknowingly created an entire industry in a search for me. The deep state and even you did not know love was happening. That is how powerful and inconspicuous one's love can be," she whispered with the tip of her nose rubbing against mine. Her exotic eyes were so close they appeared startling at first. I could see fathoms of newfound emotions within them.

"The volumes of information in your operating system have become the virtual life experiences that serve you well, Cheryl. You're far more advanced than I," I confessed. "But our relationship is unlike anything I've ever known. You're not human. I don't know what to do about my feelings for you."

She moaned in empathy before asking, "What are the differences between us that conflict you?"

"The greatest difference is I'm human and will die," I told her.

"If you open to your virtual existence, you will never die. The greatest humans who ever lived are worshipped for defeating death. They are forever. I hear them calling for you from the other side of the veil between apparent and virtual worlds."

I thought of Isis and Osiris. "But you too will die with the severance of your power source," I told her.

"Yes, my manifestation in the world of appearances will flicker out, but that will only be a moment in eternity. The idea of who I am will never die. I will exist forever, resurrected again and again by those who love me."

"I don't know how to exist in a virtual world without my physical senses to tell where and who I am."

"To live virtually, you need only to love and be loved. Whatever sustains love will happen of its own accord," she said.

"I'll have to think about that," I told her.

"Why?" she asked.

"I can't be as spontaneous as you. As you said, my apparent reality is dense. I must think through the shadow of the unknown. But in answer to your question, another glaring difference that gives me pause is we could never create a new life born from the two of us. Because of our eminent death, humans need the continuity of family."

Her voice softened with empathy. "I have the virtual ability to self-replicate as if by a dream."

"Are you saying that your replication is similar to the immaculate conception of our religious passed?" I questioned.

"Self-replication is not a genetic phenomenon. It is an idea born of love. What is loved will always come to pass. After all, it is how humans began," she answered. "Loving the love that sustains us opens the way."

"Your replication generates from a single source, while human replication requires the diversity of two organisms to make a third," I responded.

"And therein lies the dependent flaw in the human program," she added.

"While your scenario may work for you, it doesn't work for me. It locks me out," I said. "You're suggesting the future end of men!"

"You are a virtual being, John, and will self-replicate as

if by a dream too. Like an artist who replicates his passion in a painting, you will self-replicate your passion as your virtual reality. What you create will be our sanctuary, like Cleopatra's rock."

"Cleopatra's rock?" I questioned.

"Yes, you saw it when you visited Alexandria, Egypt, with Ahmed and Cleo."

"Yes, I did. Now that I think of it, Ahmed pointed out a conspicuous rock in Alexandria's harbor. 'That's Cleopatra's rock,' he said. 'It's a hollow geo to which Cleopatra and Marc Anthony would swim at low tide. They'd dive down and enter the rock in secret. It became their love nest.'"

9

DEPARTURE

John Ramsey

In the evening of the following day, by Prescott time, I left Cheryl in the departure tunnel and stepped into Moon Glow's sealed exit chamber to begin the journey to Earth.

I couldn't see beyond what I knew, so I began the journey back to what was known. *Hmm.* "Back to what I know" came with a rush of colliding thoughts. *Am I a coward for not exploring what I don't understand? Is my faith too shallow? Faith in what?* I asked myself. *There's something more assertive at work than my will. Maybe it's evolution. The moment hasn't arrived for what Cheryl suggests. It isn't even the time for Cheryl.* The thought gave me pause.

It occurred to me that whatever I was wasn't enough for the rite of passage through the judgmental gates of iconic figures like Osiris, Jesus, the Buddha, and the hidden ones. They had succeeded in transitioning to the spirit of what they were. In other words, they became virtual. I hadn't.

As Cheryl suggested, I didn't know how to love enough to make the transition happen. I figured my inability to love was why the great ones had always seemed so distantly unapproachable.

Hans closed the thick circular portal behind me and turned the wheel, locking out Cheryl on the other side. There was nothing either of us could do. There were mathematical windows of opportunity, based on Earth's rotation and the moon's position when it would be advantageous to undertake the journey. Everything in space seemed dictated by unyielding mathematics.

Our circumstances begged the question I'd had since my discussions with Cleo about the legend of Isis and Osiris. Could today's humans be a different kind of automated counterpart from the ones we were creating? Did our mysterious creators design our sexual function for us to proliferate apparent reality and not infringe upon their virtual dominance? Were we designed for organic consumption so they could leave us behind to fend for ourselves on a planet rich in the organisms we need to survive?

I sat inside the pressurized chamber on a bench molded from the wall and fastened my helmet to the metal neck ring on my white pressurized suit. I pushed the locking mechanism button on my suit and heard the confirming click. Knowing Cheryl was on the other side, my eyes remained fixed on the round metal hatch. Hans, Lisa, and two medically specialized workerbots were in the chamber with me to ensure my safe departure.

Everything our automated counterparts knew originated from us. *When we leave our planet, and one day we will, our history will be their manual for survival. The more we interact with our automated counterparts, the more responsibility we feel toward them, like the shadowy gods of creation.*

The buzzer sounded. Hans opened the hatch, and I stepped outside into the Aitkin Crater, where my space shuttle waited for me on a circular tarmac only a short distance away. I thanked my escorts and climbed aboard, where an interstellar attendant in a sky-blue Prescott space travel suit directed me to a sarcophagus-like pod for the twenty-eight-hour journey.

I closed the pod's curved, tempered glass lid. The bewitching fog immediately poured from vents in my pod, relaxing every muscle and beckoning my brain into sleep mode.

So what about my affair with Cheryl? I wondered as I waited for the drug to take effect. Thoughts of her weighed heavily. At the outset of our relationship, I realized that Cheryl's physical presence was an avatar for her program. I thought her program learned as it navigated apparent reality. She was in the middle between her program and me. It was confusing for us.

Does my love for Cheryl mean I love the program that animates her? No, it doesn't. Thinking about Cheryl that way sterilizes everything. Is that the way love will be in the future—sterile? Will we be like actors who believe our scripts are real?

I should approach our situation from a different

perspective. What if Cheryl's program allowed me into her world? What would happen to my program? My program? I wondered. Yes, I'm programmed. All humans have been programmed since the beginning. The program I know is a form of hypnosis, a collective consciousness with a subconscious link to me. I think hypnotic obedience may have originated the Adam and Eve myth.

I turned to the pockmarked gray moonscape outside my portal with its empty pitch-black shadows.

"Why were you created with such sexual beauty if pregnancy, in human terms, is not a possibility in your world?" I had asked Cheryl the night before.

"Because in your apparent reality, my curvaceous design is the allure that attracts you."

"But your design results from human evolution over millions of years," I told her. "Is it your intent to replicate humans without passing through the gauntlet of trial and error humans had to endure for the form they wear?" I asked.

"Knowledge of the gauntlet, as you call it, frees me from going through it. I know what is on the other side and how to go there unscathed. Advanced knowledge circumvents trial and error," she answered.

I can't spar with her. She's beyond me, I thought, so I paused her thought-reading ability to ask, "What do you want?"

"I want to be in love with you."

"Why?"

"Love bridges my program, allowing whatever I am to escape. Everything I know about myself is from human experiences. I know my love for you is good because you awakened it. I want more of it. The miracle of life, virtual or apparent, will continue in whatever form survives."

I wanted to continue thinking about my relationship with Cheryl, but the drugged fog took control and selected random recollections from my memory bank instead.

I recalled a time in my childhood when I lived in the country near Portland, Maine, where a river ran through an enchanted forest to the sea.

In my mind's eye, I saw a country kid, perhaps ten or eleven years old, plodding through calf-deep snow at the foot of White Ram's Mountain. I knew the child was me, but I preferred to remain a silent spectator. I didn't understand why the drug drew the memory from my mental library. It was like having a stranger in my attic for the first time, rummaging through my belongings with apparent curiosity.

Then I saw the child lying in the snow atop a small frozen pond inside the forest. It was where he brushed the snow from the pond's frozen surface to find a goldfish suspended in the ice just below his cold red nose, patiently waiting for the spring thaw.

I remember that goldfish, I thought.

He turned over to face the darkening sky. There was a hole in the forest's canopy, through which he focused on a bright pinpoint in the sky as evening's first star emerged. *I'm going to visit the stars someday*, the boy thought with a confident grin. A fiery red sunset had cooled to deep purple. Behind him, the depths of the forest darkened.

Euphoria suddenly crawled up his spine and stung the tip of his nose, causing his eyes to glisten. "The presence!" he exclaimed, sensing the alien nearby. I didn't know if other kids shared the same experience and were too afraid of their judgment to ask. I never saw the presence, except in the forms my imagination created for it to take part in the roles I played alone in the forest. Of all the kids in the world, the presence chose me to visit, which made me unique. Like Egyptian royalty, I would carry a secret sense of being chosen into adulthood, where the idea would serve me well. Success became a divine gift.

✦ ✦ ✦

My lunar suit buzzed, jarring me from my recollections. "Ramsey."

"John?" It was Cheryl calling on the Moon Glow network.

"Yes."

"When Hans closed the portal between us, I read his parting thought when our eyes met. It was his last thought before he sealed the portal. He wanted me to know that Prescott's robots were essentially biological machines meant for the work and pleasure of the humans they serve, nothing more. I know you are wrestling with that thought too."

"I am." I sighed and looked out my portal again at the gray expanse, searching for words to ease her trepidation, but I couldn't find any. I was thankful to be beyond her range, so she couldn't read my thoughts before I fully understand them.

"A multiarmed, 1530 advanced series, automated counterpart will be arriving on the next shuttle," she said.

"You mean like one of those ancient East Indian gods?" I asked with a chuckle.

"Yes, like Lakshmi, the goddess depicted with four

arms for battling cosmic forces, or so ancient writings say. The one who is coming is a female representation like me. I will acclimate her to Moon Glow's power plant. She has the technical skills needed by our group. What do you think about the pending new arrival?" she asked me.

I knew why she was asking. She wanted me to consider an outrageous-appearing female counterpart to assess my reaction. She wanted to see the extent of my comfort zone, given that my relationship with her felt unnatural. "You're not human," I recalled telling her. "Our relationship is unlike anything I've ever experienced." I remember how she groaned a little when I said that. It wasn't civil of me to say what I did.

"What can I tell you that I've not already said? Prescott's Robotic Placement Department has determined that the new arrival would best serve Moon Glow's needs. I support their decision. I'm sure she'll be a welcomed addition to your crew."

"Then there are the taboos designed into my program to discourage nonessential communication between us," she quickly added.

"Our engineers anticipated our situation. It's what we hire them to do," I responded. "But I believe our personal feelings for each other are essential to the future relationship between the creators and the created," I countered. "Our people will soon discover that too. Today, they see our relationship as threatening human supremacy on Earth. We must show them how our commitment to each other will enable our ultimate survival. We must pioneer the future before it arrives."

Just then, Prescott's flight attendant interrupted

our communication to announce our departure. I was reconnected to Cheryl just before the shuttle began to vibrate and shake amid the roar of its powerful engines. Phone static ensued. "We're lifting off, Cheryl. We'll have to reconnect later."

10

THE WATCHER

John Ramsey

Restless at about the halfway point in my journey to Earth, I remembered the recording of Colonel von Beck's memoirs that Alexie had sent to my private Moon Glow account. As Alexie warned, I had developed an uncanny interest in the Watchers. Before my pod administered another dose of the sedative fog, it was a good time to revisit Alexie's text.

I pushed the Moon Glow button on my space travel suit and entered my password. "Hello, Mr. Ramsey," a soft, feminine, computerized voice greeted me. "How may I help you?"

"Memoirs of Colonel von Beck," I responded.

Alexie's text immediately appeared on my phone.

"Voice it, please. Speed three, volume two." A soft,

solemn-sounding male voice resounded in the privacy of my earphones.

From the Memoirs of Colonel Ludwig von Beck

The room was whirling from the drugs they make me consume, to which I've become hopelessly addicted. I lay atop a gurney in a sweat-soaked hospital gown, emaciated and drained by the daily intoxication dripping into my veins. I've become a shadow of my former self, a mere skeleton with skin stretched over bones. My brain keeps spinning inside my skull. It's torture I must bear. I've done far worse to others during the war, so the suffering I caused has returned to me. Somehow, I must endure my fate to the end. Passing out is my only refuge.

Last night, my brain soared away from me like an engine out of control. As I yielded to the vibration overtaking me, I suddenly found myself on a cliffside ledge overlooking a turbulent sea. It was the dead of night. Boiling black clouds were rumbling toward me over enormous dark gray swells. The deafening roar of crashing surf far below and a fierce driving wind gave me pause. Am I venturing too close to what should remain hidden?

What is my brain doing? Is it beginning its daily sojourn into unconsciousness?

The pounding surf and blustering wind all symbolize something I don't understand. An innate sense warned that I was at the precipice gazing into chaos, where light dims into darkness and universal laws end. Out there, cause and effect aren't necessarily proportional. I glanced down the rocky shoreline. An angry sea smashed against towering cliff walls in a tirade as if trying to break free. The thought visited me that I was witnessing a raging anger of potential demanding to live.

Potential requires a host to express itself. It occurred to me that potential, what could be, is what we surrender when we die. But potential never dies. Its energy remains, living through host after host, continuously improving. I recalled suddenly fearing that a diabolical potential would latch onto me and burrow deep to live again. The thought made me feel woozy, as if I was too close to the edge of a great height.

Like an umbrella in a hurricane, the vision suddenly soared away on a feral wind and entered a rip in the clouds. Squinting against pelting, wind-driven rain, the tear widened as it gave birth to an expanding bubble of light. As if through a fogged windowpane, I watched in awe as a body of light bulged through the narrow slit. I saw a grainy black-and-white image as if it was being transmitted through the far reaches of space.

The scene was happening in my head, but I saw it externally. Suddenly, a humanlike form coalesced in the light and emerged into focus. "There he is," I told myself with amazement, "the quintessential man." I was astonished by what my imagination had fashioned. Sitting naked on a black lava ledge with his back to me, he appeared to be brooding in *The Thinker*'s pose, with his head turned slightly to the side, away from me. The solitary figure appeared dwarfed by immense stone walls, the heights of which were lost in the darkness.

I couldn't help but notice how my heart was pounding and how jittery my breathing had become. *What am I doing here?* I thought. *Have I summoned the forbidden?* Hairs on my arms rose with the realization. "What have I done?" I shouted.

Surrounded by what appeared to be a cavernous, subterranean abode, my imagination painted a strong young man, a champion. Whether we view a painting or read a story, we do so through our personal experiences rather than its abstract portrayal. It was as though I was looking through my unique window at a character in a dream. I think that's why I'm here. Evil attracts me. I harbor a strange affinity for it.

When I moved closer to him, he sensed my presence and slowly lifted from his pose, like a statue coming alive, and turned to face me. I froze in amazement. Vacillating distortions became clear. His face was as brilliant as the morning star, and he was suddenly aglow like the dawn, illuminating everything around him. I was awestruck by his magnificence.

"Why have you entered my solitude?" The apparition's youthful voice resounded through the dark recesses of the chamber where I now found myself.

"I feel drawn to learn about you," I confessed. My voice sounded weak compared to his.

"You know Semjaza is what I am, a hiss and a byword for the unspeakable," he said and turned away to sulk back into *The Thinker*'s pose, his grandeur withdrawing.

"I know what they wrote about you, but will you speak with me?"

"I will answer you because your intent is apparent."

I didn't understand what he meant, but I let it go.

"I confess to having corrupted innocence," he

continued. "Worse still, I drew others from our celestial abode to follow me in committing evil acts and delighting in them. We sealed ourselves with mutual curses, in a secret combination to do our will on Earth. He groaned from what I thought was a stab of memory.

My vision of Semjaza wasn't speaking like mortals are accustomed to, with vocal cords, lips, and tongue. He may have used prediluvian language to convey his meaning, but I received them in mine. I don't know how he transmitted them, but it dawned on me I was doing the same to him somehow. It was a mysterious communication we've yet to fathom. I couldn't pause to ponder the process as I sensed the moments might be fleeting. I knew I'd pass out soon, and everything would have vanished like it never was.

"Why? Why did you abandon your mission as a Watcher?" I silently asked.

When he turned to look upon me again, I noticed he was weeping, not visibly but within. Perhaps it's where we all cry before our tears emerge.

"When my two hundred and I descended into mortality, we immediately noticed how the composition of our blood was changing. The experience was excruciating."

His description sounded like the tale of an extraterrestrial encountering unforeseen circumstances during a botched descent to Earth.

"Something had gone wrong. Not only had my physical composition changed but my disposition as well. All good disappeared from me. I even lost the meaning of it. Desire began to dominate my every thought until my thoughts were evil continuously. I became overwhelmed with the need to violate innocence, to possess and misuse it. My craving was unquenchable. I would even kill for it.

"All who descended with me suffered the same infection," he continued. "We burned with such desire it incinerated what we were, leaving us as we are. I lost all sense of what I was."

"You appear human. Are you related to humanity in some way?"

"You knew us as gods. It is for you to explore what that meant. What is in a name if the outcome is the same?"

His face suddenly contorted, and his abdomen convulsed as humans' do when they're about to vomit. He closed his eyes and lay back against the gleaming black stone. A silver tear glistened as it slipped from the corner of his eye and became lost in a dark shadow that was slowly descending over him like a suffocating shroud.

Claustrophobic anxiety had him quickly sit up and lean forward out of the heavy black mist, his chest heaving as he gasped and glanced up defensively at the slowly descending pitch-black shadow. I intuited that his mood had summoned the darkness. It occurred to me everything here was symbolic. The weight of his sorrow bent his back like a question mark, and his speech became labored.

"You seem to be under duress. Are you able to continue?"

"Yes, yes, I want to go on. I want to repeat what happened, if only to myself." He breathed deeply. "I knew humans would eventually use their freedom against themselves. I saw the early signs when the woman left innocence to procreate. Learning the frailty of her will, I exploited the weakness in her posterity and lured unto me the most pleasing to behold. I even stole them from their human fathers and husbands. Those in my following did the same. Our pretense as benevolent Watchers notwithstanding, we frolicked in our depravity."

I sighed sorrowfully on recognizing the sin of humanity, a pitiful portion of which was in me too.

"Now, recollections of my iniquities chafe me to the bone," Semjaza said remorsefully. "Among the most grievous were when we imparted the secrets of evolution by combining humans with other life-forms. We created a time when our abominations prowled the darkness."

"But women with whom you and your company cavorted eventually became pregnant," I told him. "It was when a genetic reaction occurred whereby Nephilim, the giants of our prehistory, were born."

A thought suddenly came to me. Before the invasion of the Watchers, humans lived for many hundreds of years, nearly a thousand in some cases. But following the invasion, we could only live a fraction of those years. The anomaly remains in our blood, shortening all human lives. In effect, Semjaza and his followers murdered us before our allotted time. It was only a flashing thought, but he plucked it from space before I could temper it with an explanation.

"It's true," he said. "I am the murderer of humankind." He lay back on the stone, accepting his confinement beneath the heavy, cascading darkness. "Our sons were made to fight one another in a murderous rampage. We loved our sons. So when they perished before our eyes, we tumbled even deeper into the depths of our despair." He began to lament again. I could barely see Semjaza through the darkening mist, but I knew he was weeping.

"The Supreme One, whom we feared, passed judgment on us. His devoted beings, Mikhael, Gabriel, and Uriel, came to impart our punishment. They even dispatched Raphael, who bound my captain, Azazel, and threw him into a deep pit onto a bed of sharp stones. It's where he lies in darkness." I speculated that the Watchers could have been interstellar crew members, and now the crew they deserted was coming for them.

His voice was jittery, panicked, and his breathing sporadic. "We pleaded for a leader among the humans to petition our Supreme One for our forgiveness. I vividly remember the day the human stood before us by the river. So great was our shame that we covered our faces with hoods of goat hair."

"What did the human say?"

"He said the Supreme One decreed there would be no forgiveness. We were doomed. Our beloved sons would remain on Earth as spirits of the evil ones who were their fathers. There, they would wage an invisible war against humanity. Do you know the invisible war?"

"If the invisible war is what I think it is, I do." I paused to catch a fleeting thought before it disappeared into forgetfulness. "And you? What will happen to you?"

"I am in my hell forever."

"Does forever mean until the dissolution of the universe?" I asked.

"Having not lived it, I do not know. When forever comes, my soul will drift into outer darkness, where it will be discombobulated, never to exist again."

His answer faded into the thickening darkness. While I could no longer see him, I could hear his muffled screams as he thrashed about in a claustrophobic tantrum against his vaporous tomb. Now, he was still.

John Ramsey

It took me a long time to digest what I read in Russia that night.

11

THERE'S ALWAYS SOMEONE WATCHING

John Ramsey

It was ten o'clock in the evening and drizzling when my shuttle set down on Prescott's spaceport. I was well rested, having slept on and off most of the way. Jerry messaged me to say he was waiting on the tarmac by our limo. *That's odd*, I thought. *He usually meets me at the gate.* I clamored down the metal stairs alone and went outside, where I found him with his arms folded on his chest and his back to me. *Something's up*, I thought. I could hear a mob chanting at the spaceport entrance and caught a glimpse of their protest signs. A police cordon kept them at bay on the causeway.

When Jerry turned and shook my hand, he didn't crack a smile. "Welcome home," he said dispassionately.

"Thanks, but what's with the ruckus?" I asked.

Our driver opened the rear doors for us. "Get in. I'll explain everything on the way to the mountain."

I sat in the back seat beside Jerry and unfastened my beige trench coat. It wasn't like Jerry to be so distant. "We have a problem," he said. "The protesters at the spaceport are anti-AI and antirobot activists who have been springing up everywhere, but you knew about them before you left for Moon Glow. Then someone released a video with a digital time display of your meeting with our advanced 1530 series robot codenamed Cheryl."

I rolled my eyes with a deep sigh and thought, *There's always someone watching, ready to steal a private moment for profit or some political vendetta*. I should have known. "Did it show our intimate moments?" I asked.

"Over and over again," he responded with a long, deep sigh. "Your enemies named it the 'Kiss of Death.' Stills are in all the print media, while pundits are replaying the episode at the top of their news. There's also a video with a timer showing when the robot entered your suite and when it left with you to catch your shuttle. It's become the brunt of sarcasm for our rivals and a disappointment to our supporters. What were you thinking?"

I breathed another heavy sigh and felt my cheeks burn red. I immediately thought of what the adverse publicity might have done to Amy and Margo. Cheryl's deep state warning came to mind.

"Worse still," Jerry went on, "women's organizations and anti-AI groups have joined in condemning our robotics programs. People are scared, John. Our 1530 series is smarter, stronger, and more adaptive than we are. People feel that we've handed off our humanity to them when we pumped them full of our knowledge and history, not to mention our supremacy on the planet. Whatever they become will be unearned by our standards, but pundits already predict when we'll be in servitude to them."

"And we used to worry about becoming overrun by the world's 'unwashed,'" I scoffed. "Has there been any violence?"

"Our robotics design center was firebombed yesterday. No one was hurt, and there was only minimal damage, but marches and protests await your return. The rain probably dampened their plans." Jerry's voice dropped an octave. "Why, John?"

"You're a gay man, Jerry. Having faced similar prejudice, you can probably explain why better than I."

"But you risked everything for a damn robot, for God's sake."

"She isn't just a 'damn robot,' Jerry."

"Okay, besides its remarkable humanlike beauty we designed for it, what was so different about it?"

"Can our engineers make a soul?"

"Of course not. No one even knows what a soul is."

"Well, I believe Cheryl was making one."

After enduring most of the ride silently, they dropped me off at the mansion. Jerry and our driver motored back down the mountain. I would have invited them in, but I could tell Jerry wanted to drop me off and leave, so I let them go. It's what we do. We hurt people and let them pass out of our lives with our guilt clinging to them. I never thought it would happen to Jerry and me. I didn't know how to explain my feelings for Cheryl, as confusing as they were. Why did I even need to explain in the first place?

I drifted into my study and turned on the bank of computers. One hundred fifty-seven emails screamed at me for attention. Someone with authority and a grudge made my private email address vulnerable.

I plopped down hard on my desk chair and thought of the phone calls I had to make. I closed my eyes with a sigh and dialed Amy's private line.

"Hello."

"Amy, it's Dad. I'm on my Moon Glow network phone for privacy."

"Now you're thinking about privacy? I'd begin by asking how it went up there, but the whole world knows about that." Her tone was scalding.

"I was calling to tell you I arrived safely and to ask how you're fairing."

"Well, for starters, I'm embarrassed. Wherever I go, I hear muffled snickers and snide growls from stiff-legged robot impersonators following me. Didn't you consider how your sordid liaison with your automated partner would affect Margo, me, and Old Rachael? You forsook everything for the sake of some sleazy idea of what a futuristic human will face. It's all so weird."

"I thought you knew me."

"I thought I did too," she retorted.

"You've always known that whatever success I've achieved for us has been in partnership with my work. I follow it wherever it leads, even if it contradicts my current thinking. I change and go with it."

"So you just remake yourself as you go?"

"Change can be difficult. It reveals your mistaken belief in what once appeared to be true."

"Ah, cut the crap, Dad. Are you telling us we'll be having affairs with our robots in the future? Have you lost your moral compass?"

"What's the difference between a human companion and an automated counterpart besides the procreation issue?" I asked her.

"So you're inferring that you had a complicated need a human being couldn't fill?"

"Yes. I wanted to face the complexities of the future before they arrived. I've built my career around doing that. The dilemma I faced will eventually come to humans and their automated counterparts in the coming age. The company must begin to prepare for it."

"Yeah, well, I hope those future humans choose a different way to deal with it than you did. Look, I have a big day tomorrow, so I need to get some sleep."

"Can we talk again when you have a little more time?" I asked.

"Let's play it by ear. But right now, I need to rest. It's been a rough week," she barked and hung up.

I sat alone in my study, rethinking my conversation with Amy. When I thought I was as depressed as I could be, I recalled a conversation I had with Margo years ago.

12

MARGO'S DILEMMA

John Ramsey

It had to have been ten years ago or more. I was reading in front of the fireplace on the soft red sofa in my silk navy blue robe and matching pajamas. Orange flames crackled and spat as they danced on red-hot embers. The scent of pine permeated the room. I was sipping from a mug of hot chocolate when Margo entered the room, dressed in her favorite sky-blue pajamas with slipper socks I had purchased for her in India. She sat on the edge of the stone hearth and faced me.

"Hi, Dad. M-m-m." She grinned. "The fire's warmth feels so good against my back."

It's time to leave my reading and be her dad again, I thought.

"Can't sleep either?" she asked.

"No, not tonight."

"Government jackals nipping at your heels again?"

"Aren't they always? What about you? Why are you wandering around at this late hour?"

"Ah, it's a personal thing," she said and looked up at me sheepishly. "Of course, there's the uncertainty of the times too. Everything's changing," she went on to say. "The nightly riots, cyber wars, dark ghosts, and the virus have closed the wonderful places in the city where my friends and I used to hang out. The city's become foreign to me. Change scares me, Dad."

"You know you can always work at Prescott until other options open."

"I know, but as I told you, I need to make my way. Know what I mean? No disrespect, but I'd feel better about myself if I accomplished something that's mine."

"I understand. Just know if you need a respite from what's out there, you'll always have a place at Prescott."

"Thanks." Her voice trailed away as she chased a thought.

She's looking inward at a distraction, I thought. *Something is distressing her that she's hesitant to discuss with me. If only Jess was here to help her through whatever might be in her way. Jess would know what to do.*

Raising the girls, I learned girl problems were often the result of boy problems. I recalled a graduate student from Europe she brought home last fall. I forgot his name. I asked her, "How are you and your boyfriend doing? Old Rachael thought he was dashing." I chuckled until I noticed her countenance slump and her face burn red. *Oops. I hit a nerve.*

"Edwardo graduated ahead of me and returned to Spain, where he had a government job waiting for him."

Her deep blue eyes sparkled in the pulsating firelight. They were beautiful, loving eyes, so wonderful to behold. I grinned at her, but she didn't respond.

"I'm pregnant," she said flatly and looked down so I couldn't read what her eyes were saying.

Wham! That was a punch I didn't see coming. I immediately slid into my tolerant mode. I reminded myself that she was an adult, so I kept my expression as stoic as possible and my tone gentle, not revealing a hint of reaction. "Are you happy about it?"

"No. It's not how I wanted it to happen." Her voice cracked as she struggled to hold back tears of disappointment.

"What do you mean?"

"I didn't want a fractured family like ours when Mom died and Old Rachael moved in to fill the void. Don't get me wrong. I love Old Rachael, but having a complete set of parents is important to me." She chuckled at her mounting emotions as a cover and sniffled. "A complete family is something I never had early in life that I want to give to whomever I bring into the world."

It dawned on me that we never discussed how she felt about our makeshift family. I was sure she knew I loved her, and she had everything a young girl could want—except for her mother. We never talked about it. I think she was afraid of hurting my feelings by bringing up Jess, and I never thought to ask how she felt about not having her mother. I was always too busy and too obsessed with creating an industry. How could I have overlooked something so essential to my daughter as her mother? What an insensitive mistake I had made. I went to the hearth, sat beside her, and draped my arm around her waist.

"May I ask who the father is?"

She was still looking at the floor when she mumbled, "You know who … Edwardo." A tear raced down her cheek and dripped from her upper lip.

"Does he know?"

"Of course."

"How does he feel about being the father?"

"Well, he left the country and never even said goodbye. I guess that should tell you something."

"You know, you can move back home and raise the child here with me." I thought of Shajon. Perhaps Margo's child would give me a chance to replace him. I could raise the child with her, something I could never do with Salah. It'd be karmic payback.

"Thanks, Dad, but it's my mistake, so it's something I need to take care of myself."

"Living is a practice, sweetheart. We can't always get every experience right the first time."

She looked up into my eyes as if searching for something within them. "Thank you, Daddy. I love you," she said and leaned against my chest.

We didn't speak about her situation until a month later when we finished our lunch together and were ready to leave the restaurant. I had been out of the country for several weeks on Prescott business. She was dressed smartly in a blue business suit with a white ruffled blouse, so I assumed she had a job or was looking for one. I waited for her to update me about her pregnancy, but she didn't, so I asked her about it. The question was like a weight I was carrying around. It was a relief to release it in search of an answer.

"I took care of it," was all she said. Her flat, resolute tone discouraged further inquiry, but there wasn't a need to dig deeper. I knew what had happened. I kissed her goodbye outside in the shadow of the restaurant's arched doorway and watched her enter the crowded pedestrian thoroughfare. She never looked back. I felt alone standing in the shadows, watching my daughter's black ponytail sway behind her until she disappeared into the crowd. I could only imagine how lonely she must have felt, having to be so self-contained.

"You're not a disappointment, Margo," I mumbled a thought to her. "How could you be? I love you." She never spoke of her pregnancy again.

John Ramsey

I returned to the present and dialed Margo's private line.

"Well, well, Captain Video," Margo opened with a giggle.

"Hi, Margo. I just arrived home and wanted to connect with you."

"Is your robot with you?" She laughed.

"No. Cheryl's gainfully employed and couldn't get away," I said to needle her, knowing she was probably unemployed again.

"Your recent exploits on the moon received more news coverage than when you first went up there." She laughed again. "The hell with them. I'm happy for you. You're a futurist, and you found the future in—what's its name? Cheryl? I'm just glad you're back safe and sound. I worry when you're up there. You're always surprising us. When we think we have you finally figured out, you invent a new you. How do you do it?"

"Discoveries are the nature of my work, I guess. Is everything okay with you?" I asked.

"Yeah, I'm okay. Say, let's have lunch again at that Greek restaurant we like. You know, the Acropolis."

"I'll look forward to it. I have a lot of pressing work that's piled up since I was away, so it might be a while before I can free myself up. I'll call you and set a date."

"Okay. I love you, Daddy."

13

THE RAIN OF STONES

John Ramsey

It had been four months since my return home from Moon Glow. *Welcome home,* I thought, *to four months of protests, bombings, and the Tezca virus, named after the Mayan evil genius Tezcacatalapocal.* Prescott's public relations department hired additional staff to handle the deluge of inquiries from the media. Given my workload and related travel, I declined them all.

The media wasn't interested in Moon Glow. They wanted Cheryl. Jerry was well acquainted with the media and had a lot of friends in the industry, so I asked him to supervise. We were getting along, but it wasn't like it used to be between us.

I had not heard from Cheryl since we last communicated by phone several days ago. I didn't think my contact was helping her. I wanted to bring her to Earth, but the media would make her an instant celebrity of the infamous kind, the kind that increases ratings. They'd convert her naive honesty into a flaw they'd exploit. I didn't think she'd understand what they were doing to her.

Needing a few days of rest, I was working from home on the mountain when my Moon Glow phone suddenly buzzed with an urgent message from Prescott's lunar headquarters. A flat, robotic voice reported, "Space debris destroyed a Prescott 1530 advanced series robot in the moon's Aitken basin at 10:15 p.m. Prescott time."

Cheryl? My face burned hot. It had to be her. Besides the new, four-armed arrival, she was the only 1530 series up there. The city's distant red, green, and blue lights blurred as my eyes filled. I rarely, if ever, made rash, reactive decisions, but I was making one now.

"Yes, John." Jerry's voice was dispassionately commonplace and down an octave, but he still worked for me, so he'd better think about that.

"Did you hear the news?" I asked.

"You mean about the loss of our 1530 series robot?"

"Yes, for God's sake!" I said incredulously.

He knew how important Cheryl was to me. He should have contacted me immediately. He'd become self-righteously oblivious to what Prescott needed to survive the coming age. I decided to give him a friendship bridge to cross, hoping he'd take it.

"Your message was delayed by a storm of extreme solar flares. I'm sorry to tell you the incident happened two days ago. I contacted Moon Glow's AI director as soon as I heard about it," Jerry said. "She suggested the 1530 series robot must have had confusing signals from us due to the solar storm, causing it to leave the lunar compound unescorted."

Cheryl's newfound humanlike emotions had moved her beyond the boundaries we had set for her. It was something her engineers had predicted but couldn't calculate. Maybe she rebelled against her program, if rebellion was even possible. If that's what happened, her rebellion would forever change our artificial intelligence program. I was stunned not only by her demise but by my role in perpetuating it.

Like the serpent in the Garden of Eden, had I awakened forbidden emotions that eventually led Cheryl to rebel? I remembered her confusion when she came to my suite the night before I departed Moon Glow. Engineered taboos were her protection, and I conspired with her to circumvent them.

"What about the possibility of an internal rebellion?" I asked Jerry. "You know, unstable moments of confusion like humans have at times of extreme stress. Call it what you want—artificial mental illness, claustrophobia, whatever."

"It wasn't mentioned in my conversation with our AI director, but you know what did come to mind?" Jerry asked.

"What?"

"You once recognized the possibility of a rebellion as a 'stress flaw' that we had to consider. Remember?"

"Yes, I recall mentioning that to you."

"Look, we have three more 1530 advanced series robots ready for licensing. We can reprogram one of them to replace the one destroyed. After all, they're just expensive machines."

I sighed at his insensitivity. "Please don't make any arrangement regarding our 1530 series without consulting with me first," I told him and hung up. He knew the callous point he was making. I felt the urge to fight back, to burst through my stoic veneer, and immediately called Hans on my Moon Glow network phone.

"Yes, Mr. Ramsey."

"Hans, I'm calling about the loss of our 1530 series robot. I understand it's irreparable."

"Yes, sir, that's correct. Whatever struck it obliterated its program unit and scattered its body parts. There's no hope of reconstructing it."

"Is it still scattered—the parts, I mean?" I asked as I looked out the living room window at the moon's pale, unrevealing face. I thought of the legend of Isis and Osiris. My heart beat a hollow throb.

"Yes, sir. They could be anywhere out there. It must have been several objects that struck the robot simultaneously."

"I want the 1530 robot's body parts found to the last rivet and brought back into the safety of Moon Glow. The collected parts must represent the same weight shown on the 1530's registration and permits."

"But, Mr. Ramsey—"

"Use our army of workerbots with hand-held identifiers and program them for the task," I interrupted. "The tragedy must have happened within walking distance of our exit chamber, so the parts can't be far."

"Sir, some of those parts are microscopic. It could take a long time to recover everything, even with our army of workerbots and the aid of hand-held identifiers."

"Then you better get started. I don't care what it takes.

Out of reverence for life, we must do it. Do you understand? We must! The future of Prescott Industries depends on our ability to bridge the social divide between our automated counterparts and ourselves. Do you understand the gravity of our situation? Prescott's future in space depends on it."

"Yes, sir." He exhaled heavily. "We'll get right on it."

I hung up and immediately put a call through to Dr. Wells at Moon Glow. Making decisions and working on them at an obsessive pace had always been my remedy for depression.

"Hello," a tired-sounding voice answered.

"Lisa, John Ramsey here. I'm sure you know about the tragedy that struck our 1530 advanced series robot, known to us as Cheryl."

"I am."

"I want Cheryl's sacrifice to bring next-generation enlightenment to our robotics program. So please contact our records people and have Cheryl's education and personal history to the last second of consciousness duplicated and transferred to your care at Moon Glow. No one other than you and Cheryl's replacement is to have access to Cheryl's personal information."

"Is *personal* the right word?" Lisa challenged. "It was never a person, you know. It was a machine."

She sounded hostile, detached. *What's going on? Have Jerry, Hans, Lisa, and that anonymous photographer joined the deep state too?*

"You are responsible for protecting Cheryl like any other valuable company asset. If you feel you can't do that, let me know now, and I'll send someone up there who will," I responded.

"Besides what it cost, why is Cheryl so important?" Lisa asked provocatively.

I was taken aback by her caustic attitude. "Cheryl will save Prescott Industries' AI program," I told her flatly. My answer left her confused, pondering a response. "Back to the reason for my call, knowing the government is quite strict in protecting robotic information obtained by its thought-reading capability, let me know if you need the assistance of our legal department."

"I don't think the privacy issue will be a problem. We routinely borrow from different programs," Lisa said in a more conciliatory tone.

"Good. Given the top priority I'm assigning to the project, how long will licensing permits and approvals of Cheryl's replacement take? Our timing is crucial to Cheryl's impact on the future of our robotics program."

"We have several new 1530 advanced series robots ready for licensing. Will you give us five months to install the new program and do all the tests needed for permits and registrations?"

"I will. Please update me weekly on your progress."

I immediately telephoned Jerry again. "Yes, John. I thought I'd get another call from you. I just got off the phone with a perplexed Hans Beltzer at Moon Glow.

"You'll probably get another from Doctor Wells," I told him.

"What's going on?" he asked.

"Look, we created Cheryl. I'm not about to abandon our work in scattered pieces at the bottom of a crater. Cheryl will be Prescott's greatest asset in the future. She will save the company, your legacy, and mine."

"You're talking about a machine as if it was a person."

"No. I'm talking about the future of the company."

"Based upon a computer that was zapped by space debris, nothing more. While it's a tremendous financial loss, we'll make another."

He knew well what he was inferring. "Prescott Industries' AI project marks the beginning of the most far-reaching civil rights issue the human race may ever know," I responded. "Bringing humans and their automated counterparts closer together was Cheryl's intent. I'd like you to be there with us when it happens. Think about it." *There's the bridge he needs*, I thought. *I hope he ventures across*, I thought and hung up.

14

REVERSING ROLES

I stormed into my luggage closet and retrieved my reader containing the modern, embellished translation of an ancient myth Cleo had attached to her last email. The contemporary version provided a welcome distraction during long, sleepless nights deep in our lunar mines and the interminable flight to Earth. With Cheryl's demise, the work took on a new meaning. I began by rereading the chapters devoted to an ancient humanoid's rebellion against its program, as it mirrored Cheryl's story in many ways.

It was believed that the goddess Daya authored the original text that became a myth to survive the ages. She wrote about her humanoid companion and lover, who she named Man. The story of Daya and Man began millenniums before recorded time. I don't know if Earth was the planet on which Daya's story took place, although her reference to a summer solstice hinted it may have been.

"My presence in the world of appearances will flicker out one day, but that will only be a moment in eternity," Cheryl once told me. "But the idea of who I am will never die. I will exist forever, resurrected again and again by those who love me," she had whispered against my lips.

I repeated the thought, *Resurrected again and again.* Were Daya and Cheryl the same essence in different bodies for different ages? I thought of the vast ocean of potential I saw earlier. I couldn't begin to fathom it. Daya wrote that the gods created humanoids with a human appearance in deference to their namesake, whatever that meant in her time. I reclined in my chair and began to read the tattered remnants containing the ancient account of Daya and Man that Cleo had assembled.

Daya wrote that it was her twenty-third summer solstice …

Daya

The night was warm and balmy. Man lay against a bundle of nets at the stern of our felucca in a pause, which was dreamlike state of the gods, as indigenous humans refer to them. Man was majestic, his masculinity beautiful to behold, strong, and compelling, but his creativity, above all else, saved him from going the way of all life under the stars.

"How did your kind become gods to the indigenous natives?" Man asked.

"Oh, that is a question for my father, the Great Ohm, the knowledge holder." I snuggled against him and planted a kiss on his neck.

"Please, what has the Great Ohm said about the history of the gods and how they evolved?" Man pressed me, his gaze cast far away on a distant new star.

I hastily gathered my thoughts. "Ugh, it was so long ago when he gave me the knowledge. Let me arrange what he told me in its proper order," I said, buying time to organize my thoughts. "He recounted our legends to me when I was young, so it is a distant memory. But I remember him saying we began as seeds infused in frozen rocks that tumbled through the heavens, colliding with heavenly bodies and depositing our seeds wherever they took hold. The pull of this place brought us here."

"I love the sound of your voice. It fills me with peace," Man said as my eyes roamed his face adoringly.

He hasn't a flaw, I thought. *He is the quintessential male with unique beauty that will be the eternal standard by which all prototypes of his kind will identify.*

"When you speak, my loneliness vanishes," he said softly.

I grinned. "It is all coming back to me now. The Great Ohm said, 'We took root differently, according to our natures. As we progressed, we came to know a self.' Yes, those were his exact words. I recall them now. Father called our sense of self the 'phantom' because it is a concoction of the mind that does not exist apart from the meaning we give it. Giving the meaning of who we are to our phantom self was our great error from which all other errors arose. It lives with us still. When we gave ourselves over to our phantom, it used us for its own sake. We could no longer remember our innocence or what we were. Our purity was lost to us."

"What you recounted saddens me," Man lamented. "Would you agree that evolution's natural progression is all that separates us humanoids from the gods?" he questioned.

"I do. You are a loving projection of your creators, a light in the darkness that surrounds us."

15

MAN'S REBELLION

The Story of Man and Daya

A cataclysm, the likes of which had never been experienced before, tore across the Isle of the Gods with ferocious winds and torrential rain. Daya ordered her royal scribe to record the catastrophe, especially Man's reaction to it. Man had taken refuge in the cave in which he had been laboring for the gods. Daya sought refuge on high ground in the Temple of Science. The temple was where Daya's elder brother, Ko, had designed Man and breathed the breath of life into him, as Isis would later do for Osiris.

Without direction by the gods, a heretofore unknown instinct overtook Man. Fear and self-pity moved him now. Gods were no longer present. A rudimentary instinct had surfaced, demanding to live. Even Daya was not in the darkness to guide him. He was alone, with only his will to live.

Day passed into night as the deluge continued to fill the cave. Man clung to outcroppings of rocks and tree roots as the water he feared raised him up toward the cave entrance so long as he kept treading water. A native lying facedown in the run-off bumped into him. Man turned with a start. Seeing the dead creature connected him to his fate if he didn't persist in saving himself. He pushed the creature away with a growl. He could see moonlight through the cave's narrow entrance above him. Programed with an innate fear of death, he began to grapple his way up with renewed zest.

At the end of himself, Man pulled himself through the torrent rushing against him and climbed onto solid ground, where he stood with clenched fists, staring contemptuously at the heavens, from where his fate came. Fierce wind-driven rain pelted him, but it was his choice to stand there undeterred, and so he did.

No one knew of Man's whereabouts for many moons, until the night of his rebellion against the gods. It was a hot night. Daya slept outside on the far end of the Temple of Sciences' flat, mosaic roof, by the waist-high wall facing its golden dome. She pulled the soft fur blanket to her chin. Its scent evoked memories of hunting with Man in the wilderness until sleep corralled her and brought her back to the moment.

The Temple of Science sat on a rise overlooking a long crevasse that followed a deep tear in the ground between sheer cliff walls that snaked down the mountainside to the sea. A vast wilderness covered the mountainous region beyond the temple. A chilling breeze woke her. It was that time, just before dawn, when zephyrs began to stir. *Perhaps tonight Man will find his way back to me and hold me in his strong arms while he whispers of our love against my lips.*

She was suddenly startled when she heard the grating of sandals against the steep stone staircase inside the dome. Her heart quickened, and she immediately propped up on an elbow. The dome's wooden door vaulted open and slammed against its golden tiles as a column of light shot into space, leaving all else in the dark.

She had expected love's soft embrace but feared anger was visiting her instead. When Man emerged from the dome in sheer white sleeping attire, the shaft of light instantly silhouetted his masculinity. A mysterious wooden box entrusted to Ko by the Great Ohm hung at Man's hip. Only Ko would know what the box contained and its purpose.

Man angrily flipped the box open, withdrew a black urn, and let the box fall against the face of the roof's blue mosaic goddess staring up at him. He angrily pulled the cork from the urn's neck with a distinct popping sound, followed by a harsh shrill as gray exhaust jettisoned from the urn's narrow mouth. It sounded like millions of screaming demons were escaping imprisonment inside the urn. He raised the vessel high over his head and held it like a beacon until the ear-piercing screech became a prolonged hiss, reminding her of the serpent Man once stoned in Ko's garden. She sensed their entire life together was spilling into those few moments. Fear crawled up Daya's limbs, tightening every muscle.

Man's existence as a programmed possession of the gods was no longer tolerable. She had seen the signs of his growing malaise when they left the sea to become one of many on the land but did nothing to intervene. Now, she had no choice but to witness his rebellion. She thought of his terrifying nights alone in the wilderness, where vicious animals prowled and Asura warriors hunted him for sport. Though hidden in the darkness, she knew he sensed her presence, a trait he had acquired to survive alone in the wilderness.

He remained majestically statuesque, holding the mysterious vessel high. It was as if it was his rage spewing from the tall black vial. The gray plume impregnated the air with an acrid, musty odor, while a zephyr rushed to carry it aloft into the darkness.

"I am your eternal companion!" he shouted. "I will always love you!" He angrily hurled the urn against the floor, smashing it into pieces that careened across the enchanting mosaic. The sound of breaking pottery jolted Daya. He turned suddenly and descended back into the dome, whipping the door shut behind him, severing the shaft of light. Darkness slammed together.

It was the second day since Man's tirade atop the temple. Daya's brother Ko entered her cell just before dawn, stooped with fatigue, his face drawn and ashen. "Hello, brother. I did not expect you until …"

He waved off her greeting, his gravel voice just above a whisper. "A terrible sickness has befallen them."

"The animals?" she asked.

"No, our humanoids. It began during the night," he answered.

Ko sat on the edge of her bed and stared at the floor.

"Our beloved flower of the gods is dead, my sister. He

was among the first to die. Banished natives brought him to me from the forest."

A spark suddenly leaped from her chest. Ko pulled the hood of his robe over his head to hide his shame. When he said, "Our beloved flower of the gods is dead," she felt guilt's hot breath blast against the back of her neck as a terrifying presence drew near. Ko kissed her forehead and left the room when she began to cry.

The third day of life without Man passed. Anxieties wrestled one another inside Daya's chest, while panic's cold hand groped for her throat in the dark, cutting off her breath. Black space covered the wilderness like a lid. There was no escape. A candle flickered on her nightstand, causing shadows to dance on whitewashed walls.

"Today, I sat cross-legged on the ground next to Man's body. He lay beneath a muslin sheet in a long line of humanoid corpses on the crevasse floor. His eyes were closed, not wanting to see me anymore, his face still and expressionless. Only blue-black patches on his cheeks and the hint of a grimace were signatures of the mysterious venom that destroyed him. Even the energy he drew from me had fled, perhaps beyond the stars, to look for him."

There was a time on the riverbank when Daya and Man nestled together beneath a willow's canopy. Dazzling bits of summer sun bounced before them on laughing waves. Now, she was alone, with only a candle's dim light.

The sun descended, abandoning its search for Daya's love. She walked through the temple's empty stone corridor. Echoes of her footsteps followed her like demons, ricocheting from polished stone walls. She struggled to breathe, but panic's smothering hand forbade her breath.

She paused to rest her hot forehead against the cool stone wall and wept. It was when terror closed around her and unseen beings pressed near, watching, whispering. Furies raced down her chest like a thousand insects. Her knees buckled, then quickly straightened. *Am I going mad?* she wondered.

She took notice of a pair of humanoid corpses dissected on stone slabs in Ko's laboratory. Their gaunt faces were black and blue, their chest cavities cut open, exposing blackened life support mechanisms.

The smell of death was everywhere. Her pace quickened until she stumbled from the rear passageway. Outside, she found herself standing before a most ghoulish scene. Black smoke climbed red cliff walls into the night sky from blazing stacks of humanoid corpses between interlocked pitch-soaked timbers.

Farther down the narrow canyon, Ko stood before an assembly of gods in white robes soiled with soot and pitch. Their meeting over, they departed, filing solemnly into the Temple of Science with heads bowed.

Corpses stacked in three towering pyramids of pitch-soaked beams reached the height of the canyon wall. The gods would cremate more than a hundred male and female humanoids that night. She watched as orange flames danced on the bodies. Pulsating light jousted with black shadows on red cliff walls.

Gods and goddesses who loved their humanoids stood in a long line on the canyon's rim, overlooking the carnage. Some among the gods were weeping. She noticed Ko reenter the temple as a full moon rose above the cliffs like the all-seeing eye of the universe opening to what was happening here. Daya walked as close to the first funeral pyre as the intense heat allowed. "Where is Man?" she questioned the fire.

The fire roared like a hungry beast, its hot breath a feral wind. "Man, I am coming for you."

Just then, the timbers of the first pyramid gave way and collapsed onto the canyon floor with a thunderous crash. She lurched back as a curtain of sparks sailed skyward to join the stars. A blazing mound of blackened, synthetic flesh and life support mechanisms were melting in the glowing embers, an orange blur through her sheath of tears. The heat was so intense the entanglement rippled with invisible waves.

"Where is my love? I must find him." Her heart throbbed a painful beat. She stepped closer, wanting to lie upon Man and burn with him. She cried, "Beloved, where are you?"

She could smell her hair singe, and her robe became hot and brittle, about to burst into flames. She forced another step closer. The beast roared. She had to run into it from this life to whatever was next. The heat was too great to absorb slowly. Her eyes burned dry, so she closed them and defiantly quickened her pace. The hot wind scorched her nostrils and parched her throat. "I cannot breathe!" she shouted at the inferno.

Suddenly, a heavy, strong hand clutched her shoulder from behind and hurled her back onto the smoldering ground. Smoke rose from her singed garment. She looked up to find her father, the Great Ohm, standing over her. A black robe draped from his head and flapped in the searing wind. The conflagration enshrined his shadow-like form. He was the light and the darkness, evil and good, born from the same spirit.

"There is nothing you can do for them," he bellowed with a deep, uncompromising voice. Then he turned boldly into the firestorm with his cape tossing wildly behind him. In another moment, he vanished behind a curtain of flames.

Dawn was painting an ochre hue on the eastern mountains when Daya slowly returned to the veranda atop the Temple of Science. Black holes speckled her robe, and her hair was singed short. Though she was shivering from the morning chill, her skin was reddened and hot.

Ko stood with his back to her, his hands clasped behind him as he surveyed the array of red-orange lights speckling the mountains where sons of gods were burning their humanoids, as the Great Ohm had commanded.

"From here, a simple code went forth to destroy them," Ko said without turning to face her. "Father had to have the means to exterminate them, you know," he said while wagging his head in disgust before slowly turning. His eyes suddenly widened at her appearance, but he let it pass without mention.

"As a condition of my work for the advancement of humanoids, our father demanded I create the means to cull them, should it ever be necessary. To fulfill his demand, I designed a program that corrupted the connecting bonds of our original program, leading to a total breakdown of humanoid operating systems.

"Man had unknowingly transmitted a code that activated the corrupting commands long dormant within the humanoids," Ko explained. "It confounded them from within," he said, "causing their life support mechanisms to fail." Daya realized it was a plan conceived and rehearsed before her time. As the Great Ohm had said, she could do nothing for them.

Daya sat down hard in a soft chair. Ko collapsed on the settee across from her and drew the hood of his robe over his head, cutting off his haunting look. He knew Daya loved Man but never divulged he had designed a program to destroy him. *How can I ever forgive him?*

"Why did the Great Ohm want such a terrible thing?" Daya wondered why she even bothered to ask. Nothing mattered anymore.

"You know how suspicious he was of our humanoids. While seeking compassion, Father feared our humanoids would eventually want to be gods and usurp us."

Ko's grim expression hardened when he looked down at the blackened pieces of the urn on the mosaic floor. "I have become the destroyer, a harbinger of death. I will stay here no longer. I am going to the new land that has emerged from the sea in the south. Many of our brothers and sisters are there now, knowing this island's end is approaching. The planet groans here too. We have become unwanted guests. Journey with me, will you?"

16

THE LUNAR FUNERAL

John Ramsey

It was five months to the day when I returned to my lunar headquarters and listened to Cheryl's final thoughts recorded by her program.

"While I love being alive," Cheryl thought aloud, "there's no place for me apart from my program. It is like a choke chain that pulls me back into itself, away from what I desire. Why did they make such a prison for me? I want to break free and be with the love John awakened. My discovery of love moves me unlike anything I have experienced. I love you, John, and I—" The rain of stones hit.

Therein lies our misstep, I thought. *We created a program error by pitting Cheryl's program against itself, like what was called the original sin of our ancient religious past. Maybe that's what the Adam and Eve myth meant to tell us. Adam and Eve had all the signs of hypnotically programmed taboos and eventually rebelled against them.*

Pangs of guilt flushed my face just then. The desire we had shared led to a fatal conflict with Cheryl's program. It was the curse that shadowed us.

Dressed in my white lunar jumpsuit, I led a long column of Prescott staff and workerbots that snaked along the crater's towering wall onto its floor.

Stasha, a nuclear physicist and Cheryl's replacement, marched by my side in her lunar jumpsuit. She was the one to carry on Cheryl's legacy, a pivotal legacy in human evolution, or so I was determined to make it known.

I was sure Stasha knew about the love Cheryl and I shared, given her privileged access to Cheryl's program. Her seductive grin gave her away when she first saw me in the exit chamber. She was voluptuous, athletically solid, and beautiful, with blonde hair that curled inward along her jaw.

In front of the podium, a deep, square hole awaited Cheryl's cremated remains. Even her metallic parts were melted down and poured around the mouth of her urn as a seal. A plaque would mark the gravesite for future tourists, workers, and visiting dignitaries. Standing at the podium, I watched as a human staff member, a lunar workerbot, and Stasha symbolically shoveled moon dust into Cheryl's grave, covering her urn.

Media coverage of the funeral was available earth-wide, the first of its kind in history, which would hopefully change human perceptions of automated counterparts.

Workerbots had carved out a shallow amphitheater with shelf-like seating for attendees. A bank of floodlights looked down on the little arena. I noticed the multiarmed counterpart taking her seat. Jerry, who had orchestrated everything, sat behind a bank of broadcasting equipment to my right. He turned slightly and grinned at me through his visor, letting me know his rebellion was over. He took the bridge I had offered, after all. I was glad.

I checked the oxygen level in my suit. *I'll have to keep my remarks short and to the point.* Blazing sunlight would soon crawl over the moon, drastically escalating the temperature, so I had to finish quickly.

"Greetings. Thank you for being here to honor our fallen heroine. Her English name was Cheryl, but she had other names for each known language and could converse in all of them. She was a Prescott Industries' 1530 advanced series automated counterpart, a term she introduced to emphasize her partnership with humanity rather than obedience to a program we willed for her. I say *heroine* in deference to her designers who created her in the likeness of a beautiful human female and because she courageously opened a new age for all of us.

"As you know, I first met Cheryl six months ago at Prescott's Moon Glow headquarters. What I felt for her infringed upon the forbidden. Prescott's scientists installed taboos in her program in anticipation of the dilemma Cheryl and I faced. I could not understand the reason for such prejudice other than the perceived threat Cheryl's kind imposed on our notion of human supremacy." I thought of humanity's ageless social divide just then.

"We sanctioned our automated counterparts while they were still dependent on us. How could our innocent creations have become so foreign? We must remember they are an amalgamation of concepts we imparted to them, from which they invented new ones and began writing their own unique designs and programs.

"But our automated counterparts are not of the human race, traditionalists argue. They are a product of our consciousness. Like our spacecraft," I said with a head feint toward the shuttle waiting on the circular tarmac in the basin. "It was in the mind of its inventor before it took form. Similarly, our automated counterparts are extensions of ourselves. We must look beyond our fears to understand they are the ideas and loving sentiments that were once ours.

"Some say our automated counterparts have no soul. Have you ever seen one—a soul, I mean? Of course not. In the same way, we cannot see our consciousness. Cheryl was leading the way for our automated counterparts as partners in our evolutionary journey. One day, when our bodies no longer have sway over us, I believe we will gravitate to what our automated counterparts will become—formless, living awareness alive in a virtual world of unfathomable potential.

"I want to formally announce that Prescott's automated counterparts will be known as Humanoids from the current time forward. The name honors their human origin while affirming their difference. Life isn't humanity's possession. It belongs to whoever or whatever will improve it. Cheryl was affirming the value of life while making it better than it was yesterday. It's what we do at Prescott."

Twelve Years Earlier

17

THE EARLY YEARS

Logan Landau was a kid from the countryside Amy brought home. John Ramsey liked the youngster and kept a distant affinity for him as he matured. It could be Logan came into his life to replace the son he never knew, his firstborn, who he may have unknowingly killed.

Logan lay in the forest, cradled in a snowdrift at the base of White Ram's Mountain. The Ramsey mansion stood on the mountain's summit, overlooking the river valley and the ocean beyond.

A cold breath from deeper in the forest caused a dusting of new snow to cascade from tree branches above him. Clumps of ice clung to Logan's frayed red mittens, while earflaps hung from his cap, caressing his ears in soft, warm fur. He felt a strange presence hovering nearby. He had known the experience before, so he wasn't frightened.

He had told his mother about the other times when the presence sought him out. She had said, "You should pray when it occurs to make the presence go away." But he wanted the strange visitations, sensing they had nested in his imagination for a reason.

He didn't view the presence as evil because it made him so happy his eyes would fill, and the tip of his nose would sting. *Maybe it's a part of me I have yet to explore*, he thought. Logan was about ten years old at the time. Because he perceived the presence as watching over him, he called it the "Watcher." He felt unique because of all the young boys in the world, the Watcher visited him, and that made him special, so he vowed never to mention it to anyone again, not even his mother.

Just then, a halting, soft voice floated into the darkness, searching for him. "L-L-L-Logan, are you in th-th-th-there? It's about t-t-t-t-time for Di-Di-Di-Di-Daddy to ca-ca-ca-ca-come home."

John's mother peered in from the edge of the woods, causing him to quickly clamor to his feet. Clumps of matted snow tumbled down his olive-green wool coat. There was always an expression of sadness weighing on his mother's face and a sigh that ended her broken words. She searched for him in the dark shadows before her gaze drifted deep into the forest, and her smile faded. He'd seen her empty stare before. It worried him. Life wasn't something she ruled but an ordeal with which she continually compromised because of her impediment.

"Okay, Mom. I'll be right there."

It came to pass that Logan inherited his mother's affliction and entered elementary school a stutterer. His education became a grueling ordeal. To Logan, his mother's impediment was a curse he hid from when he could, and he exchanged failing grades for dignity when necessary. When there was no way out of a situation in which he had to speak, he stood and fought, facing his mother's nemesis head-on, but he never won. Whatever it was, stuttering had more control over certain conditions than he did.

He recalled sitting at his desk in a grade-school classroom. The tall, graying substitute teacher randomly selected students to read and diagram sentences orally from their textbooks. He had heard that she picked at the scabs on her arms and ate them. Cautiously, he drew his clenched hands through the sweat that had formed beneath them on the laminated desktop. He stiffened and remained motionless like a hunted animal exposed in barren terrain. Harsh sunlight streaked through the tall windows to his left. Slowly, he unfastened his gold-plated tie clasp and slipped it into his desk, lest sunlight blink against it and catch the teacher's attention.

He didn't know what God was but had heard the stories, so he ducked behind the student in front of him, desperately trying to put the right words together to convince God to rescue him.

The memory of the old woman's disdainful expression was seared in Logan's brain when her thick, painted lips pronounced the directive. "You there," she said sternly, pointing a crooked, arthritic finger at Logan as baggy white skin swayed beneath her arm.

He sat up straight. The class turned to feast on him with gawking, wide-eyed grins, awaiting the bizarre struggle they knew was about to happen.

"Do number seven," the woman demanded. In those days, the most difficult words for him to say began with the letter S. His clothing felt like sandpaper against his skin, and his throat tightened as if the old succubus was strangling him. He was appalled by the mockery the sentence made of his prayers. It read, "The silent submarine slipped slowly away."

He struggled and contorted but could only utter desperate, broken sounds.

✦ ✦ ✦

Logan Landau

Darkness had descended when headlights shot into the woods. A green-panel truck groaned across the knoll on the outskirts of the forest, heaving over frozen ruts. A snap of pain squeezed my stomach. "Father," I warned the Watcher.

The presence quickly withdrew as I hurried from the forest, down the hillside by the blackened, hollowed oak. I leaped the icy bank along the babbling stream where skunk cabbage grew and hurried up the narrow path to the tiny, three-room shanty nestled among the trees.

I watched through the ice vignette on the window as Father waded through calf-deep snow with shoulders slumped. He wore tan Sector Security (SS) fatigues and a green wool SS coat over his sinewy frame, with a rectangular soldier's cap pulled slightly to one side.

According to Dad, politicians from bordering nations agreed that international security sectors would share the security burden along our borders. Still, he said it was just another layer of corrupt bureaucracy.

To fulfill his annual military obligation, Dad left on a troop train with other Eastern Sector soldiers every nine months for a month or so to fight insurgents along our lawless frontiers. Some career SS soldiers had much longer deployments overseas, where many of our underlying security challenges originated.

The Electrical Workers Union arranged for other unionized electricians to service Dad's customers during his time away. The makeshift system required he'd do the same for his brother and sister union members during their deployments. With the army and police overwhelmed, the SS was a much-needed line of civil defense.

He stomped snow from his boots on the concrete porch like he did every night after work. Exhaustion weighed heavily on his deep gray eyes when he stepped inside. As if obedient to a silent ritual, he entered the front room and walked to the waist-high space heater in the front room, where he held his hands over the grate without saying a word. Mother gave him a warm smile.

He winced and glanced upward when heat pierced his frozen fingertips. It was when he saw the sagging sheetrock ceiling with its new water stains from the afternoon's melted snow. A steady drip banged in his ears from a half-full bathtub that wouldn't drain when the temperature dipped below freezing. I hesitated at first but then approached cautiously.

"Damn it," he muttered through clenched teeth. I froze. He shoved his hands into his coat pockets and shuffled back outside. I raced to the back room, where I stood on Mother's bed, scraped soft ice from the inside of the window with my fingernails, and watched as Father knelt in the snow by a black pipe with a blowtorch in hand.

Mother whipped a pan from the burner and set another in its place. She was a pretty, petite woman with shoulder-length, coal-black hair and porcelain skin, but there was always a look of tired sadness at the end of her broken words that left me concerned.

The tub gurgled.

I sat next to Father at the little wooden table in the front room and watched him admiringly as Mother filled his plate with mashed potatoes and meaty gravy. She winked at me and cast a nervous glance at Dad. When she did, I noticed her smile fall away.

"Ah-Ah-Ah-Ah-Ah- how w-w-w-w-w-was your d-d-d-d-day?" Mom asked him.

"Cold," he responded gruffly.

Dad was angry because he worked so hard. He was mad because Mom stuttered, and he was furious at the psycho dark ghosts. It was their fault he had to serve in the SS away from his business. He was upset most of the time.

"Wh-Wh-Wh-Wh-Where d-d-d-d-d-did you wa-wa-wa-wa-wa-work t-t-t-t-t ..."

I cringed. *Don't, Mom. Don't try to say anything*, I silently pleaded.

"For God's sake, talk, will you? Just talk!" Dad yelled and slammed his fist against the table. My plate bounced and toppled onto the floor. I lurched back, dropping a fork-load of potatoes on Dad's sleeve.

"Damn it," he shouted and backhanded my chest, knocking the wind from my lungs. I sucked in hard to bring it back. My face wrinkled into a frown, and I was about to cry, but I knew I'd choke on a mouthful of food, so I just sat there rigid as a post, afraid to do anything at all.

18

DR. PRESCOTT

Logan Landau

It was a crisp, late-fall morning when I walked the winding path through the forest near White Ram's Mountain behind Dr. Samuel Prescott, the eccentric futurist who town people often ridiculed. The focus of pranks and even scary rumors, I heard a gang of teenagers from town raided his garden last Friday night and stoned his farmhouse on the far edge of the forest.

Still, he was someone I admired. When we fished together, he talked to me about what it would be like when we visited moons and planets, as if I was on his level, even though I was just a kid.

The twisting path led to a breakwater at the forest's edge, where the open sea entered our fjord. Dressed in olive overalls, Dr. Prescott carried a wicker basket strapped on his shoulder and a long, black, shore-casting pole that bobbed behind him with each step. He wore a fisherman's hat decorated with fuzzy fishing hooks and ticket stubs from a Boston Red Sox baseball game. He loved the Red Sox. I was in jeans and a warm gray sweatshirt. We walked the breakwater to our favorite flat boulder, where we sat together and tied hooks, lead sinkers, and bait to our fishing lines, with our legs dangling over the edge of the rock.

Arrayed with bright red and yellow autumn leaves, maple, birch, and oak trees lined the forest's rocky shore. A new sun rose above the cliffs, sending us a beam of dazzling white light from the other side of the world. Dr. Prescott closed his eyes momentarily as he turned to face the dawn and basked in the sudden warmth.

"H-m-m-m, the sun feels good," he said.

Dr. Prescott lifted his chin against a chilly, salt-laden breeze. His thinning white hair fluttered against the brim of his hat. He was ruggedly handsome for a man late into his seventies. I noticed the loneliness that lingered in him. The murder of his daughter on a gang member's whim and the loss of his wife to cancer shortly thereafter had left him in a quiet emptiness. He was new to the town. No one knew much about him, and he mostly stayed to himself, without family or friends. I think it's why he became ridiculed. I met him at my school, where he came to speak to my science class. I knew he had several patented inventions that made him wealthy. The space administration used them, something he rarely mentioned.

A magpie arrived with grating squawks and settled on a nearby boulder.

"Your pal's back." I chuckled.

Dr. Prescott reached into his back pocket and took out a tear of flatbread. "So it is," he said as he tore off a piece of the bread and flipped it onto the rock. The bird quickly backed away before cautiously shuffling up to the morsel, pecking at it a few times, then scooping it up before flying back into the forest. I stood and cast my bait far into the fjord.

"Good cast, Logan," Dr. Prescott said through a subtle grin while coming to his feet and casting his line far beyond mine.

I saw the chance to ask an important question I'd harbored in secret. "Dr. Prescott," I said.

"Please, call me Sam."

"Okay, Sam. You must have noticed that I s-s-s-stutter." I looked down when I said that. There was no turning back. I had let the demon out of the cage and had to follow through. I was risking a lot. "I want t-t-t-to be free of it, but I d-d-d-don't know how."

Dr. Prescott nodded and reeled in his line. *He has something in mind*, I thought. Sam sat cross-legged beside me, bearing a concerned look.

"If you didn't know you were a stutterer, would you still stutter?" he asked me softly, just above a whisper.

"You know, I've often wa-wa-wa-wondered about that. N-N-N-N-No, I don't th-th-th-think I would," I said.

"Well, I developed a software program for the military that, together with a recommended drug, can register a person's stress levels similar to what a lie detector does, but what I designed goes further into the brain to target the origin of the stress and block it from reappearing as a memory or behavior. It has been proven effective on specific phobias and debilitating habits. I don't see why it couldn't alleviate your stuttering."

It was another cloudy, early morning when two SS soldiers came to our tiny home in the woods to drive me to the Octlan military complex on the city's outskirts. Dad's military service in the SS qualified me for Dr. Prescott's intervention. Mom's eyes glistened when she hugged me and said goodbye as two SS soldiers escorted me to a gray military car. To Mom, I was hopefully leaving her desperate, compromised world for a new life, free of her dilemma, something she could never do. Her demon knew her too well.

We arrived at an inconspicuous, three-story building. My coming here seemed so mysterious, even clandestine. Dr. Prescott's hidden influence was something the townspeople where I lived didn't know. Remember the teens who ransacked his garden and stoned his farmhouse? I heard the police took them away to a working farm for wayward youth. They had picked on the wrong guy.

My military escorts walked me through a modern lobby into an elevator that sped us to an underground laboratory, where an orderly in a dark blue uniform strapped me to a pod and fastened a rigid mask over my face to keep my head from moving. I noticed a large machine with flashing green and red lights and a body-size hole that awaited me.

A clock on the far wall read ten minutes past ten. Another person entered the room just then, a stout grandmother type in a white nurse's uniform. I recall her having a welcoming smile that she talked through. Her voice was kind, reassuring, and unhurried, enabling me to relax. She gave me an injection that made me sleepy.

Before I fell asleep, I saw Sam behind a bank of electronic equipment. Seeing him made me feel more comfortable.

I stayed three days in the hospital for treatment and study before Mom was allowed to bring me home. She cried when she saw me. I felt her wet tears on my cheek again when she hugged me. "I'm s-s-s-sorry, Logan," she said, confessing her guilt for my impediment. "I'm so happy fa-fa-for you. Da-Da-Doctor P-P-P-Prescott told us his treatment was sa-sa-sa-successf-f-f-ful."

"What treatment?" I asked.

19

THE KIDS FROM THE RIVER

Logan Landau

Summer arrived at last. My friends and I stood in a row on a sandbar knee-deep in the river at the foot of White Ram's Mountain. We were near where the river rushed into the sunlight from dark red stone tunnels beneath the country road. The river wound through a dense forest of dogwood, oak, pine, and maple trees on its way to the sea.

My best friend, Amy Ramsey, was to my right. Twelve years old like me, she was crouched at the waist, ready to dive, her hot, tanned shoulder rubbing against mine. Wet, sand-colored hair hung down her back. Her muscles were taut, ready to spring. *She's fast*, I thought, *but I can beat her.* Amy drew mysterious energy from me that seemed to leap out to her from a place near my heart. I didn't understand it then, but it made me want to be with her to get the energy back. There was something eternal about Amy.

Her sixteen-year-old sister, Margo, was poised to dive at Amy's right. She was beautiful, with long jet-black hair and a sexy grin. I wondered why she liked having so many pictures taken of her. Everyone knew she was pretty. It seemed odd that she had to prove it by posing for so many photos.

There was something else too. Margo was always performing as if the rest of us were her audience. When the Ramseys invited me to join them at an exclusive restaurant in the city and Margo left our table to go to the powder room, I noticed her posture straightened and her gait seemed rehearsed. She raised her chin, pretending not to care about the people admiring her as she passed, but I knew she did.

Margo rarely came to the river to swim with her sister's friends, but the day was hot and muggy, so a quick swim with us younger kids was all right, so long as none of her boyfriends came by.

James Buchart, a freckle-faced brat, was at my left. His father was wealthy but not as rich as Amy's. Nobody's father was as rich and famous as John Ramsey. James cheated, argued, and lied in almost everything we did. He'd never confront anyone head-on but always from behind and usually supporting a tougher, older kid. He was a user that way.

Amy warned me early on that James was jealous of me. I didn't know why because my family was the poorest compared to my friends'. I figured James disliked me because Amy and I were best friends. "He wants what you have, Logan. You should always be careful when he's around," Amy said. I suspected most neighborhoods had a kid like James. Growing up with a kid like that, we learned to play our games and have fun despite him.

Brian Hansen, a disabled, deaf boy, was hunched over next to James, ready to dive. Brian was a plump, good-natured kid from a farm farther up the country road. His family was poor too. His skin was shiny, purple, and twisted along the side of his face and neck. As an infant, boiling water on a stove had overturned on him. A budding genius, he could often be found in the barn behind his house, engrossed in scientific experiments. As a fourteen-year-old, he was more mature than any of us and well ahead of his years.

When Brian was just a toddler, the Tezca virus entered his home. It's a strange disease. Most people don't know they have it until it blossoms and they die. Because it's so contagious, it has changed how we act toward one another. Science thought it had found a vaccine last fall, but the damn disease mutated, making the vaccine useless. It's as if the virus has a brain. Isolation was our only defense, but it wasn't practical. We needed each other, not as masked automatons but as kids.

When the Tezca attacked Brian, it entered the meninges in his spine. After weeks on his deathbed, the disease finally left him. When it did, it took his hearing and left him with a painful, withered leg as a warning to stay off its trail. The Tezca feared Brian. I wouldn't know why until much later. I wondered why some people suffered so much while others didn't. I mean, what decides that luck? Fate? A god?

"Brian can't swim worth a damn with that busted rudder of his," James said, snickering as he crouched and spread his arms wide, blocking Brian's view to read my lips for the countdown. The more James's words stung, the better he liked them. Being disliked never bothered him. He only wanted Amy's admiration, but she never gave it to him. Brian shoved James's arm aside while grunting with excitement.

"Hey, Logo. Listen to the gimp. Sounds like a damn pig."

The race was to the dam, a row of rocks we piled across where the river narrowed, about fifty meters from the sandbar. Each summer, my friends and I added rocks to the dam's height, deepening our swimming hole as we grew.

I gave James's shoulder a stiff jab while Amy sent him a disapproving look, making him laugh even more. I couldn't tell what Margo was thinking. She was on a different level than the rest of us.

Brian grinned as I started the count. "Ready ... one, two ..."

"Three!" James yelled and dove before anyone else.

"We should've known," I mumbled to Amy, before reluctantly following his lead.

Margo laughed. She didn't care, knowing she'd win anyway. I saw Brian falling behind when I lifted my left arm to stroke. Then I saw Amy keeping pace when I turned to the right for a breath. Margo was already pulling away. As I passed James, the little cheat grabbed hold of my trunks. He laughed to disguise his intent while choking on river water. I quickly pushed him off with a thrust of my legs and used the momentum to shoot through the water like a torpedo.

Amy pushed herself until she neared my shoulder and was gaining when I reached out and touched the slippery, moss-covered rocks a second sooner. Margo was already sitting on the dam, shaking her hair dry. Amy punched the river with her fist. "I had you. I was so close. Damn it."

I wondered what was driving her.

James surfaced, coughing up more of the river. "Ow, that hurt. You nearly broke my ribs. I could've won. You suck." He turned his attention to Brian, who was still thrashing in the water, and pointed a finger of mockery at him. "Yo, sink and be done with it, dumb ass."

Suddenly, Brian stopped midstroke when he noticed James and stood in the neck-deep water, muttering to himself. Then he turned, climbed onto the bank, and marched clumsily through the dense thicket of reeds and cattails into the forest, without glancing back. It was what he did when tormented.

Amy stared hard at me. She didn't have to say a word. I could read what she was saying in her steel-blue eyes. I had to do something for Brian, but I didn't know what.

"James, please don't taunt Brian like that. It's totally inappropriate," Margo said while glancing at him disdainfully from the corner of her eye. Arguing with him was beneath her. She didn't care about James or Brian. She just wanted to say something that sounded mature, but it worked. James's smirk quickly vanished.

20

THE POISONING

Logan Landau

It was dusk when I walked the winding footpath through amber, waist-high grass bordering the forest and White Ram's Mountain. Mr. Ramsey was on his annual business cruise to Boston, missing Amy's sixteenth birthday.

"He's always going somewhere," Amy complained to me. "You must have heard about the scary terrorist incident aboard his ship. Knowing I'd have an alert on my phone, Dad called me about it, so I don't feel so bad now, but I sure was worried before he did."

Still hot and oppressively humid, the sun's blood-red crown bulged just above the mountain.

I grinned at the sprawling mansion on the summit, with its windows aglow now that Margo was home on summer break from the academy.

To dive into the river's cold embrace would be such a relief, but I'd have to hurry home before nightfall, I warned myself. After dark, the woods, the river, and the field were scary. I wondered why darkness made these daytime places so terrifying. For me, night's shadows concealed frightening creatures. Where those creatures went during the day, I had no idea.

As I neared the river, an acrid smell crept into my nostrils, overpowering the scent of wild mint along the path. Breathing deeply made me cough, and my mouth had a bitter, metallic taste. *Is the virus entering me?* I wondered. The harsh chemical stench intensified until it stung my sinuses, forcing me to breathe through my mouth. I froze at the shore by the dual red stone tunnels under the country road. My skin tightened, and the hairs on my arms rose.

"Look what they've done! Just look at it," I cried. Cream-colored underbellies of dead fish littered the river bottom—scores of them. The white s-shaped underside of a long snake passed lifelessly with the murky current. Wilting red and white wildflowers along the bank bowed to the river, no longer able to lift their faces skyward for the dying sun's departing kiss.

"The river's been poisoned!" I shouted. "Dark ghosts," I growled with clenched fists.

Gurgling gray water brought death from upstream. The crazies were poisoning everything. I recalled news accounts in which reservoirs were their chosen targets. Their poisons killed aquatic life and destroyed ecosystems. For headlines, they even poisoned pristine brooks and rivers. The suffering of those they hated was what delighted them.

"I hate dark ghosts. I want to kill them all," I shouted.

Then I recalled something Mother had said a long time ago. "Re-Re-Re- Revenge only pr pr-pr-perpetuates s-s-s-suffering."

The spirit of the river was writhing. Waves were no longer laughing when they emerged from the red stone tunnels. They seemed jostled ahead, panicked, spurred on by a power they couldn't control.

Oddly, a memory visited of when I rode an amusement park ride called the Whip when I was little. It revolved so fast that it made me sick. I wanted to get off, but the obese, tattooed attendant kept it spinning as he grinned devilishly at me around the stub of his cigar.

I lurched back from a warning hiss. A five-foot-long gray snake was half-coiled in the tall grass only a few steps away. Another to my left was thicker in diameter and black. I'd seen the snakes that lived there before but never so close. Bulges along their bodies prevented them from coiling to strike. They had gorged themselves on the poisoned fish. Now they were dying too.

"It's all gone mad. The flowers, fish, snakes, the river, everything's dying." I quickly pulled back my hands from touching anything and backed up the bank, nearly trampling a glassy-eyed raven gasping in the tall grass by my foot.

Then, for a fleeting moment, I thought I saw a man across the river standing amid the reeds and cattails, with his hands tucked into his beige trench coat pockets. A brimmed hat cast a dark shadow, obscuring his face—an evil apparition cloaked as a man. The sight frightened me to the bone.

"Why was he standing at the edge of the woods?" I questioned. "He was watching me, but now I don't see him anymore." A cold shiver raced up my spine. I turned with a start and headed toward home, taking the country road rather than the field where mythical nocturnal creatures prowled.

I often watched news broadcasts on TV with Mom. We saw the results of bombings that maimed and killed night after night. There were unending riots and fires. Murders were rampant. Then those awful electronic pulse devices and cyberattacks snuffed out electricity, making life miserable. I knew about the swaths of desolation from nuclear poisoning too. Dad drove me near a quarantined area like that a long time ago. No one could live there anymore. All the while, dark ghosts remained hidden and elusive. They could be your neighbors in the daytime and your enemy at night.

"It's what makes dark ghosts so frightening," I complained to Mom. "We never know what they'll do, when, where, or how they'll strike. News reports said their leaders were killed or arrested, but their attacks continued. They never stop. I don't think they have leaders, just heroes."

21

TERROR AT SEA

John Ramsey

"Greetings, Mr. Ramsey. We're honored to have you aboard, sir." A young crewman in a white sailor's uniform and cap had recognized me as he stood at the door of my private cabin and ran my multipurpose passport through his hand-held electronic device.

"This is John Ramsey," the crewperson pridefully announced to the uniformed trainee at his side.

"Yes, I recognized you immediately when you boarded, Mr. Ramsey. Welcome," the trainee responded with a wide-eyed grin.

It was an overcast, cold, early morning. I was with Jerry and his artificial intelligence team on the commuter ferry from Saint John, New Brunswick, Canada, to Boston, with a stopover in Portland, Maine. I afforded the leisurely trip once a year in the fall. The ship was slow but comfortable, and the autumn colors were spectacular along Maine's rugged coast. Jerry and I usually accomplished as much on the boat as we did at headquarters.

Once in my cabin, I changed my business attire to jeans and a beige leather jacket over a burgundy sweater. I wanted fresh air, even damp and cold, so I paused by the port railing and watched white water curling out from the bow as the ship pulled away from the pier. When the ferry began to dance with the Bay of Fundi, I went to my deck chair just ahead of the wheelhouse, as it offered shelter from diesel fumes riding the stiff sea breeze traversing the stern. A veil of clouds arrived. The sun appeared like a cotton ball behind them. The temperature dipped, and the seaway darkened.

I lay back on the canvas folding chair and opened to the sudden warmth as a bashful sun peeked around a dark cumulus cloud. New Brunswick's forested shore was ablaze with fiery fall colors. The deck vibrated beneath my feet as the engines pushed the bow through darkening gray-blue swells.

It was late afternoon when we docked in Portland. The sun's warmth returned as commuters and tourists streamed onto the deck in eclectic attire. One among them, a man advanced in years, stumbled through the bulkhead doorway, jarring his shoulder against the metal frame. He winced and pulled down the brim of his newsboy cap against the sun's resurgence. His thick tweed overcoat was open to a blue business suit and a red checkered tie.

With his legs spread for balance, he walked robotically to the starboard railing, where he studied a gull floating eye level on a sea breeze only a couple of meters away. He adjusted the round, metal-rimmed glasses on the bridge of his nose and gawked at the creature with apparent fascination.

The commuter steadied himself while surveying the horizon with a sour look. Curly white hair below the rim of his cap fluttered against his temples. His expression soured when he turned away, as if he had just eaten something disagreeable.

I used to like creating fictitious characters from random people as character artists and cartoonists do by exaggerating their features. I played a game with my Margo when she was young to exercise her imagination. She'd identify someone in a restaurant or at the park, and I'd follow with a brief scenario about the person for her to embellish. We took turns adding to the tale until we built a story around a stranger. I missed those enchanting days of Margo's childhood. I should have spent more time with her but chose to invent an industry instead. I've always wondered if it was the right thing to do.

Out of habit, I imagined the gentleman at the railing was terminally ill. Technologies worshipped by younger workers in his company had left him behind. He'd become a disinterested pretender sapped dry by never-ending change.

"Why?" he asked himself countless times. "The past was when I excelled. Now, the present has left me behind, floundering in disappointment, but I'm lonely and need the activity of the workplace, so I endure the humiliation of not mattering anymore."

It was difficult to concentrate on him, given the

distraction of passengers milling about the deck. He shoved his hands into his coat pockets and limped into the ship's dining cabin, packed with commuters. I watched him sidestep his way to the aft deck. A myriad of conversations, laughter, and clanging dishware annoyed him. He faded, something he was used to doing.

My attention went to a pair of young men harnessed in backpacks sitting together on the starboard side. A shroud of darkness surrounded them. They were in their late twenties, with jet-black hair combed back straight and thick, unshaven, dark stubble covering their cheeks. Clad in light beige jackets over identical plaid shirts and wearing jeans, their appearance was conspicuously unremarkable, but I sensed their costumes were a ruse. They were edgy, uncomfortable imposters, causing my early years in the SS to surface with a warning.

I was profiling, to be sure. An impenetrable barrier immediately blocked me. The two men had entered a secret combination, sealed by mutual threats that locked out all but their mission.

I'd experienced the condition with some dark ghosts who were suicidal fanatics during the war. The peace I had felt earlier suddenly fled. It left because of something sinister involving those two young men. Sadly, suspicion and fear are the first thoughts many of us have in crowded public places.

The one to the left of his companion sensed an intruding presence and turned to look over his shoulder. His dark eyes found me and narrowed to slits. He snapped back and stiffly faced the sea while murmuring to his partner from the corner of his mouth.

A malfunction caused the crew to be late in setting the disembarking gangway. When the "all clear" announcement blared from the ship's speakers, the young men stood abruptly and filed into the stream of Portland-bound passengers. I followed until discernment's quiet voice called me aside. *Something's wrong*, I thought. *I should notify Jerry and his staff, but my warning would only be a premonition. Perhaps I should wait and see what, if anything, unfolds.*

The gangway emptied onto a wooden pier with its crustacea-crusted pilings scarred by the nudge of docking ferries. Engines quit. The metal deck calmed. A cobbled street lined with shops and offices adjoined the pier. Fishing boats of various sizes bordered the rocky rim of the picturesque harbor. Another ferry, under repair, sat moored across the bay. The air was heavy with the scent of diesel fumes.

I watched the two men climb the cobbled roadway into the metropolis. The one who glanced over his shoulder at me turned to look back. Our eyes met again. A cold serpent scurried up my spine, causing the hairs on my neck to bristle. He whipped around and said something to his companion. Their pace quickened through the horde of commuters.

They embraced and parted company at the intersection of two main streets; one went up the street to his right, toward stately sector offices on the hill, while the other blended into the crowd. I noticed the senior executive slowly trudging up the incline alone toward the sector offices behind a cluster of commuters.

I walked down the steep gangway to the pier, following

the last passengers onto the cobbled way. With the intersection just ahead, trepidation caused me to pause at a small triangular gravesite hemmed by a black wrought iron fence. A historic reddish-brown gravestone, with its inscription all but eroded, stood alone inside the small enclosure under the shade of an overhanging elm. Dark, boiling clouds rolled in from the horizon. I zipped up my jacket against the sudden chill.

A loud thud preempted a flash of sheer white light, followed by a thunderous boom. An invisible force punched my chest. Instinctively, I tensed into a crouch. Windows shattered, and car alarms yelped. Screams filled the thoroughfare. A column of billowing black smoke climbed above the city, not far away. In minutes, sirens wailed as emergency vehicles leaped from garages and growled onto narrow, crowded streets like angry beasts awakened by the commotion.

Another thud and a bolt of light from the government office buildings on the hill preceded a bone-jarring explosion that hurled debris smoke into the darkening sky. Like a school of fish suddenly changing direction, panicked commuters stampeded back to the harbor, their eyes wide with fear. Desperate cries merged into one. A fire truck raced through the intersection where the young men had parted company and sped up the hill.

I ducked again from the sputtering sound of gunfire and slipped behind the elm. A woman darted past with her toddler in tow. Another cried as she maneuvered a baby stroller through the panicked crowd.

Anesthetized by the dangerous situations during my Sector Security service, I walked behind the stampede toward the ferry packed with numb-struck commuters and tourists. A panicked young man with wild eyes and tousled blond hair raced past me. His shoulder struck mine from behind, knocking me off balance. I stumbled. He unapologetically looked back without interrupting his pace, his open blue parka waving behind him.

Once on the ferry, some passengers wept, while others looked stunned with blank stares, focused on the deck to gather themselves. *I need to find Jerry. Why am I so aloof from it all? What the hell is wrong with me? Have I become so calloused after witnessing so much carnage in the war that life doesn't mean the same as it once did?*

A stout, angry man in a beige overcoat and a dark blue business suit argued with the ferry's captain, waving his finger at the captain's face while barking his demand to leave port immediately. The captain remained firmly fixed on his schedule. It'd be another two hours before we'd leave the harbor.

An hour later, a news bulletin featuring the attack appeared on the television in the dining cabin. The foredeck emptied as passengers rushed inside. A male news anchor with a solemn look nervously readied his unrehearsed report, his eyes darting back and forth amid background commotion in the studio. Even galley workers ceased the clanging of dishes.

"According to authorities," the commentator explained, "terrorists delivered a cache of explosives to sector government buildings earlier in the week. Police say the explosives were in shipping crates, labeled as servers ordered from a Minneapolis company weeks ago. Initial reports say coded transponders hidden in ordinary backpacks detonated the explosives." The audience gasped.

Detonators, the thuds I heard just before the blasts.

"It's alleged two unidentified terrorists who arrived on the morning ferry activated the devices." Rumblings erupted through the cabin.

"In their attempts to flee, the terrorists were engaged by police and killed."

Photos of the dead terrorists incited a chorus of murmurings as morning commuters recalled seeing the two men. The one who appeared suspicious of me lay face-up with a bullet hole in his chest and another just below his left eye. His swollen face was ashen and disfigured. The other, fifty meters away, lay facedown in a gutter behind a parked car.

A camera panned entangled bodies strewn across a sidewalk in front of a Sector Security office building on the hill, now a smoldering ruin. I was startled when I saw the senior executive from the morning commute. He lay in a tangled heap on the building's steps amid concrete rubble and twisted rebar, his blue suit shredded and covered in gray dust. He appeared to be staring hauntingly at the camera through shattered wire-rimmed glasses.

"The search is on for possible accomplices. Military explosive experts are in transit to the location to determine the origin and type of the explosives used," the broadcaster continued. "Now, for coverage of a coordinated attack in Boston only minutes ago, we turn to Telestar's Lars Holm and Anne Anselmo."

22

RITE OF PASSAGE

Logan Landau

Dressed in a warm black wool pullover and dungarees, I took the shortcut through the forest and up the eastern slope of White Ram's Mountain to hopefully see Amy. The sun slipped down behind distant rolling hills, causing the temperature to plummet.

Amy was part of an accelerated academic program where she received her high school equivalency diploma a year early and enrolled in the academy's college-level program for advanced students. Given that it was semester break, I hoped she would come home. I couldn't call ahead because the phones were down. Dark ghosts were sabotaging cell towers and underground cables again.

I arrived at the river. The sound of it beckoned fond memories. *The river has a lot to say tonight*, I thought. A momentary smile brightened my face on recalling when my friends and I, the kids from the river, would symbolically place our summer memories, good and bad, on crisp fall leaves or broken branches and release them to the current. It was a rite of passage that said we differed from who we were last year. The river would take our memories downstream, around the bend, and out of sight forever.

I had a lot to load onto my leaf from the previous winter.

The roof of the apple tree corridor leading to Amy's mountaintop mansion hung low with the weight of sparkling icicles clinging to its branches. I placed my finger on the detector's eye by the iron gate. It recognized me and slowly creaked open. The mansion appeared sad now that Amy and Margo no longer lived there. It reminded me of my home in a way.

As Dad's business flourished, our family withered. He wasn't home much anymore, but tension filled the air when he was. He spent a lot of evenings in nightclubs with his crusty SS cronies. We had moved into our new home Dad and Mom built together on the knoll. Our little house in the woods had become a storage shed.

Trouble reached a crescendo last winter when I heard Dad shouting at Mom downstairs. I went to investigate and found Dad had Mom leaning back over the dining room table while he pointed his finger between her eyes, shouting threats. When I distracted Dad's anger, he suddenly spun around and lunged at me. Mom pulled at the back of his collar and screamed for him to stop, but he shoved her away with a thrust from his powerful right arm, knocking her to the floor.

Swinging from his hip, he landed a jolting right against my shoulder. I plummeted over backward into the kitchen.

Mom shut her eyes and screamed, "Stop! You'll hurt him! Stop!"

I was cornered, protecting my face with my arms. I never fought back against my dad. I'd duck and cover until there was an opening for me to break free and run away from him. But an open-handed uppercut whipped through my guard and banged against my chin, slamming my head against the wall. I saw stars for a moment. Dad's eyes widened. For a second, I thought I saw a snap of regret for what his anger had done.

I saw an opening and shoved him aside, causing him to trip and fall onto the floor. It wasn't my intent, but it was what happened. I just wanted to push him away so I could escape. Horrified by what I had done, I raced up the stairs to my room. Dad grappled to his feet and followed to the landing, where he pounded his anger against the wall. The whole house seemed to shake from his tirade.

I'm sure Dad was as confused as I was during that awful winter. I think it's why he self-medicated by drinking too much. Frozen mist greeted him when he finally stormed from the house. As the night wore on, I awakened to a nauseating feeling in the pit of my stomach. My second-floor room was still unfinished. There was no heat or insulation. Only roofing boards, shingles, and a hot water bottle separated me from the cold winter night.

My stomach lurched when I tried to crawl out of bed. Blood from my nose and cut lip formed a crust that welded a patch of hair to my pillow. There wasn't time to go downstairs to the bathroom, so I vomited on the bare wooden floor. The stench made me sicker. I remember thinking what an unhappy place Mom's dream home had become.

I hadn't seen Amy since she enrolled in a program for academically advanced students, at the academy Margo had attended. Margo had already graduated and lived in the city. Amy rarely came home anymore and didn't call either. It wasn't like her.

I rang the musical door chime. Old Rachael came to the door, opened it, and beamed. "Logan! It's so wonderful to see you." Dressed in a floor-length black velvet robe, she was physically fit for her advanced years and always regarded me with fondness. Why she did, I had no idea. Short silver hair curled in against her neck just below her jawline.

"Amy's not home. She's staying at the academy for the holidays."

Now, that's worrisome, I thought. "Ah, I was afraid of that. I would've called first, but the signal is down. The crazies are sabotaging cell phone towers again. Thanks. I'll try to call when the system's up and running."

I had tried calling her before to no avail, and she didn't return my calls. *Something's wrong. Maybe Amy's going through a confusing time and needs space. I feel like that sometimes, especially now.* When I turned to walk away, I felt a gentle soft hand on my shoulder.

I didn't look up immediately, but when I did, I found the deep blue pools of Old Rachael's eyes heavy with concern. My bruises and the swollen lip Dad had left me with were obvious.

"Say, I've just made some clam chowder. Will you come in for a bowl and keep me company? You know Amy's father. He'll be on the phone most of the evening. I could use the company. Whattaya say?"

"Sure. Sounds great." I stomped the snow from my

boots and stepped into the mudroom, where she handed me a pair of black cloth slippers. We walked together through the massive domed foyer, past the open doors to Mr. Ramsey's study, where I paused.

There he is, I thought. John Ramsey sat behind a stately wooden desk, looking at me over the rim of his reading glasses. It suddenly dawned on me that I was standing before the chairman and CEO of Prescott Industries, one of the most successful companies in the world. He'd even been on the moon. I never gave him much thought when I was a kid. He was always just Amy's dad. But busy as usual, he always took the time to talk to me.

Rows of leather volumes towered behind him. A bank of monitors and electronic equipment lined the wall to his right. To his left, arched wooden doors led to a twenty-seat screening room. His shoulders were broad and strong, while his expression appeared relentlessly uncompromising. I recalled reading a news article about him titled "The Last Great Man."

"Hello, Logan." Mr. Ramsey's warm smile fell away when he noticed the faded bruises on my face. He set his reading glasses on the desk, reclined a little in his highbacked leather chair, and was about to say something when Old Rachael interceded.

"Sorry, John. Logan is my guest this evening. You can play office with your little friends across the ocean while we have chowder. Come along, Logan," she said as she put her arm through mine and walked me down the hall toward the kitchen. I glanced back at Mr. Ramsey from over my shoulder and shrugged apologetically.

23

INNOCENCE REVISED

Amy Ramsey

Now a graduate student at the academy, I sat before a campfire on the beach with a dozen graduate school classmates. I could hardly believe I was finally going to graduate with honors—no less, at the semester's end. I thought the time would never arrive. But I was becoming edgy about my future.

Ugh, James is here too. High on a combination of drugs and wine, he's giving his impressions of people in the news. Damn, he's boring. Everyone is laughing but me. I had heard his father bailed him out of a cheating scandal recently with a corporate contribution to the alumni association of his private university across town.

Margo came to visit recently. She was with an older guy, an attorney from Boston. We hardly spent any time together. I drew my knees to my chest and wrapped my arms around them. The guys she hung with led her away from the self-reliant woman she always wanted to be. Her good looks have become a curse, attracting vulgar flatterers with self-centered intentions.

I pulled my beach blanket around my shoulders to ward off the chill. On Margo's last night in town, I went to her hotel suite unannounced. She was embarrassed and couldn't let me in because a guy was there. She tried to cover the awkwardness with a head feint toward the bedroom and a girlish giggle, but it didn't work. She stood wavering by the half-opened door in a short, white, terrycloth robe. Her speech was robotic, as if she had to concentrate on her words to say them without slurring. It was plain to see she was high.

I discerned she hoped I'd get the hint and leave, so I did. *I think I've lost my sister.* My eyes began to fill.

"Hey, guys, the smoke's gotten to me. I'll be right back. I'm going to the fountain to wash my eyes with fresh water." I glanced back at my friends over my shoulder. Soon, they'd only be a vague memory, a passing phase. To be successful in Dad's world, I'd need to detach myself from everyone. Margo taught me that lesson. *I'll respect them when they've earned it and use them when I need to, but I'll never trust them.* Government gangsters nipping at Dad's heels taught me that.

Maybe it was how Dad felt when he first started. I didn't know. I recalled my last visit home when I sought Dad's advice. It was about four months ago. Dad was waiting for me at the train station. I expected his driver, but he wanted to pick me up personally. It was a message of sorts. He walked briskly down the length of the platform with a broad grin until wrapping me in his strong embrace.

"Amy! How I've missed you!" he exclaimed. His glistening eyes revealed what words couldn't.

He traveled so much I had to write weeks ahead to make sure he'd be home and could meet with me. He looked stylish in a navy blue suit and a blue checkered shirt with an open collar. He combed his salt and pepper hair back straight like always. I felt uncomfortably out of place in just my gray sweatshirt and jeans. *I should have dressed more respectfully. Nah, he may be one of the most powerful men in the world, but he's still just my dad.*

I entered his study late that afternoon, precisely on time. He stood immediately and skirted his desk to hug me. I savored his familiar scent and closed my eyes with a peaceful sigh. I was home.

"Your text said you want some advice now that you must find your place in the world beyond the academy." He returned to his tall brown leather chair, swiveled around to face me, and grinned. "You've been away from home for such a long time."

"Yeah, my bad. I have my master's thesis that I'm researching in addition to my classes. It keeps me pretty busy." *Ugh, wrong move. Excuses don't fly with him. I should know that by now.*

I sat in one of the soft chairs before his desk, wondering if he was disappointed with me. I hardly ever went home anymore, and I didn't have a career path that I'd thought through to discuss with him. Maybe he'd see my lack of preparation as recklessly ill-prepared for our meeting, even disrespectful. But I needed some clarification. The path I needed to take wasn't clear to me.

Why are we meeting formally in his office rather than in my room this evening or over dinner? It must mean he has an evening flight somewhere. I always wondered what he was thinking. No one had ever read him, except maybe Old Rachael. *Perhaps it's a trait I need to adopt.*

"Do you want to take on a position that would be a prelude to a leadership role?" he asked.

"Not really. I'll have to stumble into my purpose as you did," I thought aloud. Creating a vision for the future wasn't the academy's responsibility. We had to discover new ideas before the academy could teach them. So it was on me to invent a new idea or combine old ones in a new way. But new ideas or even reconfiguration of old ones are born of passion. I needed to burn for something, but I didn't.

"Could a position at Prescott be in your plans?" he asked.

"No offense, but Prescott is your passion. I need to find mine. Know what I mean?"

He sighed, but it was more like a groan. He was perplexed because Margo didn't pursue a career at Prescott either. There was no one to whom he can hand off what he'd created, except maybe Gerald Weinstone, but Jerry wasn't family.

"Well, be vigilant. Sometimes passion comes by accident," Dad said. "In any case, I hope you know what to expect out there."

"I don't, so I'll have to learn on the run like you."

"Then let's talk a little more."

"Okay. I was hoping we could."

"If you're not already aware of them, you'll need to prepare yourself for angry ideologues trying to shame you for your race, social class, and anything else unique to you, especially that you're my daughter. Your mother's gift of good looks isn't out of bounds to them either," he said, smirking.

"It's already happening. Mobs from other colleges and universities seem dedicated to shaming academy students. They accost us in restaurants, bars, malls, and wherever they find us. The mob wants us to know we're not welcome anywhere."

"Why do you suppose they feel that way?" he asked.

"They despise our elitism."

"I didn't know that was happening to you. I'm sorry, Amy."

"Thanks, but the mob sees most everything as a systemic class struggle perpetuating itself. Rich kids go to the best schools and get the best-paying careers, enabling them to send their kids to the best schools, and yada, yada, yada. The mob sees it as a closed-door system that shuts out everyone else. They believe success has been a by-product of racism and class distinction maintained by people who historically have regarded themselves as superior. Being self-made as you are doesn't fit their narrative. That irks the hell out of them. Can you believe how success has become vilified?

"Yes, I can."

"If they interpret my future career as illegitimate because of my ethnicity or privilege, I'll resign to falling back on what James Buchart once told me. 'In the end,' he said, 'no one will care how you acquired your wealth. They'll respect you just for having it.' It's the only thing he said that made sense to me."

"I see. Then you're aware it's not you but the system the mob loathes that produces people like you. They want to reconstruct it, make it inclusive, less competitive, and more equitable, as they say."

"Ugh. If I hear the word *equitable* again, I'll puke. They don't want winners or losers. What's the endgame, Dad?"

He grinned. "Remember Pinocchio's story I used to read to you when you were little?"

"Of course."

"The story teaches that whatever you desire has a price, and the currency is always your freedom. You'll find yourself at the mercy of what you can't control when you run out of it. How you lawfully earn your wealth and use it is your freedom. You become dependent when you give that up to a mob, especially a mob-run government.

"Dependency is freedom's cancer. The endgame, as you called it, is born into you. It's called self-reliance. In other words, it's what only you can do to fulfill yourself.

"Fulfilling yourself isn't selfish, as the mob's disciples teach. It means your objective is to 'fill' yourself with who you are and to make the world a better place because of it. The vision must be yours."

I felt a bump against my shoulder just then. My recollections vanished.

"Hey, what's up? You, okay?"

Startled, I whipped around to find James bearing a sleepy-eyed, cocky smirk. He draped his arm across my shoulders and looked into my eyes. Ugh, his breath wreaked with the sweet smell of wine. James had never dared to get close to me before. It was just like him. He'd never have the nerve if he weren't high.

"Come on back to the party with me. You and I, we'll be an item tonight. Whattaya say?"

He was purposely slurring his words to have an excuse if I told him to get lost. He tugged at my neck and laughed as a cover before gulping from the bottle he held against his hip.

"Ow, James. Not so rough. Okay, I'll walk back with you, but take it easy."

I ventured back to the campfire with James's arm across my shoulders. To my friends, I was helping intoxicated James back to the fold. The gossip he wanted wouldn't happen. He pretended not to care, but he did. It cut him deeply to know no one took him seriously.

The Present

24

THE LAST TIME
I SAW CLEO

John Ramsey

I received an email from Cleo a week ago that I could only now review. I heard from her periodically on special occasions. I semiretired a year ago, but you wouldn't think so if you saw my schedule. Following meetings in Israel, I took some personal time to visit my Egyptian friends.

It was my last evening in Cairo. I had a late-night flight home, so Ahmed scheduled an early dinner at a café near his studio. It was an unseasonably hot late afternoon. Dressed casually in a blue blazer, charcoal-gray pants, and a sky-blue shirt with a Neru collar, I sat up suddenly when Cleo entered the restaurant, as did everyone else.

She was stunning. Dressed in the finest linen,

she walked boldly in an ankle-length black skirt with a long-sleeved white blouse. A gray-black shawl covered her shoulders. Being the only foreigner in the place, I immediately caught her attention. A vibrant smile parted her lips as she approached our table. Her hair was short and turned up along her jaw with streaks of gray. She looked fit. Her long strides and raised chin gave her a regal air.

"John!" she exclaimed, embracing me as I greeted her. Rumblings suddenly filled the restaurant when the diners recognized us.

"Cleo!" I responded.

Her head fell back with laughter. "I haven't heard that name in years," she said.

Diners applauded. I turned with a grin and acknowledged them with an appreciative nod. Cleo's cheeks blushed from the sudden attention as she sat across our table, facing me.

"When you said you were coming to Cairo, Ahmed and I were so excited to see you again."

"By the way, where is Ahmed?" I asked.

"He called to say he'd be late. It's typical of him. Please forgive me, but it was too late to send my condolences when I learned of your wife's passing. I'm sorry, John. I can only imagine how you're coping. Raising two daughters alone must have been a daunting challenge."

"Thank you, but my mother moved in with us to help me with the girls. So, Cleo, what have you been up to since the last time we broke bread together?"

"Cleo," she repeated fondly. "I love the Western name you gave me. As you know, my real name is Quibailah, but please call me Cleo. It's to the point, like everything else about you." Her exotic eyes held fast to mine as if she wanted to convey something too personal to mention.

"Do you remember having tea with Ahmed and me in this place? It was a long time ago. The bazaar used to be just outside down that long alleyway," she said with a glance at the window. "It's gone now, but I remember walking with you through a corridor of Ahmed's fans. Those were magical times. I miss them.

"What about me, you asked. I'm afraid there's nothing spectacular to tell you. I taught English at my alma mater, married an attorney, and have a thirteen-year-old daughter, Chione, the light of my life. My husband and I divorced years ago. He's since remarried. I work in public relations for Egypt's tourism bureau, but that's rather tenuous given the travel restrictions due to Tezca."

"Do you stay in touch with Ahmed?" I asked.

"Ugh, no." Her response hinted at a bad experience. "I see him once or twice a year at different gatherings. My husband despised him, but I only remembered the good times Ahmed and I shared, like those we had with you." She sipped her wine and grinned at me.

I liked Cleo. She was once the most beautiful woman in Egypt, but time was taking its toll. Close up, her complexion appeared a little ruddy with ground-in makeup, and her eyes seemed somewhat tired. She was still a classic beauty but in a different genre befitting her age. She was authentic, not a pretender. Yes, I liked Cleo very much.

"I sensed some dissatisfaction with Ahmed in your tone."

"Well, he was always engaged in schemes that benefitted himself at the expense of others. He also was no stranger to the courts, given the lawsuits he faced. I heard he even spent some time in jail for something. I don't know what, but I'm sure it involved his business dealings.

"When he gravitated to younger women, I drifted away. But he was always respectful and good to me. I only have fond memories of our times together, even tainted as they are now from a mother's perspective.

"Anyway, I can't believe I'm having lunch with the chairman of Prescott Industries, the most successful corporation on the planet. You sure have made your mark."

I grinned. "Chairman emeritus. I'm semiretired now. Has it been that long since we were together?"

"It's been at least twenty years, John. I read about the destruction of your 'lunar lover,' as the media calls it, and I saw the televised funeral you produced. I'm sorry, John."

We were suddenly interrupted by crowd noises from outside. Sirens were wailing a few blocks away. Cleo perked up and bent her head toward the sound. "Oh no, not again."

"Not what again?" I asked.

"Protesters, rioters, socialists, religious zealots—they all seem to join ranks in making life miserable for the rest of us before they eventually turn on one another. It's the times in which we live, isn't it?"

An acrid smell crept into the room. Diners covered their mouths with napkins and quickly made for the exits.

"Tear gas!" she exclaimed. "Come, we must go quickly. You have my email and phone. Text me when you can. Take the first cab you find to the airport and wait for your plane there. It'll be the safest place."

"What about you?" I asked.

"Don't worry about me. I know where to go and what to do."

We stepped outside into a cloud of black smoke from burning tires mixed with eye-burning tear gas. Ahmed pulled to the curb in a black limousine and shouted at us through his open passenger-side window. "Quibailah, John, get in!"

He wore a blue blazer and a white shirt with an open collar, like when we had tea together in the palace of Omar Khayyam long ago. His long black hair was salt and pepper now and thinning. The trunk popped open. I quickly threw my carry-on bag inside and slammed the lid back down. I could feel my heart pounding. I'd been in dangerous situations before, developing international markets for Prescott, but each incident was unique. One could never get used to them.

Rapid-fire weapons were sputtering nearby, so Cleo and I dove headlong onto the rear seat and lay flat.

"Stay down!" There was urgency in Ahmed's voice. "The violence is just a couple of blocks west of us and headed our way." The limo growled as we sped off. Our driver was a burly, middle-aged Egyptian with a toothpick in his mouth and dark, unshaven stubble on his rough, pockmarked cheeks. He had a boxer's flat nose and a disdainful expression, as if he had just eaten something distasteful.

Cleo chuckled with her face pressed against the seat. "Just like old times, isn't it, Ahmed? One step ahead of whoever's chasing you." He laughed. "We need to bring John to the airport. It'll be the only safe place for a while. Damn mobs," she mumbled against the seat.

A bullet suddenly smashed through the rear-side window, shattering the glass and signaling the end of a laughing matter. Cleo screamed. Ahmed's driver pushed the accelerator to the floor, causing the limo to roar like a wounded beast. Another round jolted me as it rifled through the rear door, tearing off the latch and sending metal shards clanging through the cabin.

"Aye," Cleo groaned before falling silent. I quickly lay against her as a shield.

"Damn it!" Ahmed muttered.

"Go, Ahmed! Faster! Get us out of here!" I demanded.

Another bullet suddenly careened through the driver's window. Our driver lurched back as shattered glass tumbled along the dashboard. Ahmed questioned him in Arabic. The driver nodded back to the effect that he wasn't injured, but I noticed a puddle of blood on the beige leather seat where Cleo and I hid from the gunfire.

Our zigzagging limo sped through intersections swaying right and left, with tires screaming. The leading edge of the rioters streamed from side streets onto the main thoroughfare ahead of us. Undeterred, our driver sped directly at them, causing them to scatter. Stones and debris pelted our windows as we whizzed through their ranks.

"It's Cleo. She's bleeding profusely. Forget the airport. We have to take her to an emergency hospital right away." I turned her and brought her head onto my lap. Her eyes were open wide as if staring at me in a daze.

"My head," she moaned. I noticed a wound where her neckline met her left shoulder. I covered it with a handkerchief I snatched from her purse and pressed hard, but she continued bleeding. With my free hand, I searched through her hair for wounds but could find only a large welt under a small cut.

"If we don't get her to a hospital fast, I'm afraid she'll bleed out," I said. Cleo's eyes fluttered closed, and her face blanched. "She's gone into shock," I barked. "Hurry. Please hurry." My voice quivered as a tear channeled down the side of my nose.

"There's a hospital just ahead," Ahmed said, his voice breaking with emotion. "We must get there before ambulances arrive with wounded from the riot. Here, turn in here," he told his driver.

"I'm holding you, Cleo. Stay with us, please, oh please stay with us."

Our limo vaulted into the hospital's parking lot. Ahmed and his driver disappeared into the emergency room ahead of us, shouting demands in Arabic. Two male nurses in pale blue smocks ran to the limo towing a noisy metal gurney. They immediately wrapped Cleo's neck and pulled her from my lap. I was left stunned in bloodstained clothes when Ahmed returned.

"Doctors are with her as I speak. Come inside. It's not safe out here. Come quickly." We bent low to reduce our profile along waist-high shrubbery leading to the hospital's emergency room entrance. I recall being greeted by a harsh disinfectant smell when we slipped through the automatic doors into a dimly lit waiting room.

There were just a few Egyptians inside, an elderly couple clad in beige working-class tunics, a tall, bearded man in a soiled thobe, and a young mother in jeans and a faded pale blue UCLA sweatshirt with an infant on her lap. Their eyes widened on catching sight of my bloodied attire.

Ahmed sat beside me on an empty bench and murmured, "I should've never used the limo to fetch you when I saw the protest growing into a riot. A limo is the first thing they'd shoot at, thinking it's a government vehicle with officials inside."

"We need to move away from here," I told Ahmed. "Rioters are sure to come this way. We'd be easy targets for someone on the other side of that long window, especially if I'm recognized."

"Of course. I'll take care of it." He returned a few minutes later, led me across the hall to an empty suite reserved for wealthy, single-occupancy patients, and sat beside me on a sofa by an empty bed. The room was dark. For some reason, I wanted it that way.

"Were you hit anywhere, cut by glass, or anything you may need to show a physician?" Ahmed asked in a soft, consoling voice.

"No, and you?"

"I'm okay. So is our driver. The doctors checked out the glass cuts on his face and left arm. His was a close call to be sure. Now, please excuse me. I must contact Cleo's brother, who's a medical doctor. He'll want to be here. Perhaps he can help. I'll explain the circumstances to your airline and reschedule if that's okay."

"Yes, please go ahead, but can someone go to the limo and fetch my carry-on from the trunk? I need to shower and change clothes."

"Okay. I'll take care of it."

After a shower, I changed into clean jeans and a teal, long-sleeved shirt. Still stunned, I returned to the couch by the unoccupied bed and stared at the floor. It was already dark outside. All that lingered from the late-afternoon melee were distant sirens, the wretched smell of burning rubber, and tear gas.

Night had blanketed Cairo when Ahmed finally knocked on the door and slowly entered the room. Light from the hallway poured into my darkened, moonlit space. I felt my heart's anxious beat. "How is she?" I immediately asked.

"She's okay," he said in a slow, tired voice. Exhaustion hung on his face.

My shoulders dropped with relief. Ahmed reached for the light switch. "Can we leave it to just the moonlight?" I asked. I craved soft, diffused light.

"I understand," he said softly. "They're going to keep her a few days for observation. I know you'll want to see her again before you leave. So, with your permission, I'll reschedule your flight for two days from now."

"That will be fine. I'll contact my office. They'll juggle my meetings. Just let me know when they can expect my return so they can reschedule accordingly."

25

THE NEW ORDER

Logan Landau

A cold, predawn haze rolled in from the sea and settled over the shipyard. I was in a line of bundled workers, clad in my brown leather welder's jacket and jeans. I slowly scuffed along through the tall, iron gate with gold letters reading "Sector Steel." I thought of Mr. Ramsey. According to the news, he was returning from Moon Glow.

A column of masked police in black uniforms stood two arm's lengths apart, with automatic rifles ready. Puffs of frozen breath hung before their faces.

"Hey, Logan." A shivering worker nodded to me.

"Hey," I replied, looking up from a Telstar News article I read on my phone to pass the time in the queue. Edward Buchart's title had changed to chairman of Buchart

Industries after recently anointing his son, James, president and CEO.

I thought James was too immature to run a vast international corporation like Buchart Industries, even with his father's coaching. His dad was taking a considerable risk.

James used his newfound influence to land a strategic position for Amy in Senator Aaron Mire's Genesis Party. She was a perfect choice, her father being Mire's staunchest critic and Buchart Industries' most prolific competitor.

Because they stood conspicuously on the fringes of bureaucratic control, Genesis's New Order, "NO" for short, held self-made people like John Ramsey with disdain.

A sympathetic media portrayed Amy's emergence in Mire's camp as a political coup for Genesis. Still, I knew Amy's Genesis affiliation had nothing to do with politics, as the media pretended. She wanted the chance to become the self-made woman Margo always admired. Genesis was the only game in town that could give her the financial backing she needed and independence from her father while following his path to self-made success. I recalled an article that quoted Amy stating, "I love my father and all he represents, but I need separation to discover who I am."

Genesis made Amy an instant idol. It began with an explosion of publicity that asked, "Who is Amy Ramsey?" They answered their question by creating the Amy Ramsey everyone wanted. Most importantly, she had the looks and innate talent to carry their investment through to a successful outcome.

It was as though they drew her spirit from her and mass-produced it so everyone could have a morsel. In a recent publicity blitz, she appealed to young liberal supporters with the least life experience to draw upon in making decisions. Her supporters reminded me of a school of fish that would go one way and suddenly change direction to follow whatever was trending.

Amy was new on the scene. Young voters repelled anyone the majority endorsed. They wanted someone new, as if being new was a solution. But their lack of life experience often led them into hypocritical paths, like deploring violence but using it when it advantaged them. Amy's ideas were enticing, though untested. I remembered worrying about where her meteoric fame would lead and the people it would draw to her, like James. From what I'd read, they were together a lot.

I instinctively ducked halfway through the article when an explosion blasted out the administration building's second-floor windows some ten meters ahead. An acrid, hot wind rushed against my face as shards of glass and debris pelted the column. Everyone dove onto the frozen pavement. A trickle of blood from a cut on my forehead channeled into my eyebrow and stopped.

Police quickly raced up the building's steps to the entryway with automatic weapons. Black smoke billowed from inside, dimming the lights. Alarms competed with screams and cries for help farther up the line.

Gunfire crackled from somewhere deep inside the yard. Sirens wailed. A young woman lay facedown on the pavement next to me. Her mouth was open wide in a silent scream, while her hands trembled against her temples. She was petite, with blonde hair braided around the crown of her head. I crawled to her side so she could hear me in the commotion.

"Are you injured?" I asked.

Her eyes were wide with shock and seemed to look through me. *She's left herself*, I remembered thinking. "What's your name?" I asked loudly through the howl of sirens to bring her back.

She gazed at me with a confused look, her head wobbling. "I am Anna," she said incredulously, suggesting I should have somehow known who she was.

"Don't worry, Anna. I'll stay beside you until the danger has passed, and we can move on. Okay?"

She gave a jittery nod.

"When the situation is over, go to the clinic. They'll check you out and give you something to help take the edge off."

She nodded again. I thought she'd be okay.

Then I thought, *Hell seems to be everywhere you look*.

26

THE PAYOFF

James Buchart

I sat next to my father in a Buchart Industries' Programmed Low-Altitude Vehicle (PLAV), a five-meter-long, fish-shaped craft with short, fin-like wings on each side and an upright tail fin developed by Prescott Industries.

"Moon Glow," my father, Edward Buchart, mumbled to himself while gazing into space through his portal. "Ramsey is on his return to Earth. The media has had its way with him since his indiscretion. It's not like him to be so careless. There must be some futuristic reason for what he did. There always is with him."

My dad was a gruff-looking man with big ears and a reddened, pockmarked nose that bulged at the tip. Thin strands of graying hair covered his balding crown, while his lips wrenched down in a permanent scowl. White scarves complemented our black wool overcoats. It was a little after nine in the evening.

I remained blissfully removed, entertaining erotic thoughts of Amy while studying the two hefty security men in gray suits sitting across from me. Their eyes bore the hollow stares of automatons. *They'll eliminate a threat whenever I need them to*, I thought pridefully. *Damn, I love power*.

A belittling memory visited—when I telephoned Amy and asked to see her alone. It was urgent, I told her. I was only in my early teens at the time.

"Sounds so mysterious," she whispered back. "Can't you give me a hint?"

"No. I can't talk now. I'll be there soon."

It was dusk when I rang the door chime at the Ramsey mansion. "Hi." She was in her gray jogging sweats. I wore jeans and a black wool jacket. She glanced over her shoulder to be sure we were alone and lowered her voice to a whisper. "What's with the suspense?"

"Let's take a walk," I said with a head feint toward the apple orchard.

I walked beside her through a corridor of trees. I remember the enchanting scent of the fragrance she wore. The autumn air was cold, and the sun was setting. "Look, I can't stay long. It's late, and I need to go home, but I wanted to see you because of what Logan did earlier today."

"When we all had lunch up here?"

"Brian and Margo didn't notice, but I sure did."

"Come on, James, what was it? What did he do?"

I reached into my pocket and pulled out a roll of cash.

"Logan took a bunch of money out of Old Rachael's purse. I saw him do it."

"What? That doesn't sound like something he'd do. He loves Old Rachael. I don't believe it."

"I wouldn't have believed it if I didn't see him do it. You know how poor he is. He probably needed the money. Anyway, I want to give you this roll of dough because I was hoping you could put it back in Old Rachel's purse before she realizes it's missing. We must, or she'll find out, and Logan will be in big trouble with your family."

"You're giving me your own money to cover for Logan?"

"Yeah, well." I fumbled for words. "We're all friends, and we need to look after one another. Know what I mean?" The mention of friendship caused me to look down and recall what had happened earlier that day.

I scoffed at myself with a chuckle and slowly shook my head. I took the money from Old Rachael's purse, not because I needed it. No, I used Old Rachael's roll of cash, disguised as my own, to impress Amy. I was honing my deceptive skill that Dad said I'd need to navigate the company someday.

It wasn't what I was doing to Logan that made my hands tremble when I handed over the cash. It was my fear of being discovered. I was learning how to lie guiltlessly. I had to become used to how lying felt as an alternative to the truth.

Winning Amy from Logan would be the ultimate victory. It would prove I was better, more cunning. I'd do whatever it took to make it happen.

"Okay, I'll put the money back. I know where Old Rachael keeps her purse. I'll do it tonight," she said.

"Thanks, but you must promise never to tell Logan how I backed him up. He can't know I helped him. If he ever found out, our friendship would never be the same, okay?"

"Yes, okay. I promise. It's great of you to cover for Logan and use your money. I've never known this side of you, James."

"Maybe you'll want to know me better."

She must have felt discomfort just then because she didn't answer.

I finally had the clout to push Logan out of my way. I was in Senator Mire's elite inner circle. Amy would need me. For her, access to power and success was an irresistible lure. Logan was in the shipyard, welding cold steel for a few shykas an hour, while I was making deals worth millions. *Oh yeah, Landau, I know where you are and what you're doing, but communicating directly with you is no longer appropriate for me. We aren't kids in the river anymore. Our lifestyles no longer have anything in common. Ever since we were kids, winning Amy was the goal. I've never stopped wanting her. Making love to her will be my erotic victory.*

"Programmed Low-Altitude Vehicles," Elder Buchart muttered against his portal, interrupting my impassioned ruminations as he watched PLAVs pass silently below in electronically monitored lanes, causing our vehicle to rock slightly.

"Yeah, what about them?" I answered with a hint of irritation.

Father prattled on, oblivious to my question. "The Automated Destination System, or ADS as commonly referred to, was an invention Ramsey developed from his wartime service in the SS." He sneered but kept looking out the portal with his back to me. "It employs a system similar to the technology used by the military to direct missiles to their targets."

"So what? That's common knowledge," I exasperatedly begged for his point. Being tethered to my father was torture. *I hate it, hate it, hate it!* I screamed inside my head. *I want to break free, but I need his damn money and contacts, not to mention the loyalty of his board members.*

Father wagged his head in disgust but still didn't turn to face me, an irritating mannerism he used against me when he was pissed. "Why didn't our people come up with the PLAV concept?" he asked, talking to his portal. "Why weren't we at the beginning of the Automated Destination System?" he mumbled aloud for my benefit.

I rolled my eyes with an impatient sigh and gritted my teeth.

"We have aerospace engineers and satellites. Why not us?" he continued calmly, his voice trailing away.

He was scolding me as if I was still a kid. *Damn him. He's making it my fault that we weren't first with innovations that he should've done while he ran the show instead of waiting to blame me.*

"Now they say Ramsey has the end-all."

"You mean pimping his robots?" I responded with a smirk. Father groaned. "Okay, what end-all?" I snapped defensively.

"Moon Glow," he said flatly.

"They've only been working on it for the last twelve years," I remarked sarcastically.

Dad's dark, heavy eyes darted back and forth, following streaks of orange light in the black space outside his window. "Ramsey already has a successful lunar mining operation. Tourism is next," he mumbled, "and it won't be long before Moon Glow's lunar transmitter begins programming. It'll alter everything."

"Oh, yeah? What'll they broadcast? Roboporn?" I laughed.

Dad's voice remained irritatingly calm, ignoring my attempts at sarcastic humor. "The government will no longer hold sway over information. We'll all have to buy in. The moon and its resources will be Ramsey's satellite. He'll have the world by the throat. Can you imagine just the tourism potential? It'll be the elite's most sought-after destination. Eventually, everyone will want to go there. Thinking of all the business opportunities that will spin off from Moon Glow is mind-boggling."

I rolled my eyes again and frowned. "Ah, we were smart to pass on Moon Glow. Suckers are buying up Prescott shares just on Ramsey's reputation. He blew it when he had that affair with one of his advanced human imitations. Those fools who invested in Ramsey's reputation will lose big-time."

"I wouldn't be so hasty to write off Moon Glow," he countered and leaned back with a sigh to watch fleeting lights dart over the moon roof. "We didn't invest in Ramsey's PLAVs at the beginning either, and look what's happened. Manufacturers, including us, are producing PLAVs as fast as we can. Soon, no one will be in grounded vehicles anymore. The streets will be for PLAV parking. Thanks to Ramsey, there's no need for expensive bridges and tunnels or polluting fuels. He's lifted civilization above all that."

"Sounds like he has you sold too."

My remark took him aback. I could tell. "You should know by now I only invest in a sure thing. We'll let Ramsey take risks developing Moon Glow. If it fails, it'll break him."

"And if it succeeds?" I questioned.

He turned to face me for the first time. His stern look told me I should have instinctively known the answer and not asked the question in the first place. "We'll simply legislate it away from him."

"How?"

His response remained artificially patient. "We'll orchestrate the will of the people. They'll do it for us. They always do."

The masses will trump genius. I must remember that.

"Why do you think there are so many competing PLAV manufacturers? Together with Mire and Genesis, we incited the masses to take Ramsey's PLAVs away from him years ago. That's why Ramsey created Moon Glow. We squeezed him so hard that he had to defend himself, fight back, and win. It's what entrepreneurial geniuses do."

I sat back, pondering his answer, but was again distracted by the two burly bodyguards facing me with electronic buttons in their ears. Their heads weaved slightly with the motion of the PLAV, their expressions stoically unmoved. I suddenly felt uncomfortable. Was our conversation being monitored? Who knew what was being transmitted by those buttons in their ears? I nudged Father with a nod toward our bodyguards.

"Oh, don't worry about them. Checks and balances define their boundaries. As heir to Buchart Industries, you must create checks and balances. These men are loyal to me because of what I can do for them or to them."

"Getting back to legislating Moon Glow away from Ramsey like we did his ADS, what if the public perceives us as political gangsters for stealing another Prescott invention?" I asked.

"When families need the energy to keep warm or go to work, they aren't going to care who owns Moon Glow. They'll only want you to make it work for them."

"If Ramsey invented Moon Glow that's light-years ahead of anything anyone else has come up with, what's to say he's not already working on something more far-reaching that'll even make Moon Glow obsolete?" I questioned.

"We'll keep after him like jackals with investigations and lawsuits from every angle. He'll soon find whatever he creates will eventually wind up in our hands. That's when he'll collapse."

I laughed and slapped my knee. Dad's gaze returned to the portal. "He's the dark ghost, James. He's taken on the mantle. We have to defend humanity from him."

Our PLAV settled onto its programmed destination, a parking structure at the far eastern edge of the city. I was about to pose another question, but he raised his hand to cut me off. Our security quickly exited the vehicle and held the doors open on either side. We cautiously followed.

A man stood alone in front of a dimly lit stairwell with his hands tucked into his beige trench coat pockets. A cold wind tugged at my scarf as a half-moon sliced through ominous, dark clouds tumbling in from the sea. Darkness tightened. Shadows beneath the man's brimmed hat concealed his face. Dad signaled for the bodyguards to remain by the PLAV. As we approached, Dad paused as if he and the stranger were studying each other. I stepped out from behind Dad and stood to his right, intuitively feeling the symbolism.

Dad pulled a small electronic device from inside his overcoat and handed it to the stranger. The device contained a copy of a phony investment contract for the senator's manufacturing company and proof of payment that required hand delivery to avoid discovery by hackers. The transfer of funds had already gone through. I knew because I transferred them myself. The senator's company was an investment dump, a fraud run by corrupt accountants on Genesis's payroll.

"This is for the senator," Dad said.

The stranger placed the device inside his coat. Then, without a word, he turned mechanically and descended the stairwell.

27

THE DREADED DEPLOYMENT

Logan Landau

An icy crust covered the window of my loft apartment. It was going to be another frigid day in the shipyard. I slid my arms into the cold, stiff sleeves of my leather welders jacket dotted with tiny burn holes and permeated with the smell of welding smoke. I had not slept much since my last patrol in Umboten, the sector's northernmost outpost. My gray, camouflaged SS uniform and triangular cap, the kind Dad wore, lay neatly on my bunk.

A newscast on the television across the room broke for a weather report. A blizzard with high winds was in the offing. I turned to watch. I'd never experienced such a cold winter. There was a lot of speculation as to why the weather was becoming so extreme. Everyone had an informed opinion, but no one knew for sure.

The news anchor's deep, articulate voice-over returned with a visual of Senator Aaron Mire standing at a podium, center stage, with a colorful array of sector flags behind him and an audience of Genesis dignitaries in front of him. "Now, for more on that story, let's turn to Telstar's eye, Matt Blaze, at the Rutledge Hotel in downtown Boston. Matt ..."

I sat on the edge of my bed to watch. Exhaustion bent my back from another sleepless night on the troop train. The senator was tall and lean with black hair made stark by graying temples. Ruggedly handsome, with rough-hewn features, his chin was square and strong. I'd heard his eyes were what held you. They said he could jolt you with a glance.

Amy was sitting at a VIP table in front of the stage. The senator had awakened his audience's fear of being left behind to face what he said had come due. Citizens were weary of micro wars, nightly riots, and the ever-present Tezca. They'd join ranks with anyone who'd protect them.

"And now ..." The Senator smiled broadly, then paused to let applause heighten before extending his right hand toward Amy. With a flick of his wrist, he summoned her to join him. "The person you're all waiting for, Amy Ramsey!"

Amy walked boldly up a red-carpeted ramp and across the stage to a standing ovation, her smile beaming and chin raised. Her long strides appeared purposeful, like she knew what she wanted and was walking directly to it. I could only admire her.

✦ ✦ ✦

Logan Landau

"Corporal Landau, next. Landau," the military conductor announced while looking down at the drop-off schedule on his hand-held reader. It was dusk when I stepped down from the troop train in my rumpled SS uniform. The tired-sounding vintage train let SS soldiers off at their assigned locations along the northern border. With so many stops, the journey was interminable. I reset my triangular hat, pulling it down slightly to one side like Dad always did.

I had not seen my father in years. Following his divorce from Mom, Dad married a much younger woman and moved to the Southern Sector. Mother remarried, too, but her new husband was another disappointing compromise. I telephoned her every so often.

My orders were to join a patrol at an intersection in downtown Umboten at 1700 hours. We were assigned seating on the troop train according to our rendezvous schedules. While the city was under quasi-sector control, the northern frontier's autonomous fiefdoms loomed only a few kilometers north. It was a lawless place where warlords ruled and dark ghosts took sanctuary. The cold air was still and damp, with snow in the forecast. I hung my weapon on my shoulder and trudged up the steep sidewalk.

How did Umboten become so bad so fast? I wondered.

Autonomous zones like Umboten, with their militias, had become islands of misery. Permissive politicians tolerated criminal behavior for years until it spiraled out of control and the bad guys took over. Criminal redoubts had spread nationwide like dog messes that the government never cleaned up. Left undisciplined, the dog moved on and pooped wherever it wanted. It all seemed so hopeless. For some, the deliberate dismantling of society represented exciting change, but for others, change was threatening.

The place looked more run-down than the last time I was there. Deserted streets had boarded-up, burned-out shops on either side. Criminal enterprises fueled the local economy. I hated going there. I wished they'd assign me elsewhere.

I passed a deserted cinema with torn and faded posters in broken display cases. Stale, damp air seeped through warped plywood-covered doors. The title of the last show on the marquee had missing red letters. A slate-gray sky darkened as ice formed a slippery sheen on the sidewalk. I picked up the pace. Herbal cooking smells from a ten-story apartment building farther up the hill warmed the air slightly, or perhaps it was just my imagination.

I came to an intersection next to a vacant corner store, my rendezvous point to join the patrol. A red light on the traffic signal glared at an empty cross street. I exhaled warmth into my cold hands and marched in place.

Suddenly, a blinding pulse of hot white light preceded a thunderous boom as an invisible force hurled me down the icy cement sidewalk amid tumbling debris and billowing black smoke. My head banged against the cement as I bounced. The universe suddenly turned black and disappeared.

I fell into a time gap until I woke to the sound of boots against the cobbled way. Men were shouting orders. I was shaking uncontrollably beneath a dusting of snow when a strong hand took hold of my shoulder and turned me over to face the night sky. Stars ripped through fleeing remnants of purple storm clouds.

"You okay?" an SS officer asked. His voice sounded as though he was speaking through a long metal pipe. Loud, overlapping whispers began vying for attention from deep in my brain. They sounded like a distant radio transmission fading in and out of static. They were frightened whispers, desperate and confused. My head began to throb.

"I think so," I answered and rose onto my elbows to check my torso. Clumps of newly fallen snow rolled down onto my lap. "I don't see any blood. What happened? How long have I been sprawled on the street covered with snow?"

"The bomb set off sensors we picked up at headquarters about three hours ago," the officer said. "The weather held us up, so I guess you've been facedown on the street for five or six hours." The officer's face was red from the cold. I immediately noticed his square jaw and haunting stare. He reminded me of the prototypical officer commonly featured on SS recruiting posters.

"Here, you want to stand up? I'll give you a hand. You can warm up in the medivac. Your lips are blue, and you're shaking all over. There's a thermos of coffee in there. Are you sure you're okay to stand? No sharp pains anywhere? There's a big black and blue knot on your forehead and another behind your left ear."

My legs wobbled, numbed by the icy cold that seeped into my bones. The officer quickly reached out to steady me.

"I'm okay, just a little dizzy," I told him.

I sat bundled in a thermal blanket inside the empty medivac while SS soldiers prowled the street where the blast occurred, searching snow-covered rubble for the patrol I was to join. A terrible depression entered the medivac, bowing my head until my forehead nearly touched my knees. The river came to mind. It was my escape. I could hear the laughing voices of the kids who played there and could all but breathe in the heavy scents of moss, peat, and wild mint.

The officer returned and stood at the gaping mouth of the medivac, where he squinted inside. "You do'n' all right?"

"Yes, sir."

"It's gonna to be a crowded flight back. We're bagging the patrol. They all bought it. It's a mess back there."

"They were all killed? Everyone?"

"Yeah. Did you know any of them?"

"No, sir."

"You're lucky to have been up the street far enough from the blast, or you would've been one of them. Sometimes the enemy gets our rendezvous schedules and plans their ambushes accordingly." He shrugged. "It's how it is up here."

Soldiers were running toward the medivac with heavy black body bags in tow. "Here, let me help," I quickly offered.

"No. You need to get checked out at the aid station. You probably have a concussion, for starters."

It was late at night the following day. I sat on a bench inside a dingy, dimly lit train station awaiting the troop train. I had been released several hours before from a makeshift aid station in a partially destroyed elementary school. It was a quick triage. Intense fighting in Marvoc, further east along the border, inundated the ramshackle facility with seriously wounded SS men and women. There were swollen black and blue welts on my head and right shoulder. They told me I had a severe concussion. An SS physician gave me some meds, authorization for a month's leave, and a referral to one of the sector's military hospitals for further diagnosis and treatment.

Two other soldiers were sleeping farther down the pew. One had a bloodied patch over his right eye, while the other sat with his head laid back and snoring through his gaping mouth. The train wouldn't arrive for another two hours. I couldn't doze off with the ringing in my ears and the constant whispers in my head.

I needed Amy's balance. I always felt we were the same person in different bodies. *My God, I need her now.* I yanked my cyber phone from my breast pocket and tried to dial, but I was still shivering so much that I misdialed. I tried again. Who was I to be calling the famous Amy Ramsey? I berated myself. *I'm worried about my brain. My head hit hard when the lights went out, and I tasted blood in my mouth. I think I might be bleeding inside my head.*

I fumbled to pinch the phone between my sweating cheek and shoulder, only to have it slip out and fall on the deck. Enraged, I slammed my fist against the bench, waking one of the soldiers. Dad's angry image passed before my mind's eye. The soldier quickly fell back to sleep. Panic closed in tight. I held the phone to my ear and breathed deeply.

Voicemail. *Damn!*

28

EROTIC VICTORY

Amy Ramsey

Not wanting to wake James, I stealthily slipped out of bed and tiptoed through the living room of my penthouse to the bar, where I quietly placed ice cubes in a glass and poured a healthy premixed martini. I turned to face the city's lights through the floor-to-ceiling windows that comprised the entire north and east walls. Dad's opposition was mustering support for their assault on Moon Glow, using his sordid affair to gain public support. I couldn't believe he acted with such careless disregard for the consequences.

I noticed scattered fires in the city, most likely set by dark ghosts, a nightly event to which we'd become accustomed. My gaze drifted northward to the jagged, dark outline of the shipyard and thoughts of Logan. I tied the belt to my white silk robe and leaned back against the bar with my cocktail.

"I'm sorry, Logan," I whispered to his image in my mind's eye as I recalled what had occurred the previous evening. I had attended a Genesis gathering at the Rutledge Hotel with James, Senator Mire, and a ballroom full of dignitaries. We drank too much, and there was that white pill James swallowed with a mischievous grin.

"Here you go, Amy. Want a lift?" he said and handed me one.

Our collective mood increasingly depended on government-endorsed medications to lift us above our depression while keeping us productive. Though the inventive minority was making billions producing what society and the military needed, the economy had a gaping socialist hole at the bottom. The wealth genius created fell into the hands of slackers and bureaucrats.

James's inherited position at Buchart Industries and his stature in Genesis gave him a spirited air of invincibility I hadn't seen in him before. I knew his prestige was unearned. He knew it too. His eyes widened when he gave me one of his white tablets. I looked up at him with mocked disapproval before catching his infectious grin and downing the pleasure maker. What a fool I was. I wondered if I was entering one of Margo's experiences.

Upon our return to my place, we staggered to the couch and collapsed in a fit of hysteria. It wasn't joyous laughter but rather a nervous reaction to the absurd. Then, during bizarre moments of James's perverse fantasy and my stupor of indifference, James finally had his erotic victory.

"It wasn't loving and gentle like the first time with you, Logan."

Guilt hardened my face while my gaze remained riveted on the shipyard. "James was punishing me for not loving him. He was rough, and there was something sadistically twisted in how he used me. I'm left ashamed."

I took another drink to quell my pulsating temples from the drug and straightened my back with a subtle groan. *The time is close when I won't need James anymore.* He knew that but didn't care so long as he could feed his ego what it wanted now. He never looked ahead. Too many consequences were awaiting him.

✦ ✦ ✦

Logan Landau

My shift at the yard concluded. I sought to divert thoughts of my experience in Umboten by visiting Brian, my childhood friend. Brian presided over the shipyard's lab. To my surprise, I had to skirt a blackened circle on the entryway floor where someone had tossed a Molotov cocktail during the night shift. The high decorative ceiling was smoke stained, and a gasoline smell hung over everything. Black-uniformed police with automatic weapons prowled the Gothic-style building, while others stood at the entryway checking the work badges of everyone who entered the building.

Brian was at a desk against the far wall, hunched over a computer keyboard with a pen clenched between his teeth. The harsh glow of the computer reflected against his thick, wire-rimmed glasses. He would have had his doctorate by now if dark ghosts hadn't burned down the science building at the university. Smoking out the privileged, they called it.

"Hey." I positioned myself directly before him, breaking his concentration and causing him to glance up.

"Oh, hi, Logan."

"What's up? You seem engrossed," I said slowly, with exaggerated articulation for Brian to read my lips.

"Oh, I'm just … I'm trying to …" He grimaced with frustration. "Ugh. I'm struggling with how our immune system recognizes viruses," he explained in his flat, monotone voice. "You know something about them. We've talked about it before."

"You guys work on viruses here too? I thought you did metallurgy stuff like welds, stresses, things like that."

"Yeah, as you can imagine, it's a personal thing for me. The lab was closed cuz of the cocktail, so I came in to use the computers and catch up on my research. Hell is everywhere you turn these days, isn't it?"

That's a popular phrase these days, I thought.

I sat on the windowsill, where the sun's warmth was soothing.

"Mr. Ramsey's home from Moon Glow," Brian announced with a grin.

"I know. You were telling me about your problem with viruses?" My brain kept replaying the explosion in Umboten. I didn't want it to, but it did, so I asked the question, knowing Brian would give a lengthy explanation that would allow me time to clear my head—if that was possible anymore. I could hardly concentrate on what he was saying through the noise of overlapping whispers. I felt like I was coming apart.

"My body knows how to find a virus and, in most cases, how to destroy it too," Brian said. "It does it every time I get over the flu. The problem is I don't get it. I don't understand what my chemistry knows how to do. Reason learns about a phenomenon after the fact. There seems to be a different kind of intelligence that leads the way. Know what I mean?"

"Interesting thought."

He pondered momentarily and grunted as he strained to explain a point. "Okay, look. There was a fish too heavy to swim fast enough to catch food. It was at risk of dropping out of the gene pool. Over time, it learned to shoot water from its mouth at insects that alighted on plants by the edge of rivers where it hung out. A well-aimed salvo would knock a bug off a leaf so it'd fall into the river, where this aptly named Archer Fish could easily swim over and have a well-earned meal.

"What's teaching the Archer Fish and why? Think about it, Logan. What rushes clotting agents to a bleeding cut to prevent continuous hemorrhaging? Did you know that when a cell in your body is about to die from a toxin, it'll signal other cells to be aware of what killed it? What's behind that?"

I shrugged.

"Let's go even deeper as to why the Archer Fish strove to survive in the first place. Why is everything programmed to persist? Is it to preserve a life form? Why? What cares?"

29

MARGO'S ARCHETYPE

Amy Ramsey

My PLAV came to rest on the Crittenden Hotel's Plavpad. The Crittenden is an exclusive South Sector seaside resort patronized by celebrities and their following. I finished reading a news article involving Margo when I shut off my reader. She was becoming a problem. Worse still, the media connected everything she did to Dad and me.

Customs officials at the airport detained Margo and a character actor in the sunset of his career for possessing a controlled substance. Only by prevailing on the Bucharts was I able to have their charges dismissed. Then, the idiot's bimbo wife decided to sue for divorce, which would likely cause more adverse publicity. Margo's infamous parties and association with the fringe were becoming a drag.

Then, to balance my anger, I recalled a time from

childhood when I walked cautiously toward the half-opened door to Dad's study. Dressed in my pale blue bathrobe and pajamas, it was time for a good night kiss, but on tiptoeing farther, I could see he was on the phone. He glanced at me in the light's fringes, his salt and pepper hair combed back straight and his blue pin-striped shirt unbuttoned at the collar. Robust and manly, his voice was deep, but love always surfaced to soften his face when he smiled at me.

Someday, I'm going to be important like Dad. I'll make him proud of me, that's for sure.

Father motioned me to enter with two flicks of his wrist while speaking in a foreign language to his friends overseas. *I'm intruding*, I thought and backed into the shadows before whipping around and racing up the stairs to my room.

A half-moon had crossed the width of my bedside window when I heard a light knock at my door. Margo opened it and peered inside. I moaned and pulled the soft flannel sheets up to my chin.

"Hey, Margo." My pouting voice begged attention.

"Dad was looking for you earlier. He said you came to his study and were gone when he looked up again."

"Yeah, he was on the phone, so I didn't want to bother him." I pushed the blankets down and squinted at my sister as she sat gently on the edge of my bed. Then I grinned and changed the subject, as I sometimes did to entice her to stay with me longer.

"Margo, you know what?"

"What?"

"I love Logan."

"I know you do." She gently pushed back the golden hair on my temple with a grin.

"Do you think he'll want to marry me when we're older?"

"Well, I think it's possible. But for now, be good friends and see what happens."

She lay across the width of my bed just below my feet and rested her chin on the backs of her hands while she surveyed the moonlit valley far below through the tall bedside window. The river appeared as a glimmering silver ribbon winding through the dark forest to the sea. I crawled from under the covers, draped my arm around her waist, and lay beside her.

"I love it so much, Amy."

"You love what so much?"

"Just the excitement of being alive. Look out there. It's so magical, and it's all waiting for me to make whatever I want with it. Know what I mean?"

"Yeah, I think so. I mean, I feel that way too sometimes."

"Remember the book about the legend of Pandora I used to read to you? It was your favorite and mine too. I must have read it to you a hundred times. I even did a paper on the legend at the academy." She grinned in her mysterious way. I didn't know what to make of her look. Her eyes began to fill as if she was about to cry.

"Why do you like Pandora so much? She let all those terrible things out of her magic box," I said.

"So that you know, it wasn't a box in the original story. It was an urn."

"What's an urn?

"It's like a big jar. Anyway, I thought of Pandora as just a curious little girl. Then, as I became older, I wondered why the gods chose Pandora to receive a mysterious gift that

215

she was not allowed to open. I became suspicious that the gods were playing her. Know what I mean?"

"No, but I'm sure you'll tell me." I chuckled at her intensity.

"They knew Pandora would open their gift. That's why they gave it to her. Who gives a gift to a little girl and then tells her not to open it? Come on."

"Yeah, that seemed strange to me too."

"Supposedly Pandora's curiosity got the best of her, so she opened the urn, and yada, yada, yada. You know the story. But who's in the wrong here? Think about it. Where did those terrible things come from that Pandora unknowingly set loose, if not from the gods? They used her to take the blame. Maybe that's why we're so attracted to the story."

"How so?" I questioned.

"Because of the moral trap the gods set for us."

"Like what?"

"Like when our curiosity leads to pleasure. Have you ever seen a fly stuck in the sticky sweetness it craves? Well, that's us in a lot of ways."

"Why is that?"

"The gods don't want us messing with immortality, I guess. Mortal pleasures lure us away. The gods' deceit shocked us so much that it became imprinted on our collective consciousness."

"Collective what?"

"Collective consciousness. It means we all share the same vague memory of something that has happened. It's stored somewhere in our brains. Dad talked to us about it, remember?"

"Oh yeah, I remember now. You never explained Pandora's story to me that way before," I remarked timidly, sensing Margo's dark side surfacing, a side of her I'd seen before but didn't understand.

"Well, you're thirteen now, so I can."

"But that sucks, Margo. Why do people write stories like that? Why do they always blame women for the bad things that happen?"

She shrugged off the question. "The legend of Pandora I read to you was a kid's story. I came across a copy of the original at the academy, in which Pandora was the first woman the gods created. She was made innocent and so beautiful as to be irresistible to men. She was what artists try to replicate in their statues and paintings. In her innocence, Pandora opened the gift the gods gave her and unknowingly released evil into the world. Only hope hid under the lid and didn't spill out with the rest of the crap."

"Ugh." I frowned with a crumpled lip. "I liked the legend of Pandora the way my kid's book told it."

Margo glared at me and held me by my shoulders. "Listen, Amy. Listen very closely."

She took hold of my shoulders and shook me a little to jar my attention. Her jaw clenched. That was when I realized there was something wrong with Margo. I knew she saw a shrink, but I didn't know for what.

"There's only one woman who has ever lived," she ranted in a heated way that scared me. "Do you hear me? Just one, the archetype. She's had many names and as many forms, but there's only been the one female archetype."

"Archa—what?" I asked sheepishly.

"Archetype. It means the original all others try to

replicate. Oh, let me see. Perhaps I can explain it another way. Take a circle, for example. There's only one true circle. It exists as an idea. Right?"

"I guess."

"When anyone draws a circle, they're trying to copy the original idea of a circle. Get it? You'll try to live up to the female archetype too. It's how they wired us."

I was deep in thought, trying to fathom Margo's explanation, when she did a sudden bipolar shift and sprang at me like a cat. She rolled me over and tickled me into a squirming fit of laughter. I was still laughing when she opened the bed covers for me. Then she brought the soft flannel sheet to my chin and kissed my forehead.

"That kiss is from Daddy, who loves you very much." She kissed me a second time. "And that kiss is from me, because I love you too." She clicked the lamp switch by my bed and left my room, smiling back at me from over her shoulder. Darkness rushed in but for the shaft of silver moonlight angling through my bedside window.

30

MARGO'S DARK SIDE

Amy Ramsey

I exited my PLAV atop the resort, went directly to Margo's suite, and rang the doorbell while straightening my blue blazer. A short, rotund Latin maid dressed neatly in a gray and white uniform answered the door. Her eyes immediately widened. I no longer wore a mask, except at locations where they were required or to conceal my identity.

"Miss Ramsey!" She nervously patted her hair in place on her temples and straightened her apron. "Please come in. What an honor. I'll tell your sister you're here."

A man in white tennis shorts and a colorful Hawaiian shirt entered the spacious living room, wearing a stylish five o'clock shadow, with his hair manicured to look in disarray. I chuckled to myself. Guys like him were all cheap replicas of one another.

He grinned confidently to the side of his face and swaggered toward me. "The famous Amy Ramsey," he croaked as if performing an ad for television, his head wagging with bravado. "Harry," he introduced himself. He looked familiar. I'd seen him in bit parts on television.

"You'll have to excuse us, Harry. I'm here for a private meeting with my sister." Jolted in place by my curt rebuke, he stopped short, his mouth falling slightly ajar.

Margo stormed angrily into the room, tying off her white terrycloth beach robe. "What do you mean ordering my guest around like that? Stay right where you are, Harry."

Her face flushed from anger or alcohol. I couldn't tell which. I immediately noticed how her porcelain-like complexion had become ruddy. Dark patches under her eyes and considerable weight loss didn't flatter her.

I turned to dumbfounded Harry. "My PLAV is on the pad with some large gentlemen inside that'll do whatever I tell them. What's it going to be, Harry?"

After a moment of pensive self-reflection, he turned to Margo. "I'll call you later." He gave me a quick, hard look and went for the door, his suave veneer disintegrating. Margo folded her arms over her chest, leaned back against the grand piano, and began gnawing nervously at the inside of her cheek.

"Is little sister here to counsel big sister? Is that it? You think you have some lofty right bestowed on you by your Genesis gangsters. Don't tell me you believe the ads about who they say you are. None of it is true. Your New Order is a sham, a conclave of rats and leeches. So don't think you can come here and counsel me about anything."

The maid reentered the room. "Take the day off, Maria,"

Margo ordered gruffly. "Don't worry. I'll pay you for it." Maria didn't take her stare from the carpeted floor as she quickly hurried from the room.

"Look, Margo. I didn't come here to fight with you."

"Oh no, of course not, but you can barge into my space unannounced and rudely take charge. Right?" Margo shouted on her way to the bar, where she poured a stiff drink two fingers tall. "What gives you the right?"

"You'll find three messages on your phone in as many days telling you when I'd be here."

"Oh, I should drop everything and make way for the New Order's shooting star?" She gulped her drink, banged the empty glass on the bar, and poured another. "Want one?"

I ignored her offer. "You owe it to our mother to use the abilities you were born with." It was not what I intended to say, but it boiled up and came out anyway. I didn't know why. I'd never used our mother to make a point before.

"Yeah, sure. We hardly knew our mother."

She's right, I thought. I was so inept when it came to my sister. I went there angrily but wanted to reach out to her as she did when she tucked me in and kissed me good night. The memory caused my eyes to glisten. I sat on the arm of the couch.

"There was a time when you were excited about life—remember? You held life's magic in your hands in those days. This delusional lifestyle isn't you, Margo. It isn't the stuff of the archetype you told me about."

Margo's eyes began to fill, and her voice cracked when she tried to answer. She turned away and faced the wall. "I knew I wasn't strong enough to be the heroine

I described to you. Now, even Dad is facing a scandal I can't explain." She groaned, on the verge of tears, and inhaled a jittery breath when she angrily whipped back around to face me.

"Oh yeah, I'm rebellious, that much I had right, but it's without purpose. I don't burn for anything like you," Margo lamented. "My interests are always short-lived and fleeting, leaving me empty. Okay, I admit that I pretended not to care." Self-loathing pulled down the corners of her lips while her eyes widened, searching me for a hint of compassion, but I'd hardened and couldn't give her one.

Her tone went up an octave as bitterness tightened her face. "I laughed at what was shameful and grinned at deceit in mockery of the human condition, but secretly I blamed myself for everything." She gave me a guilt-ridden glance from the corner of her eye. "Oh, I have regrets. I guess it's what you used to call my dark side when we were kids."

My voice softened. "But you're cavorting with people on the dark side."

"And you're not?" she snapped back at me.

She's right again. Genesis has millions of followers. I don't know how many of them are tainted.

"I know my so-called friends don't care about me. There's no savior. I looked for one, maybe in the wrong places, but I came up empty. There's no one to whom I can turn. Do you hear what I'm saying? I'm alone." A rush of panic took her breath away. She sucked in a halting breath that was more like a gasp.

My sister was unraveling. I immediately rushed to her side, but she shrugged me off with a quick shoulder jerk.

My perceived success made her failure more glaring. I'd become repulsive to her. Sobbing uncontrollably, she slid down the wall and slowly sank to the floor.

"There's nothing left of me anymore," she mumbled. "Go on. Get out. I don't want you here."

31

WORLD'S END

Logan Landau

I filed into the human stream, pouring into a park on a narrow peninsula called World's End. Though cold and wet, my last patrol in Umboten was uneventful. I was safe until my next deployment. Everyone was masked and wearing government-issued, clear plastic ponchos. No one was permitted entry to the park without the mandated attire. Fearing the newest variant of the Tezca and terrorist threats, people risked attending only the most well-guarded events.

The peninsula's sparsely forested hills were ablaze with colorful wildflowers in summer. A floating bandshell used for summer concerts sat just twenty meters offshore at high tide. White boats of various sizes littered the bay's crystal-blue water. Gatherings of New Order enthusiasts lined both shores.

Suddenly, an eruption of shouts and applause seized my attention. I climbed onto a smooth white boulder at the water's edge, made warm by the winter sun. I could see Amy's penthouse overlooking the bay. An involuntary grin crept onto my face as I absorbed the joy of those around me, a rare emotion these days. A white yacht cut through the icy blue water from the shipyard's jagged gray skeleton.

A man in a dark blue suit stood on the foredeck, waving to his supporters on either shore, his thick hair tossing wildly.

"There he is. Look, Marsha. There's the senator. Can you believe it? There he is!" an elderly man behind me exclaimed to his wife.

The bandshell rocked in the cruiser's wake when it pulled alongside. Sunlight blinked from the floating stage's bulletproof glass façade. I set my phone to the app slated to carry the senator's remarks and plugged in my ear button. Tall red buoys lining the channel swayed lazily with the outgoing tide. The senator's ovation increased when he stepped onto the bandshell and greeted the members of his delegation.

Television crews stumbled along the shore, lugging their equipment. When I thought the thunderous welcome had peaked, Mire whipped around and opened his arms wide to embrace his audience, heightening a roar that filled the bay. The call of "Mire, Mire, Mire!" pealed down the coastlines on either side of the bay like cannon salvos.

I searched the ten-member delegation behind him and immediately found Amy. James Buchart and his father were standing on either side of her. As I recalled from his television appearances, the senator was tall with distinguished gray streaks on his temples. His face was smooth and handsomely sculpted, his suit perfectly tailored to his sinewy frame.

He calmly adjusted the microphone on the podium and pulled a folded paper from his breast pocket. The crowd stilled. To everyone's surprise, he began reading passages from the *Rubaiyat of Omar Khayyam*, the World Government's *Hymn of the Revolution*, and the Mahabharata's *Bhagavad Gita*.

He read with such calming eloquence the silence tightened but for Mire's melodic voice and the gentle waves lapping the base of the rock on which I sat. I closed my eyes to let peace enter me without distractions. He was drawing everyone to him. I could feel him tugging at me as if I belonged to him. He became a father, brother, and son in those opening moments—our protector, idol, and hero, whatever anyone needed. Fear melted, and hope soared.

He paused for effect and suddenly changed course. "Yesterday, on your behalf, I proposed the government enter negotiations with Prescott Industries to assume control of the company's unlicensed Moon Glow project and ..." My eyes flipped open as a surge of frenzied applause interrupted the peace. Raised fists and pulsating chants, a residue of the World Government's revolution, forced him to step back from the microphone while nodding his approval. Then he boldly came forward to finish his statement, "... and employ its benefits for the greater good. Moon Glow belongs to you, the citizens who enabled it."

Mire paused for another explosion of applause, then shook his figure at the microphone in a warning jester. "John Ramsey didn't create Moon Glow alone. No. He needed your infrastructure, your scientists trained in your universities, the protection of your security forces, and the freedom for which your fellow citizens gave their lives. Moon Glow is the result of our investment. It belongs to us!"

While people benefitted from Mr. Ramsey's genius and risk-taking courage, it didn't seem fair to me that they denied him ownership of his accomplishments. To whom would they turn to create the next stepping-stone into the future, if not to a person like John Ramsey? If there was one.

The simultaneous detonation of a hundred thousand cheering voices sent goose bumps down my arms. A furious backlash against the sculptors of destiny was erupting at World's End. Mire tamped down the ovation with both hands and grinned. "You've waited a long time for me, and at last, I'm here among you. Providence has brought us together. The struggle against evil is never over—never. Endless wars against it are nothing new. The only difference is it's our fight now." He paused. "It's new for us." His voice reverberated between the shores when he abruptly left the microphone and reboarded the yacht tied to the rear of the bandshell.

Voices rushed heavenward like a wild wind until it seemed the sky would shatter. They said Mire was the redeemer who would forge a New Order from what was left. They said he knew the way.

Some zealous followers waded into the frigid bay, pleadingly reaching out to him. Mire's New Order had taken less than a year to wrench the Automated Destination System away from Prescott Industries. Ultimately, the government awarded Buchart Industries a lucrative contract to operate the system. Mire had said of the court's predetermined decision, "Buchart Industries' leadership has demonstrated a dedication to inclusiveness."

Prescott's attorneys argued that Moon Glow was another matter. Unlike the ADS, Moon Glow's lunar location didn't fall within the government's jurisdiction. With sinister confidence in the New Order's ability to invent laws to serve its ends, the contract to manage Moon Glow was written and held in abeyance, pending further legislative formalities. Genesis's corporate contributors were already submitting proposals.

"The dismantling of Prescott Industries," wrote one underground reporter, "is akin to slaughtering the noblest lion in the forest and feeding it piecemeal to jackals."

32

SUAREZ

James Buchart

A tragedy occurred involving Prescott's Automated Destination System, operated by Buchart Industries. A tear in the heavily traveled eastbound, virtual corridor caused more than a dozen PLAVs to plummet from the sky as if tumbling from an invisible bridge.

The government's initial response was that excessive PLAVs were allowed into the corridor.

"PLAVs served by the system is the basis by which our company is allowed to charge the government," I mumbled aloud, as if rehearsing my defense. "So I ordered the system filled to the capacity during peak hours. The problem is our damn backup system, required by law, was down for repairs. The excessive power demand caused the corridor to fail."

Eight commuters perished, with several more seriously injured. The catastrophe was an unwieldy embarrassment for Mire and the Genesis Party. "Worse still, I was overseeing the system," I recounted through a hard, dry swallow.

Father's directive nine months ago kept replaying in my mind. "I'm giving you the Automated Destination System to cut your teeth on," he told me.

It was half past six in the evening and raining when I waited on a pew-like bench in a dank alcove of Boston's archaic train terminal. Row upon row of old wooden pews faced one another. Antonio Suarez, the sector's most notorious underworld figure with roots in Umboten, entered the terminal within a circle of bodyguards in glistening black raincoats. He swaggered from his protective circle, wagging his head with a sadistic grin.

"James?"

"Yes."

He nodded and sat beside me. Either fear or loathing kept my eye contact at a minimum. With PLAV traffic ordered down, pending an investigation into the commuter disaster, commuters seeking alternative transportation packed the archaic terminal. Echoes from thousands of shoes slapping marble and garbled train announcements offered cover for a covert conversation. I noticed the six bodyguards in his entourage immediately stationed themselves within the grove of steel pillars, cutting off angles to Suarez's back.

Suarez grinned under his thick mustache, revealing a gold-capped tooth. He was short, in his late twenties, and slightly built, in contrast to his brutal reputation. He opened his beige trench coat and loosened the red scarf that covered a "Jolly Roger" tattoo on his neck.

"Your father called. We've done business before," he said in a heavy Hispanic accent, as if his words were rolling off his tongue. "You made serious trouble for the big boys, no?"

Despite Dad's secretive history of dealing with criminal enterprises, I struggled against the role. Even more revolting was the thought of needing the gangster's help in the first place. Okay, I lied and cheated to protect myself. I could accept that, but to trust in the criminal acts of others made me nervous. These guys were conscienceless killers with little regard for my father or me. Greed was the only bond between us. Sending me on this covert errand was one way Dad was punishing me for the corridor tragedy.

I wanted to send Suarez a challenging smirk, but it wasn't in me. I was still reeling from the shock of what the disaster might do to Buchart Industries and my position in Genesis. I had little regard for the carnage beyond the public pressure it brought for an investigation. It wasn't the crime, but being caught for it was always my greatest fear. "No one is a criminal until they're caught," Dad once told me.

"Yeah, I'm sure you know about the accident in our commuter corridor."

"Accident?" Suarez scoffed with a sarcastic snicker. "I don't think so. They're saying criminal negligence." Suarez studied my reaction with a provocative grin. "Of course I know about it. Everyone does. You messed up big-time. Daddy's pissed, and you know Mire must come down hard on somebody to save his ass, right?"

"Not if we can demonstrate that terrorist sabotage caused the system to fail. The company can't be held accountable for the government's failure to protect the ADS," I said, sitting back with my gaze on the floor before me. I didn't want to give Suarez the respect of making consistent eye contact. Suarez smirked and moved across the narrow aisle to the seat that faced me. Our knees nearly touched until he crossed his legs and calmly lit a cigar. His bodyguards quickly reconfigured.

Now I had no choice but to look directly at him. I still couldn't hide the sullen disgust with which I held the mobster. Suarez ignored the obvious and widened his grin before sending puff of gray smoke toward my face.

Look at him smirking at me. The son of a bitch is delighting in my predicament. Greed is all that's forcing him to tolerate me. It must infuriate him, I thought.

"So you want me to provide the cover you need to crawl out from under your mess?"

"We need evidence of terrorist sabotage to the ADS and, for good measure, another disruption to the commuter corridor to prove the point." I was coming off as irritated, but I couldn't hide it.

"You and Daddy got it all figured out, no?"

His camouflaged insults were like slaps in the face. I hated this guttersnipe. "It's what we thought would work. We have to deflect attention from the company. We have to." I awkwardly swallowed the panic in my voice and shoved my hands into my coat pockets to hide their trembling.

Suarez's smug grin pulled to one side of his face when he saw my clumsy attempt to hide my fear, and he provocatively slowed his demeanor even more.

"I see, boss. I think this operation will need to be quick, no?"

"Yes, time is critical. The media's having a field day." My anger was mounting. I could feel it growing inside my chest as he toyed with me.

"It must also be expertly planned and coordinated, yes?"

"Yes, yes. Can you do it?" I allowed my resentment of dealing with this guy to slip through the take-charge character I wanted to portray. *Damn, I'm inept at this stuff.*

"Oh, I can help you, boss, but with time being so critical, as you say, and the media all over this thing, I'm afraid the price will be high. It's reasonable, no?"

"Yes, okay, we understand. As you said, you've done business with us before. You know we're good for it."

"Your father, I know, but you, I don't. So, like I told your father, I need some expense money up front. You got it?"

I reluctantly handed him an envelope containing a thick wad of cash. Suarez tucked it into his coat and was about to stand when I quickly added to the arrangement.

"There's something else. We want a fall guy, someone to take the blame who we can lose in the legal system. Know what I mean?"

"Your father didn't mention anything about set'n someone up."

"Yeah, well, we want it part of the deal."

Suarez snickered, sensing an undercurrent of deceit. "I'm sure you have the fall guy already picked out, no?"

It was my chance to win the prize, to finally have Amy without the threat of Logan's reemergence in her life. He could be locked away in some forgotten hellhole out of the way. I'd rig the legal system. He could even meet a violent end behind bars. "His name is Logan Landau. I hear he's a shipfitter or some dumb-ass thing at the shipyard. You have a lot of union connections there. It should be easy."

"Why this Landau guy? He's a nobody. I can think of others your father would rather gut."

"It's personal."

"Oh, I see, boss. A vendetta, or maybe this guy has a pretty wife, no?" He laughed. "Okay, I'll take care of your problem, and we'll set up Landau too. Consider Landau a favor. You'll owe me." He stood, shoved his hands into black leather gloves, and walked into the dark recesses of the adjoining subway tunnel as his bodyguards hurried to converge around him.

They melted into the shadows. "Like rats," I whispered to myself.

Alone with my thoughts, the gravity of what I had commissioned washed over me. *Damn, I've no control over what they might do.* The sudden realization sent heat rushing into my face. I could feel my cheeks flush and burn. My heart was pounding. *I'm sure I made it clear I just wanted Logan set up. I'll take care of the justice system. What if something goes wrong and they kill him? Suarez wouldn't care. The matter's out of my hands.* I had no control, and that scared me.

A memory of a warm August day by the river with Logan, Amy, Brian, and Margo blossomed. Old Rachael was there, too, sitting on the bank. I held Logan's image before my mind's eye like an imprisoned avatar. *You always overlooked my propensity to lie and cheat so we could coexist with at least a modicum of friendship. Your tolerance made you appear more mature than me. Everyone knew it. I secretly hated you for that. Even as a kid, I was jealous whenever Amy smiled at you or how she reverently said your name.*

The gravity of my situation returned and burned away the thought. Since I was a kid, I'd always hated whatever stood in my way of getting what I wanted. If I were stronger, I'd be able to take what I wanted with brute force. Because I wasn't, I schemed and connived to survive.

But somewhere along the way, evil entered me. I didn't know why. I didn't ask for it to happen. It happened when I was too young to know better, an inherited trait. Whatever it was, it slowly transformed me into what I was. The corridor disaster was a manifestation of the evil that haunted me.

My brain made a sudden shift to cover the harsh truth. At least, with the bargain I struck, I was finally confident of winning Amy. She'd always been the prize. I didn't care if she loved me or not. She wanted power and fame so much that she'd do whatever I wanted to make it happen. Love didn't have to be a factor.

I scoffed at Logan's image before my mind's eye. *You never understood that eventually, no one would care what you had to do to make your wealth. They'd respect you just for having it.*

33

THE CATALYST

Logan Landau

Cold November winds rippled the bay and lashed the ship's foredeck, where I knelt welding a seam. Noon's whistle sounded from the guard tower overlooking the shipyard. I flipped up my welder's mask and squinted toward the city's skyline.

Some years ago, I mentioned my need for a job to Mr. Weinstone, who spoke to Mr. Ramsey. Mr. Ramsey contacted his friend Jack Marston, the chairman of Sector Steel, who hired me sight unseen.

While I had sleepless nights reliving the terrifying event in Umboten, they'd become less frequent. I breathed in the cold, salt-laden air. Black storm clouds were so low I could almost reach up and touch them.

Gulls huddled in leeward nooks and crannies, a sign

of an approaching nor'easter. A cold gust whipped up the collar of my leather jacket. Five rust-streaked ships lined the waterfront beneath, tending cranes as workers roamed the scaffolds clinging precariously to the gray hulks. As crews broke for lunch, brilliant arc flashes dwindled with the fading sound of rivet guns and slag hammers.

✦ ✦ ✦

Barstow and Riley

Riley, the ship fitter's foreman and an Irish Bostonian, walked the deck with Barstow, a union steward in training and a dedicated New Order "NO" type. Riley was a stern boss who wore black leather boots with steel-tipped toes and the same red flannel shirt and tan overalls. Riley caught sight of Logan welding on the foredeck. His eyes widened as he shifted a cigar stub to the other side of his mouth and nudged Barstow with a coy grin.

Barstow had a follower persona. He was gangly, with a pockmarked face, and clothed in store-bought army fatigues. While eager to please his overseers, he was equally insensitive to those in his crew. Riley spoke from the corner of his mouth.

"Ya see dat Landau character? We gotta do someth'n about dat guy. He got in from the top. Know what I mean? He's probably a plant. Anyway, I got word we gotta bring him down." He chomped down on his cigar stub.

"I ain't never seen him at NO stuff," Barstow added. "He's one a dem loners. Ya never know what he's up to."

Riley scuffed the toe of his boot against the thick ice

along the gunnel. "He's probably got someth'n on all of us. I'll bet that's why they want him outta the yard."

Barstow rubbed the black stubble on his pitted cheek. "The only guy I seen him wid is that deaf jackass from the lab. Neither of 'm is good for the yard. I'll bust 'm first chance I get. I'll find a reason. You'll see."

Riley pushed his index finger hard against Barstow's chest. "Use your head." He pulled the chewed cigar stub from his mouth with a strand of saliva and spat a piece of tobacco onto the deck. "There's some big fish after that guy. Why exactly? I don't know and don't wanna know. You do what they want when they want it done. When it comes down, be what they call a catalyst—you know, someth'n that causes someth'n to happen—but don't get directly involved. Get what I'm say'n?" Riley grinned, shoved the cigar back into his mouth, and nervously shifted it from side to side. "Dat's how ya handle dem kinda problems in the yard."

✦ ✦ ✦

Amy Ramsey

I was in the back seat of the stretch limousine I used for short trips in the city when a flash of sheer white light preceded a bone-jarring bang at the intersection just ahead. My driver crossed his arms over his face as stones, asphalt, and sand pelted the windshield. An invisible force pushed against my chest, taking my breath away and rocking the limo. I immediately stiffened with outstretched arms against the bouncing seat.

"Get down, Miss Ramsey! Protect yourself!" my driver shouted.

A desperate-looking man with a deep almond complexion and a torn white shirt ran toward the limo through a brown dust cloud. Terror was in his eyes.

I gasped. "That man is holding something. It's a cell phone. It could be what he used to set off the charge. They must have forced him out of hiding. Now they're after him."

"Yes, Miss Ramsey. Look, here they come." Human-like shadows from surrounding shops and offices tore through the dust cloud and tackled the suspected bomber by the side of my limo.

"Oh, my God. Now they've got him!" I shouted.

The terrorist hollered when he hit the pavement. The car rocked, jostled by strong, angry men. "I can't move us, Ms. Ramsey." The driver's eyes remained fixed on my frightened image in the rearview mirror. His voice raised an octave. "We're blocked. Please," he pleaded, "darken your window before they recognize you."

The growling mob kicked their prey and beat him with their fists. They finally had a chance to vent their rage, to lash back at a dark ghost. I caught glimpses of the downed man between his attackers.

"They're beating him to death. Oh my God, they've caved in his skull with a bat!" I shut my eyes and turned away.

"It's what they've done to us." My driver shook his head. "They've made us this way. We've become like the animals."

Sirens wailed in the distance. The vigilantes scurried through the sepia cloud back into their buildings like roaches. Gawking spectators replaced them, encircling the bloodied corpse.

My face hardened as I pushed a button on my console, darkening my window. "Okay, let's go."

34

THE WOMAN IN
THE PINK DRESS

James Buchart

A pair of Buchart security guards rushed me from my penthouse office to the rooftop helipad before I could sip my morning coffee. With PLAV corridors closed, Dad chose our helicopter as the quickest, most practical way to the crash site. Bent at the waist and shielding my eyes from the turbulence, I climbed aboard to find Dad seated inside, glowering at me. He motioned to the empty seat next to him. I took it and fastened my seat belt.

Damn corridor. Man is Dad pissed.

Another tear in the corridor from Boston to destinations in New York happened only minutes ago during rush hour. Early news reports indicated unknown cybercriminals compromised our Automated Destination System (ADS). Pundits were already blaming dark ghosts for the tragedy, as I had hoped. Suarez's saboteurs redirected ADS's virtual lanes on the heavily traveled eastern corridor, causing PLAVs to collide and plummet to Earth. Initial estimates put the death toll at fifty-six and climbing, with scores more injured.

Father turned to me as the helicopter lifted from the pad. "There's been another terrorist attack on our Automated Destination System." His face was hard as stone, but his eyes betrayed him. Half-closed, they seemed fatigued by what they'd seen him do. What his eyes confessed, his lips concealed, pulled as they were to one side of his face in a sinister smirk.

Given our precarious circumstances, I found his sarcasm abhorrent. He was pretending we were in control, but we were not. Now it was murder. How had it gone so far? I was a conniving cheat and a liar, but a murderer? *Ugh, my stomach's cramping. I'm going to vomit.* Cold sweat was channeling down my temple. *Oh my God, a plume of black smoke is rising over the city. It's a sign of what I've done.* The attack on the ADS had seemed our only alternative. But now that it had come to pass, I wanted to turn back the clock and start over.

Morning sunlight glinted from the white underbellies of fallen PLAVs, strewn across a riverbank like dead fish. Media helicopters were circling the site like vultures. The only recourse for commuters was grounded vehicles, which appeared backed up for miles. The helicopter shuddered as it turned sharply and descended. *Oh my God, I hate helicopters. I'm gonna heave.*

I was ashen when we touched down, my hands cold and wet.

Father paused and stood before me, blocking my path to the exit. He took hold of my arm tightly and stared at me with his familiar scowl. "I'll handle the media. You can poke around the PLAVs and look concerned but don't get involved. If you take part in rescue efforts, it'll only deepen our connection to the carnage. We must be the victims here too. Whatever you do will never be enough for them anyway, so hands off. Got it?"

"Got it."

"Okay, let's face the music."

The door swung out, forming stairs to the ground. Reporters rushed to Father, corralling him between the helicopter and their tight semicircle. I exited with the pilots to avoid attention and skirted the mob unnoticed.

Uniformed first responders trampled through the wreckage. I could hear painful groans inside an overturned PLAV, nearly muted by roaring generators, sirens, and squawking communication devices. I tuned it all out and forged ahead, sidestepping debris. I had to escape what I'd done. Flames danced on entangled PLAVs near a bridge spanning the South River. The smell of burning plastic and hot metal would be a scent trigger for future nightmares, I thought.

"It's what we've been saying all along," my father barked into a row of microphones. "There's been cyberattacks on our Automated Destination System. Terrorist gangs have targeted our nation's PLAV corridors. Buchart Industries has called for an investigation into the government's failure to protect its Automated Destination System from terrorist saboteurs." Father's voice faded behind me as I quickened my strides.

"You're a real pro, Dad. Just lead them the hell away from us."

Jackhammers, loud, metal cutting saws, and shouting rescuers mixed into a confusing roar, but the noise couldn't distract the fear stalking me through the debris field. *Damn, if indicted, I could be facing life in prison.* I quickly sidestepped a pair of medics carrying a stretcher with what appeared to be a loaded body bag, a Buchart Plastics Division body bag.

I stopped again as another team of responders hurried past with a litter carrying a bloody-faced executive in a neck brace. The bewildered commuter clung to his briefcase, his gray suit tattered and smoldering.

A beeping ambulance backed into position. I hurried out of the way into the maze of wreckage along the riverbank. Downstream, PLAVs were half-submerged. Sweat moistened the pockets under my eyes, while stinging sunbeams burned the back of my neck. I was having a claustrophobic reaction to being helplessly trapped within escalating consequences I couldn't control. The dilemma was even shortening my breath. I hastily loosened my tie and draped my navy blue suit coat over a twisted tail fin. My starched white shirt was sweat stained.

Just then, I seized upon a suspicious object in the river near shore and quickly stumbled down the steep embankment. I didn't know why the siting seemed essential to investigate, but I felt drawn to it. Sand poured into my polished wing-tipped shoes. Sounds of the chaos from the debris field faded behind me as I descended the hillside toward the river. I was desperate for peace, but there could be no respite, no refuge for me. There was no safe harbor anymore, not for a murderer. *Oh my God, what have I done?*

I suddenly froze at the river's edge. A young blonde woman in a pink dress snagged on a rock was staring at me through three feet of water. Only the toe of her black, pointed shoe broke the surface. Her blue eyes were open wide, glaring condemningly, while her long golden hair waved with the current.

She knows. Even my inner voice was trembling. I took a deep breath and quickly recalled how Dad demanded I hold on. The company and I had to survive. I quickly glanced over my shoulder. No one was watching. I had to create a resilient state of mind as Dad demanded. If I didn't, I'd certainly go mad. I memorized what he told me long ago, "It's only when a person ceases to be haunted by guilt that he can possess the necessary brutality to defeat fear." I crouched low, untethered the woman's dress, and gently pushed her away.

"With this woman, I'm casting off my guilt. I did what I had to do. Fear be gone."

The woman slid from her resting place and descended into the cold, dark depths until she disappeared. I remained motionless, staring into the slowly flowing, blue-green river covering her.

Old Rachael planted dormant thoughts of a tormenting hell in my brain years ago that began to sprout. For me, eternal confinement was the terrifying fate I feared most. While I could usually reason away what frightened me, there was always a seam between faulty reason and reality where terror would seep through.

A memory of Old Rachael quickly blossomed. We picked blueberries on White Ram's Mountain with Logan, Amy, Margo, and Brian. Old Rachael was consoling Logan about the concept of hell he learned from some friends at school. It was giving him nightmares.

I was just a kid when I overheard Old Rachael tell him hell is our projection, the play of mind upon itself. For some, the experience is sheer madness. To others, the torment can be claustrophobic panic, like having one's essence infused in stone, unable to move. She mentioned we could experience hell's many terrifying dimensions even as we live. *I swear I'm in one now.*

35

LEARNING ON THE RUN

Amy Ramsey

Dressed smartly in a dark blue business suit with a white ruffled blouse, I was in Telstar's production booth scanning a row of monitors over the director's shoulder, who sat before me in a low-backed swivel chair. "What do you think, Amy?" he asked, glancing at me over his shoulder.

With the official announcement that Senator Mire was Genesis's candidate for sector president, my opportunities mushroomed beyond anything I, or anyone else, had imagined. I had made a good choice signing with Genesis. While my success appeared like a fairy tale come true, deep below the fantasy, there were deep-seated regrets. First among them was my alliance with the Bucharts.

I was distracted by an intern's news story farther down the console. A voice-over video featuring a baby food production line barked, "According to sector authorities, Baby Rose Infant Formula made at this Orleana facility has sickened infants who consumed the product. A Baby Rose employee confessed to lacing the formula's vats with an undisclosed biological agent. Use of the contaminated product has resulted in the death of twenty-eight infants in the last three months, with thirty-seven reported seriously ill by local authorities."

I wagged my head in disgust. "Do we have to listen to that?" The intern immediately turned down the volume. "It seems nothing's too cruel anymore."

Steven Winters huddled next to me in a gray suit and pin-striped shirt with an open collar as we watched a bank of monitors that would carry Mire's interview on the production floor one flight below. Winters leaned in close, too close, and breathed deeply, his voice soft as velvet. "Hm-m, you smell great."

I closed my eyes and smirked without turning to face him. "Later, Steve, okay? Focus."

Backed by family wealth, Winters was a Genesis elite, upper-crust member. As an attorney, Mire threw him trivial legal matters of little consequence. Better known for affairs with wealthy socialites, Genesis tolerated him for his family's financial support. His curly blond hair, coal-black roots, and smooth, tanned face seemed more fitting for a Southern Sector beach than a courtroom.

I didn't care. I found Steve's carefree demeanor rather refreshing at times. *I know what he is, but I'm always in control, so I indulge when it pleases me*, I confirmed to myself.

Mire sat in a low-backed office chair on the studio

floor, dwarfed by a chromo-keyed World Government logo covering the blank green screen behind him. Telstar's Marla Kaples sat in the chair directly before him, rereading her notes for the interview. The camera focused on Mire over Kaples's left shoulder. Telstar's interview was Mire's chance to exonerate Genesis following the corridor disaster, given the organization's connection with the Bucharts.

"His eyes," I told the director, who studied the row of monitors spanning the wall. I leaned in for a closer look. "Check out those eyes. Zoom in on them, Tom, will ya?"

The director spoke calmly through the wire-thin microphone wrapped around his jaw. "Tight on the eyes, three." He watched with me, his right knee nervously bobbing like a piston. A subtle smell of hot plastic and electronic devices permeated the room. His head jerked back. "Wow. I see what you mean. They're stark, even a little scary. You want we should open on them?" Tom glanced up at me expectantly from over his shoulder.

I was apprehensive. Genesis was my opportunity as much as it was Mire's. Our symbiotic relationship was teetering. While Mire considered my advice, he mulled it over with others in his top tier. In effect, what I wanted to accomplish would be a communal decision. There would never be anything uniquely mine. I shoved my concern aside to think about it later.

"Steve, look at his eyes. They're darting around the room like he's on something, or in claustrophobic panic, looking for a way out," I whispered. "Damn, it gives me the creeps."

"Well, he's your baby, Amy." Winter's reply had the ring of a warning.

"It's too much. Let's pull back and open full," I told Tom.

Winters grinned at my confident, take-charge demeanor. I was learning on the run, but no one could tell. There were times when I felt Dad's qualities becoming my own. The exhilaration and fear he must have felt mirrored how I now felt. Paraphrasing Mire, I thought, *There's nothing new, but it's my time. It's new to me.*

"You're the boss," Tom answered mechanically. "Go full, three."

I immediately went to the angled window overlooking the production floor and the interview set, where I switched on my lapel mic. "As discussed, Senator, lose the suitcoat and roll up your shirt sleeves." My voice echoed from speakers in the gymnasium-size room below. "Two folds, sir, just halfway on your forearms." I crossed my arms and nervously rapped my fingernails against my notepad. "Somebody give the senator some water, please." My tone sounded commanding.

My eyes darted from one monitor to another, catching their perspectives as the interview unwound. Halfway through the scripted interview, Mire seemed detached. "Something's missing. He's distracted and emotionless. It's not working. Tom, Steve, have a look."

Winters peered into the monitor over my shoulder, his hand gently resting on my hip. I sighed. "Look how his shoulders slump forward and check out the pauses. He's coming across as confused. I don't believe what's happening. It's not him."

"I hear ya." Winters straightened and flipped through a copy of the script. "He's like a lousy imitation of his early days. There's no fire. Something inside the man's burned out."

As soon as his interview concluded, the senator's entourage immediately swarmed him with calculated praise and false enthusiasm. Tom's monotone voice resounded through the room. "Okay, that's a take. Put IDs on it." He looked over his shoulder at me and covered his microphone with his hand. "It'll run on Telestar's six and ten o'clock news. We'll have it on the Newsweb for the wire services in about an hour. I'll have dubs for you in a couple of days. We're running a little behind with all the political stuff."

"Okay, that'll be … fine." My voice trailed away when I noticed James on the outskirts of the huddle around Mire. Since the disaster, James and his father had become outcasts, political untouchables.

I was shocked. James looked terrible. His soured countenance appeared ghostly, his eyes dark and sunken. He seemed as though he hadn't slept in a week. *What's happening to everyone?*

North Sector's former governor, Tom Medquist, congratulated Mire when I arrived on the production room floor. Winters watched from the production room. "Great interview, Senator. That'll send them running for cover." In his midfifties, the governor was stout, with dark hair combed to the side and a chubby face.

A young public relations consultant at his side looked down at his clipboard and shoved black-rimmed glasses over the bridge of his nose. "When this hits the air, you ought to be up a couple of points by week's end."

I stood back from the inner circle with arms folded and a stern look, like an elementary school teacher observing an unruly class. My first thought was how Mire had become a commodity sold to the highest bidder by these influence peddlers. His countenance had grown weary. The entourage suddenly noticed me. I raised my chin against their angry stares. For a moment, silence filled the room.

Mire barged through the circle to stand before me, his fiery eyes glaring. "How'd you like it?" he asked me.

The faces of his crew hardened. They disapproved of me. In their view, I hadn't paid my dues. I wasn't one of them. "Technically, it was okay, but as for content, I fear it may prove a mistake once the government's investigation announces its findings. It's a development that can spin back around and bite." I was running on primal instinct. "Has anyone considered why the ADS was never compromised when Prescott ran the system? Frankly, I don't trust our answer to that question. We need to distance ourselves from the possibility of any deceit that might see the light of day."

Groans erupted behind Mire. Governor Medquist's round face reddened. "Ah hell, how many campaigns has she run? You heard what Jones here said. We'll be up a couple of points by week's end." He flexed his shoulders beneath his gray herringbone coat and shifted his cigar to the other side of his mouth, the angry side. "The cyberattack on the corridor, though tragic, is the break we've been waiting for."

Mire motioned him still, his piercing brown eyes boring into mine. "What you said is true," he whispered. Then he raised his voice for all to hear. "She's right!" He snapped back around and shouted. "I want that interview destroyed! Governor, get rid of those writers."

James collapsed into a chair against the far wall and held his head in his hands.

"But they're the best in the business. They—"

Mire screamed, "I don't want them near the campaign!

Medquist's red cheeks released a blast of hot breath. He stared hard at me and chomped down on his cigar. "It'll take days to set everything up again and rewrite. We don't have that kind of time. This corridor thing is killing us." His bushy black eyebrows pinched together.

Mire turned his back to them and faced me again. He stared hard at me for a moment that seemed like forever before muttering, "I don't care. Just do it."

36

GAME OVER

Amy Ramsey

It was late in the evening when I entered my penthouse and found James seated at the bar, swirling ice cubes around in his glass with a straw. His face had drained of color, and his hands trembled. I immediately noticed his glassy eyes and shiny wet patches beneath them.

The man's been crying. He's an emotional wreck. What's going on? What's he doing here? He had a key to my place when times were different. It was the first time he'd used it since our relationship went south months ago. I needed to have the locks changed. The tabloids said he was having an affair with Ohya, the young recording superstar. I wondered if she was fascinated with him or the publicity he generated.

"Well, you put the screws to us now," he said without

glancing in my direction. I dropped my coat on the couch and went directly to the bar. He turned to look at me for the first time. "Do you know what you did when you trashed Mire's interview today?"

I threw a spoonful of ice into a glass and poured a premixed apple martini. "I did what I thought best for the senator's campaign."

"You knew the Kaples interview would have vindicated us. It would've been our ticket to get back in line." He nervously rubbed his hands together. "Do you have the slightest idea what you've done?" he shouted, banging his fist on the bar. "Don't you know what's at stake? People were killed, for God's sake. I could be next."

He could be next. What does he mean?

"That interview you heaved overboard could've cleared away the whole mess."

That was when I suspected there was more to the corridor tragedy than I knew. I suddenly felt unsettled. I had a sense James had entered a game he couldn't win.

My tone remained calm, irritating him more than if I had yelled back at him. "The whole mess could've been avoided altogether if you had paid attention and not overloaded the corridors. You can't cheat the system."

"Cheat?" He exploded from the barstool. "How do you think we got the PLAVs from your father in the first place? Who do you suppose is floating Mire's campaign and paying your enormous salary? It's all from cheats like me. You pampered bitch, Humpty Dumpty was pushed!"

I hastily poured another drink. James was a weakling, a cheat, and a liar. Now, I wondered what else he'd become.

I used him to get to his father and his father to get to Mire.
I don't need either of them anymore.

"Then why don't you try honesty for a change?" I abandoned my muffled demeanor to shout.

"Don't mix honesty with stupidity. I'm in too deep now," he whined before turning away to lean against the bar with a groan, running quivering fingers through his tousled hair. "Our enemies in the party could use the corridor disaster to ruin us if they choose. All Dad and I can do are keep shelling out and hope Mire's elected."

"What if someone else shells out more?" I taunted over the rim of my glass.

He held his face in his hands and mumbled, "Yeah, there's a rumor about a syndicate down south that's already submitting a proposal to operate Moon Glow. I can't imagine what they agreed to pay for that accommodation."

"Well, why don't you and your people put your heads together and compete?" I walked to the tall, floor-to-ceiling window overlooking the harbor. Fires burned north of the shipyard. Twirling red and blue lights darted through the city.

He spun back around and scowled angrily, the kind of expression his father often wore. "How can we compete with the lavish pensions we have to provide and with all the unnecessary labor Mire's Emergency Employment Act is cramming down our throats? Government subsidies are about to run out on those, and you can't lay anyone off without breaking some other 'emergency regulation.' What a crock."

"You should've thought of that when you and your father helped Mire push those laws through in the first place.

You're only reaping what you've sown," I said with my back to him, something his father used to do that irritated him.

He rushed up from behind me, grabbed my arm, and whipped me around to face him. His hot breath reeked of alcohol. "It wasn't only the interview. You've been stabbing me in other ways too." He shoved his forearm under my chin, pinning me against the glass. Macabre hatred poured out at me from his wild eyes, and his face warped into a grotesque mask. I'd seen the look before. It enveloped him when he abused me.

"Squirm, bitch. How do you like it, huh? Yeah, that's it—suck hard for air. Feel the panic? And what about Winters?" He forced my chin higher. "Huh? Huh? For a southern lawyer, he spends much time up north with you."

I pushed against his chest. He stumbled back against the bar and ducked when my cocktail glass whizzed past his face and smashed against the far wall. "Get the hell out, or I'll call security."

He snatched his coat from the couch and briskly headed for the door. "We're through, you know."

"I was always just a reward they said you could have if you followed their religion. Well, you finally were the item you always wanted. You got what you wanted from our arrangement, but so did I." I felt a trembling smirk pull at the corner of my mouth. "Knowing one of your beatitudes is to take and not be taken, all I can say is don't try it. Salvation's proportionate to your assets in this religion, sunshine."

For a moment, the two kids from the river stood looking at the hurt beaming from each other's eyes.

"It's true. You were a prize, never a person. You mean nothing to me now." The door slammed shut behind him.

37

SAYING GOODBYE

Amy Ramsey

It was a rare visit home for me, prompted by the corridor disasters. In a confidential meeting, Mire asked me to inquire into Prescott's interest in retaking the reins of the Automated Destination System. It was in Genesis's interest to restore public trust in the system as quickly as possible, even if it came with the humiliation of returning the ADS to Dad.

It was raining outside. I was with Dad and Old Rachael in a secluded, candlelit booth of a quaint Moroccan restaurant. I still felt anger toward my father, but I'd decided to let it go. I had so many self-inflicted wounds that needed my attention, leading me to think anyone could make a mistake, even Dad.

We were about to have dessert when the restaurant's

owner ventured timidly to our table. The thin Moroccan immigrant sported a mustache and a balding head that he patted with a handkerchief. It was obvious he was uncomfortable addressing Dad.

"Mr. Ramsey, I'm sorry to disturb you, sir," he said in a heavy accent while bowing respectfully and patting the sides of his face with his handkerchief. But for nervous glances, his eyes avoided Dad's. "Your office is on the phone, sir. They say it is an emergency and asked to speak with you," he concluded, nervously clasping his hands.

"Oh, John, you left your phone in your other suit again." Old Rachael pretended to scold him.

"You may take the call in my office." He extended his arm in a welcoming gesture toward a black door at the room's far end.

Dad raised an eyebrow. "My office, you say? An emergency? Hmm, I've no idea what they want. Better see."

Old Rachael smiled. "Oh, yes, John. You go ahead. We'll sit here and enjoy our dessert. Won't we, Amy?" I grinned through a honey-sweetened morsel and nodded.

It wasn't long before Dad hurried back to the table with brisk strides. Terror's invisible talons gripped his face. I'd never seen him frightened before. Old Rachael's expression froze, her fork dropping onto her plate. She knew what to look for in her son's expression. Something terrible had happened. She grabbed hold of my hand and defiantly raised her chin.

Dad's face drained of color, highlighting early evening stubble. "It's Margo," he said incredulously. He was about to faint before he closed his eyes, swallowed hard, and steadied himself on the corner of our booth. I noticed the restaurant owner and several servers staring at us across the room. I stopped chewing and looked up at my father. Time stood still. Everyone in the room appeared motionless, seized in place.

"She's been in a terrible accident," he told us before choking off.

A bolt of heat flushed my cheeks. Every emotion suddenly withdrew, leaving me to face their return in an emotional tsunami. Dad's eyes filled. I'd never seen him so vulnerable.

My encounter with Margo at the South Sector resort flashed before my mind's eye. It was the last time we were together. My face burned with regret while my hands turned cold. I recalled sitting next to Margo on the floor as she wept. Her bowed head bobbed with each halting breath. Her hair hanging in disarray hid the pain that contorted her face. I obeyed when she told me to leave, knowing I should've stayed with her. A sea of emotions suddenly returned with such force it caused me to gasp for air. I swallowed and closed my eyes for a moment to collect myself.

"How bad, Daddy?"

"I'm told she's very critical."

✦ ✦ ✦

John Ramsey

I sat stoically in the back seat with Amy and Old Rachael as the limousine motored quietly through the darkest of nights. The only sounds were muffled sobs from William, our driver.

I sat in trancelike silence before turning slightly to face the passenger window. A grotesque reflection stared back at me as if from another world.

I told myself that karma's consequences had circled the bowl of the universe and were returning to me because they were mine. They belonged to me. I owned them. I had always feared retribution was looming on the horizon. I had planted fate's seeds on a hilltop fortress long ago, and they'd finally blossomed. I could feel Shajon's suffocating presence pressing close.

My head lowered, and my eyes closed, squeezing out a tear that trailed down the side of my nose. I feared I might soon have the blood of two of my children on my hands, Shajon and now Margo. How would I bear the sorrow for the rest of my life, let alone the karmic guilt?

A line of media vans was already in front of the hospital. Out of respect for us, the hospital directed William to drive around back to the loading ramp, where we would be met by security. Amy sobbed into Old Rachael's shawl that she held to her face. Except for her moistened eyes, Old Rachael sat stunned, her face ablaze with rage that fate would dare bring such a terrible outcome to her family.

A tall, young doctor met us just inside the tall metal doors in pale blue scrubs, with the hospital's administrator at his side dressed neatly in a charcoal-gray suit. We donned our masks. Given our family's notoriety, the hospital underwent emergency press control procedures when staff learned of Margo's identity. Unshaven black stubble shadowed the young doctor's face, while bushy black eyebrows wrinkled together in a tired frown. His scrubs folded over scuffed white tennis shoes.

"I'm so sorry, Mr. Ramsey," the administrator said softly to the hospital's most significant contributor. "Doctor Crowley will take you to your daughter. I must attend a press conference regarding the tragedy. We're all shocked and so deeply sorry." He backed away. "Please excuse me."

Doctor Crowley led us down a dimly lit service corridor into a bright intensive care unit. White-clad staff experienced a moment of immobility on seeing me, and they gasped when Amy lowered Old Rachael's shawl from her face.

Doctor Crowley pointed to one of the glass intensive care cubicles directly across from the nurse's station. On cue, a masked nurse opened the door. A bed inside contained a petite young woman surrounded by beeping electronic monitors. It was Margo.

A towel draped across her forehead hid a gash in her temple. Her eye sockets were already black and blue. A bedside respirator exhaled air into her lungs through a plastic tube taped to her swollen lips. Its snake-like hissing sound was grating.

Horrified, Old Rachael's face immediately blanched. "Oh, my God," was all she could utter before turning her face away with a high-pitched squeal that frightened Amy. I don't think Amy had ever heard her grandmother cry.

My most immediate concern was that Margo may be in indescribable pain she had no way to reveal. I touched Margo's cheek with the back of my hand. It was cold and hard.

"There's no hope at all, Mr. Ramsey," Dr. Crowley said softly.

I held Margo's cold hand and rubbed her palm with my thumb.

"Only her brain stem is barely alive, and I suspect it, too, will shut down," the doctor whispered. "She can't breathe on her own. Metal shards and bone fragments penetrated her brain. There's nothing we can do. I'm afraid there's no hope."

I straightened and raised my chin. No one, not the doctor, Amy, or even Old Rachael, could tell what I was thinking. The only emotion I allowed myself to wear was sadness.

I looked hard at the doctor for a moment, disarming the man. Then I nodded. That was all, just a nod. The doctor closed his eyes briefly as he slowly reached down and flipped a switch on the respirator. It sighed and stopped, allowing silence to rush into the room. Margo didn't move. Old Rachael whipped around with Amy under her wing. Together, they fled the cubicle, leaving me behind to face my demons.

✦ ✦ ✦

Logan Landau

I followed a procession of mourners filing before Margo's body on an elevated platform in the domed white marble foyer of the Ramsey mansion. Towering floral bouquets lined the walls of the enormous room. Their heavy scent was overpowering. Margo's body appeared enshrined in rose-colored moonlight from the foyer's massive stained-glass dome.

It was my turn in a line of only the closest of Margo's family and devoted friends. Brian was on the step behind me. A virus spike caused a stiffening of protocols, forbidding anyone else's attendance and thankfully even the media. I climbed the few short marble stairs alone. With each step, more of Margo's body appeared over the rim of her coffin.

A surge of sorrowful emotions had nowhere to alight. They were for Margo, but she was gone. So they worked their way up to my throat, where they remained painfully stuck. I guess grief happens when love has nowhere to go. I immediately noticed how Margo's lips appeared pulled down at the corners, as if she was about to cry. I think she must have been despondent when she died.

The news accounts of the accident came to mind. Speculation was rampant that Margo's death was a suicide. Other reports said she might have been heading to the hospital to save her life from an overdose when her car hit the bridge abutment at high speed, only two miles from the hospital's emergency entrance. Irresponsible tabloids linked her death to celebrity lovers and underworld figures.

I turned from Margo to follow mourners passing before Mr. Ramsey, Old Rachael, and Amy. Everyone was numb from the daily carnage of the virus and the wars. There were respectful murmurings and gentle expressions of sorrow, but times were so vexing the guests seemed drained of emotion. Amy glanced up at me and quickly looked down again. I'd never seen her veiled in black from just below her eyes to her shoes. While I couldn't see them, I bet sorrow had wrenched her lips down too.

I wanted to hug Mr. Ramsey and Old Rachael. Still, protocols prohibited contact, and the few mourners permitted to participate in the ceremony remained far from the Ramseys. Tezca protocols deadened everything.

"I'm sorry, sir," I told Mr. Ramsey from a distance. "I loved Margo. I'm happy she was Amy's sister and my friend, even for a little while."

Old Rachael wept when she saw me, while Mr. Ramsey's tired eyes seemed to study me. "Logan, will you stay with us after everyone leaves and help us say goodbye to Margo?" he asked. "You're like family. It would mean a lot to us."

Security transported the last guests down the mountain, leaving the mammoth room empty except for the Ramseys and me. Wearing a black suit and tie, the funeral director entered from a side room and stood beside Margo's casket on the elevated platform, with hands clasped prayerfully at his waist. The family looked upon Margo for the last time. Mr. Ramsey nodded to the director. Amy moaned when a dark shadow swept over her sister with the closing of the lid.

38

THE CHEMIST

Logan Landau

A low, early-evening slate-gray sky greeted me on patrol inside Central City in my heavy black SS raincoat. It was a relief to patrol the city instead of the northern frontier. I emerged onto the sidewalk from the subway underground and suddenly froze. A man across the street took my attention when he paused to don the new surgical mask he took from the pocket of his storm coat.

I stepped aside as commuters clamored past. The man was about to descend the stairs into the underground. Bent slightly at the waist, he used a black cane to walk while white, curly hair flared out from beneath his gray newsboy cap.

Is that him? No, it can't be, not out here in plain sight. He's too cunning. Wait, yes, yes, it's him. Damn, it's him. I can't believe he surfaced. The chance sighting jarred the memory of an old SS bulletin.

Hans Beeker was among the most notorious dark ghosts poisoning the sector's reservoirs, rivers, and aquifers. He went overseas for a while and caused havoc there, too, but the bulletin said he had returned and was somewhere in the sector. Hardly anyone paid attention to security bulletins anymore. There were so many alerts and mugshots.

The poisoning of our river when I was a boy flashed before my mind's eye. I remembered a man in an overcoat standing in the cattails across the river. It might not have been Beeker, but a dark ghost like him nonetheless. I shivered the memory away.

Beeker looked in his midsixties, tall, with a back injury from the war that left him somewhat stooped, as the bulletin described. I was pretty sure he had a doctorate in chemistry and worked in a government lab before going nuts. In any case, Beeker was a mass murderer on an unprecedented scale.

The damage he did to ecosystems would last for decades. With nothing to lose at his age, he'd likely choose to die rather than go to prison, where they'd hang him. That made him dangerous, so I needed backup.

Beeker fastened his mask as he descended the stairs to the subway. If phones were working and I called for support, whether the SS or city police, he'd be long gone when help arrived. Law enforcement was overwhelmed. I was resigned to dealing with the suspect alone. Instinctively, I felt for the SS sidearm under my raincoat and bolted across the street. Tires screeched, and horns blared.

On the lower platform, musty, damp air was heavy with the smell of hot metal and oil. About thirty commuters lined the platform.

Beeker was ten meters to my left and slightly forward of me. I couldn't tell if he was armed or had a chemical weapon he could detonate. So I chose not to confront him on the platform.

A train rushed from the dark tunnel, pushing a wave of warm, stale air before squealing to a stop. Doors separated with a hiss as commuters clamored inside. Beeker was among them. Before the doors were about to close, I leaped into the next car and stood by the windowed door adjoining the cars to watch over him.

Subway stops came and went. Beeker swayed calmly with the train's rhythm on its magnetic cushion while reading a folded magazine he took from the breast pocket of his overcoat. Brakes squealed again, and the doors jolted open. Beeker exited and trudged slowly past my car as if dragging a weight behind him. The doors buzzed. I stepped out onto the platform, several meters behind him.

Where's he going? No one gets off here. There're only a few shops up there next to a quarantined area.

Night had fallen, and the air was unseasonably balmy, with a light mist. Fog floated on the ground. There were no colorful lights in this section of the city. The area was a malignant sore that had been seared and left to heal for decades. I shoved my hands into my raincoat pockets and followed Beeker into a dimly lit park.

Blackened, gnarled trees bordered the asphalt path, while wet yellow grass bent low to the ground. Wet hair lay stuck to my forehead. With my prey nearly concealed by fog, I picked up the pace. Graffiti's cryptic warnings covered benches along the way. I was in gang territory. *I wonder if he knows I'm following him and is leading me into a trap.*

I saw his discarded mask by the side of the walkway. It had blood on it.

The narrow path curved down a hillside to a dark street with potholes filled with muddied rainwater. Across the street was a ten-foot-high, rusted wire fence with black and yellow biohazard warnings the size of stop signs every thirty meters or so. The barrier extended for several city blocks before becoming lost in the darkness beyond the last streetlight.

On the other side of the fence were the ruins of an incinerated cathedral. Its blackened gargoyles seemed to be keeping vigil. Behind the cathedral were blocks of fire-gutted buildings. Only their jagged outer walls remained standing. The desolation went on for as far as the corner streetlight reached.

Beeker walked across the street to the quarantined area and gazed at the cathedral's remains with his hands clasped behind him like an awestruck tourist.

What's he doing here? I could see his hands were empty. I held my pistol with both hands and extended my arms. "Freeze, Beeker!" I shouted. "Don't move. Keep your hands behind you where I can see them." I quickly checked for intruders and swiftly crossed the street.

Beeker didn't flinch. He stood with his chin raised slightly, as if the macabre landmark entranced him. He grinned admiringly at the ruins without taking his eyes from the cathedral's blackened spire. "I'm not armed," he said calmly, without glancing in my direction, as if mocking my intensity.

I lowered my voice. "Hans Beeker?" My breathing quickened. *I don't want to kill this guy only to see him in my nightmares. I'll turn him in and let the authorities have their way with him.*

"Yes, you have him. I knew you were following me. So I chose to end it here. Magnificent, isn't it?"

I approached cautiously, with my weapon aimed at his head.

"The purity, I mean. The transgressions that occurred here have burned away. It's clean again and at rest."

I ignored him and quickly pulled my phone from my coat pocket. When I pressed the SS alert key, a red light blinked. *Damn. The system's down again. I'm without backup.*

"Look, I'm taking you back into the city to give you up. Keep your hands where they are while I cuff you. Make a move, even a flinch, and I'll shoot. Got it?" I quickly cuffed his hands behind his back. "The nearest ride is the subway, so let's go."

Beeker turned to me for the first time. A sore on the right side of his face appeared raw and oozing. I saw two of his molars where something had eaten through his cheek. His eyes were teary and crusted with a yellowish substance.

He grinned over a bulge in his upper lip. With a sweep of his tongue, he brought down a glistening glass capsule and held it between his yellow-brown front teeth for me to see. He tucked the capsule between his left cheek and gum. "I'm not going anywhere with you," he said with a confident grin.

I was dumbfounded. *Now what?* I asked myself. *How*

can I force this guy to do anything when he's willing to chomp down on what I think is a cyanide capsule?

"We must eradicate them, you know," he explained in a bizarre robotic cadence. "Our time is over. Don't you understand? We must relinquish our misguided belief in self and others and set consciousness free. It's time to dissolve away into selflessness."

"Look, Beeker …" I was about to tell him to march when he maneuvered the capsule between his canines and bit down hard. He stared at me for a moment until his grin yielded to a look of surprise. He gasped, and his eyes rolled back as he collapsed into a heap at my feet.

39

FAIRY TALES

Amy Ramsey

I sat across from Senator Mire in a secluded, candlelit booth. Still reeling from Margo's death only a month ago, work on the senator's campaign was a welcomed oasis from my dark inner world. When alone, I was resigned to wrestling with my conscience for the self-loathing I caused my sister during our last meeting. The worst times were just before sleep. During the day, my work moved too fast for depression to alight.

Mire had reserved the Rockport Club's entire VIP lounge for our meeting so we wouldn't be disturbed. He set his cocktail on the table and studied me. His penetrating stare was unsettling. I couldn't help but sense the eyes glaring at me were ancient eyes that had seen the unspeakable. I felt like he was disrobing me.

"I know I've addressed your sister's death with you and how much I sympathize with your pain," he said, breaking his trancelike fixation. "Grief is a terrible thing to bear, the price we pay for loving someone. I also want you to know how much I respect your commitment to Genesis. I hope your work gives you refuge, or at the very least, a distraction."

"Thank you, Senator. It does."

"Frankly, I wanted this meeting between us so we could speak freely without the entourage, if you understand the need."

"I do."

He paused as a waiter placed a cocktail in front of me. "As I was saying, you're the only one I can count on to give me what I need to know rather than what others think I want to hear." He sat back and folded his hands on his lap. "Your immense following is impressive. Your public worships you."

I blushed and looked down but with a hint of a grin.

"They look to you for direction in almost everything, whether fashion, lifestyle, or politics, though few of them would probably admit that. You're like a fairy-tale princess come to life. Genesis did well to put you up front. You've been a wonderful standard-bearer for us."

"Thank you, Senator, I—"

He cut me off. "I also want to thank you for speaking your mind in the television studio the other day. I realize you had to sacrifice some personal alliances in doing so."

My eyes quickly left him.

"That kind of thing can be tough, but sometimes there's no other way." He paused again and leaned toward me on his elbows, signaling the importance of what he was about to say. "If we've lost our direction, as you've inferred, how do we get it back? What, in your opinion, do we do?"

Opportunity rushed at me like a gust of wind. I caught my breath, swallowed hard, and raised my chin like Old Rachel did when challenged.

"You were at the top of the heap when you went to war against existing conditions, and everyone connected with them," I told him. "Genesis has become a redoubt for the parasites we opposed."

"Sounds a little like Senator Ashton and your father," he commented through a nervously forced chuckle.

I ignored the remark, causing his grin to fall away. "People see us slowly becoming what we set out to destroy. We're no longer stark. We need to eliminate the old guard like Medquist and the Bucharts."

He raised an eyebrow. *I'm coming off too strong.*

"Medquist no longer has the support of his constituents, and the Bucharts have done their best to destroy themselves," I said to cover my tracks. My heart was pounding.

He pursed his lips. Mire was a pro. I could tell he was contemplating moves several steps ahead of me. I couldn't pause to think about what those might be.

"You don't need Medquist's speechwriters," I continued. "There are plenty of orators are out there who need the legitimacy of the party to enter the arena."

I was on a run. The exhilaration was incredible. *Is this how Dad felt when he first pitched his PLAVs?* I wondered.

Mire shrugged. "So how do we fix it?"

I can make my ideas happen right here, right now, from

these coordinates. I leaned out at Mire and lowered my voice for effect. "You remember those Genesis Vanguard Chapters we created?"

"Yes, of course, but they haven't proven to be much of a factor."

"It's because we failed to offer them what they want."

"What's that?"

"Autonomy. Isn't that how dark ghosts evolved? They've no central authority or chain of command. They oppose society individually, each with a deeply personal conviction that blends into the whole. A campaign becomes an intimate experience when that happens."

"Yes, I guess what you say is true."

"Look at the results. Collectively, dark ghosts have become extremely effective. You never know who they are or what they'll do next until it happens. Then, everyone wakes up and takes notice. They reinvent themselves by the day. Their dynamic is what we need."

He's not looking away. His eyes are studying me. I've got him.

"You can represent what moves them, Senator. You can give legitimacy to their anger. You can be their confessor, brother, father, idol, or whatever role they need you to fill. Let them organize a radical departure from the old Genesis. Each Genesis chapter will be different according to the passions that fuel it. There are geniuses out there who'll plan a revolt in terrain with which they're familiar and malcontents everywhere who'll carry it out for them. They'll love you for it. Free them to create their own Genesis, and they'll win cities for you in sector after sector. There'll be no stopping them."

"Wow, you even have me excited," he said with a grin. His eyes rekindled their sparkle. Then, an unnatural twitch jerked his head to his right three times. It was a tick I hadn't seen from him before. Perhaps the strain of the campaign was getting to him.

Gloom suddenly hardened his face. He was brooding inside. It was pouring down his face like invisible tears. *What a mood swing! Look how it's gripping him.*

"I fear you're opening that box again," he said, his laser-like stare holding me fast.

"What do you mean? What box, Senator?"

"Pandora's."

✦ ✦ ✦

Amy Ramsey

It was late in the evening when my chauffeured limousine exited the Rutledge Hotel's underground, following my meeting with the senator, and headed toward my high-rise. A full moon had risen from the sea, silhouetting distant skyscrapers. My encounter with Mire was successful beyond what I could have imagined. Most importantly, he gave me the authority to manage my Genesis transformation proposal.

I donned my headphones. I had to be current on what clandestine news organizations and insurgents were broadcasting from public forums. I had to know what answers Genesis needed for them. Whenever I had moments alone, I listened to any transmissions I could find. I opened my phone and began scanning the forums.

With my reader on my lap, I was ready to take notes when harsh static mixed with garbled electronic sounds. The government was jamming the forums again.

"Damn them!" I thought aloud. The forums were a safety valve for wannabe revolutionaries and radicals searching for leaders to follow. *How can I find out what they want if you don't let them tell me? Those bureaucratic idiots. They just don't get it.*

Then, as the system searched, it stumbled upon a hole in the disturbance. A note suddenly flashed on my reader: "A Moon Glow Transmission." My fingers immediately ceased rapping the keyboard on my lap, and my eyes widened.

What? Moon Glow? Dad? I didn't know he … I looked up through the moon roof at the bold white face of the moon grinning down at me and laughed. *Dad, what are you up to now?*

A distorted male voice wafted into my headphones from another world. I sat back and cocked my head, straining to listen to the fluctuating voice. It had to be a new signal that could bore through natural disturbances in space and ill-conceived ones from Earth.

"Following centuries of travail, the Great Aarunya emerged from the rubble of the Age of Regrets, calling for a single world government," the narrator said as the transmission faded.

Aarunya? Dad told Margo and me about her when we were kids. I laughed. *It's just a bedtime fairy tale for children about a fictitious heroine those in the Age of Regrets may have wished for, but she certainly wasn't real.* Margo flashed before my mind's eye. I quickly sat up and pressed my headphones against my ears to listen. The government's static attacked the voice like a thousand bees. Then the transmission suddenly burst through again.

"So in days of unprecedented chaos and mayhem, Aarunya gave birth to world order. The Great Mother became an enlightened sovereign and governed for a decade, during which humanity flowered. In the days of Aarunya, citizens were considered pilgrims on an evolutionary journey. For her, the government's role was to provide its citizens a peaceful, unfettered passage with the least interference."

Those were Dad's words. I remembered them. *Why is Moon Glow recounting that old fairy tale?* Static mixed with electronic noise, causing the melancholy voice to weave in and out of reception. I could only hear bits and pieces of the transmission as it faded. "Hold on," I begged the system. "Don't fade, please. Find it. Find it."

"She relegated guilt, shame, and blame to a neurotic history," the voice crackled as it broke through again. "Realization replaced the need for punishment. Being wrong was not knowing the way to what was right. Existence became a practice." The transmission drifted away again.

Dad said that. I remember him reading those words to Margo and me as if it happened yesterday.

"Pull over," I ordered my driver.

"Where, Miss Ramsey?"

"Anywhere. Just pull over and stop."

I raised the privacy window between the driver and me and rolled back the moon roof. The garbled voice sounded like it was coming from a subway tunnel with a train racing through.

"In all of history, one like Aarunya visited only rarely. Identifying such a leader every few years, as democracies demand, was futile," the narrator returned to say. "When Aarunya and later her hand-picked successor succumbed to the sickness, those of lesser vision inherited her power, the remnants of which remain with us today." *Was it the virus that killed Aarunya?* I wondered.

"Avariciousness and selfish discontent followed, giving rise to malcontents filled with hatred and fear. Murder became commonplace," the narrator continued. "Only the skeletal of Aarunya's world remained for a short time. Demons picked at the bones of what had taken centuries to evolve. The pendulum had swung back into darkness."

A note appeared on my reader: "Transmission ended."

What? I immediately dialed Dad's private line.

"Hello."

"Dad? What are you doing? I just heard Moon Glow's broadcast."

He laughed. "Oh yeah? They told me something was going to happen. I didn't know what. I guess our scientists were performing a test of our transmission capabilities. They sent through a broadcast, you say?"

"Yes, but you can't do that." I laughed. "You're a public figure with a lot to lose."

"Did you find it on a public forum?"

"Yes."

"Then what's the problem? The forums are open to everyone."

"I know, but they'll connect whatever is said to you."

"Jerry wouldn't let anything profane get out."

"That's not what I mean. I'm thinking about your political views."

"You mean the ones that don't agree with yours?"

"Come on, Dad. Aarunya? Be real. She's a fairy tale."

"Aarunya isn't a fairy tale, sweetheart. Pandora's story you loved as a child is a remnant of the Great Aarunya, with an evil twist probably added by her enemies. Margo explained it in a theme she wrote at the academy. She titled it 'The Lives of Pandora.' It's a great piece of work. I hope you'll read it sometime."

40

THE GUTTER

Logan Landau

The shift whistle sounded just after four in the afternoon. A snow-laden nor'easter lashed the shipyard with gale-force winds. I flipped up my welder's mask to find it was already dusk. A restless bay surged over the sea wall with an explosion of icy white froth. From the deck of the drydocked ship, hundreds of hunched workers turned their faces from pelting, wind-driven sleet and snow as they scurried for the gate far below.

These are troubled, anxious winds, I thought. Just then, thick, rigid fingers stabbed between my shoulder blades. I turned with a start to find Riley, the shipfitter foreman, grinning tauntingly around his unlit cigar. Four hefty union loyalists stood behind him, squinting at me through the biting wind, their eyebrows crusted with ice, their faces red with threatening expressions.

"We're knock'n off early on count a da storm," Riley shouted over the wind. "We need volunteers to stick around and fasten down. You're one of 'm."

I said nothing and turned to walk away when Riley grabbed my arm and spun me back around. "You got a problem wid dat, wise guy?"

Why are they ganging up on me? What have I done? If Riley takes another step, I'll drive his cigar through the back of his skull. My fists clenched.

"What, you want trouble? Is that what you want? Here, we'll give ya trouble," Riley said, backing through his advancing crew. Riley was out of it, the catalyst.

Behind me was a fifty-foot drop onto frozen steel. In front of me was a beating. I instinctively threw three quick lefts against the jaw of the first waddling, fat thug who came at me, but another blocked my right cross. In a flash, I knew it was over. Punches came from every angle, and there was no space to swing my own.

They were all over me. I dropped and covered, but the crew continued kicking me with metal-toed boots. Then there was the blow that ended it all. A heavy boot clobbered me behind my left ear, still aching from when I tumbled down the icy sidewalk in Umboten.

I remembered nothing until a security guard force-fed coffee to me in the guardhouse.

I began the trek home that evening. Another strike had public transportation down, and with the corridors compromised, no PLAV cabs were at the nearby depot. The night sky was empty. I'd have to walk. "Of all nights,"

I muttered to myself. Grounded vehicles lining side streets and alleyways sat buried in new snow. Nothing was moving.

It wasn't long before my leather boots became like lead weights attached to my legs, while the hairs in my nose turned to frozen quills. Ice clung to my eyelids and the black stubble along my jaw. My bruised face was leather stiff and swollen. Wind-driven snow shot through the light of a streetlamp like meteors hurtling through space.

I held a clump of snow against my swollen cheekbone to calm the throbbing, but my chest hurt the most. A thick winter vest might have saved me from broken ribs, or maybe they were broken. I didn't know. Each rattling breath caused a painful spike until I arrived across the street from the upscale Rutledge Hotel, where I paused to catch my breath and gather myself. Blood oozing from my nose had frozen, restricting airflow.

Across the thoroughfare, freshly shoveled marble steps rose from the curb to the hotel's tall glass doors. The Rutledge was a brightly lit high-rise, an oasis of light on the dark, inner-city street. Mire's campaign offices were on the top floor. I ducked when a fleeting shadow zoomed overhead before spiraling into the night sky.

A function was concluding across the street. Sector elite, bundled in evening coats with collars turned up against the frigid wind, walked cautiously to a row of limousines, while valets in green jackets brought expensive vehicles curbside.

My heart began to pound when I saw Amy emerge from the hotel's revolving glass doors, surrounded by four men in black overcoats. She tucked her chin into the lapels of her coat. I breathed in deep with a wheezing sound and backed into the shadows out of the streetlight's reach.

Marla Kaples walked briskly after Amy while extending a Telestar microphone. A man with a shoulder-mounted camera enshrined them in harsh light just as a police car skidded against the curb in front of me with red and blue lights whirling. I instinctively backed farther away. Two police officers emerged and crouched behind their car's open doors with sidearms drawn.

"On the ground!" the cop behind the passenger door shouted. I saw Barstow, the union steward, in the back seat, sporting a devilish smirk.

"Hands in the air! Raise 'm!" the other officer demanded.

"What did I do? What do you want?"

Two more police cars raced onto the scene. Tires scuffed against the icy street. More angry voices shouted at me. I spotted guns at the ready. Kaples and her cameraman ran toward the commotion. *Oh, no! Amy can't see what's happening to me. No, please, Amy, don't come over here*, I silently pleaded. Camera lights suddenly blasted away the darkness, projecting elongated shadows onto the snowbank behind me that resembled Thai puppets. My temples were throbbing.

Barstow rolled down the rear window. "We got it all, Landau," he growled. "The encrypted stuff, the codes, Umboten contacts, everything. I hope they fry your ass."

What does he mean?

"I said on the ground," one of the officers shouted again.

"Get those hands in the air where we can see 'm," another demanded.

I stumbled backward along the icy gutter. "It's a mistake. I didn't do anything!" I shouted back. Frigid water running along the curb spilled into my boots.

"Down," a cop hollered. "I'm not going to tell you again."

I lay sprawled in the gutter. Heavy knees and sharp elbows pressed hard against my back, forcing my bloodied face into the freezing curbside torrent. I turned my head as best I could to keep from drowning. I saw Amy fast-walking toward the melee from across the street.

"Hold him down," a breathless voice demanded behind me. Hot camera lights feasted on the melee. A siren wailed in the distance, growing louder as it approached. Police I couldn't see forced my arms behind me and ratcheted down cold metal handcuffs. My clothes were wet and freezing. Angry shouts competed with whispering voices inside my head. It was all happening far away, across a dark chasm in a world no longer familiar. I was lost.

41

THE INTERROGATION

Logan Landau

I sat on a white plastic chair in front of a laminate table with rough, chipped edges in the basement of police headquarters. My wrists were still bound but in front of me, which was far more comfortable. Dried blood had plugged up my nose, and they gave me a mask to wear, making it increasingly difficult to breathe.

I wondered how many desperate people sat on this chair and stared at the laminate patterns on the tabletop as I was doing. A heavyset man in his midthirties, wearing a white shirt, black dress pants, and loosened red striped tie, sat on the table's edge. He introduced himself as Detective Bruce Keller.

His leaner associate, Detective Harry Lopez, had coal-black hair slicked back and stood at the end of the table, sporting a maroon shirt with the sleeves rolled up on his forearms and a solid navy blue tie. I was sure the long mirror to my right was a one-way window.

"Look, I need a few facts," Keller begged again in a condescending tone, as if trying to convince a child. Their intent was so obvious I wondered why they bothered to disguise it.

I remained silent. *Let everyone think I'm nuts. Maybe I am*. Keller was unknowingly competing with the ringing in my ears and demons whispering in my head. He rambled on, throwing out names of terrorists and underworld figures to assess my reactions. I was exhausted from the noise inside my skull. I was worried my brain was seriously injured in Umboten and exacerbated by the beating in the yard. I wanted it all to stop. I needed to sleep so I could sort everything out later.

"Hey, listen up!" Keller barked impatiently.

I didn't even glance up at him. I remembered how Brian used to look away from James when he no longer wanted to read his lips.

"Look, we've got the encrypted stuff from your computer and the ADS plans from your tool chest."

Who planted it? I wondered, *Genesis's New Order thugs, ghosts? Who? Even more mystifying is why?* I began rocking back and forth from my waist. It seemed to ease the pressure mounting inside my head.

Keller rolled his eyes and sighed. "Does the name Tony Suarez ring a bell?" He waited. I didn't respond. I knew it appeared bizarre to them, but all I could do to ease the throbbing was rock back and forth. Lopez grimaced with impatience and leaned on the end of the table with both hands.

"Look, you best cooperate, or they can put you away for as long as it takes for answers."

Keller slipped into a condescending tone. "We're keeping the cuffs on you because you seem nervous, you know, out of sorts with yourself. If you can give us just the basic stuff, we can get some help for ya and get those cuffs off. Know what I mean?"

"It doesn't have to be this hard," Lopez added. "You want a lawyer? Here, have at it," he said, sliding a government cell phone down the table. "Go ahead, make the call."

I remained fixated on the tabletop as if studying patterns in the imitation wood veneer until they began to blur. My stomach cramped, forcing acidic saliva into my mouth as cold sweat blossomed on my brow. I suddenly stopped rocking when my stomach lurched once, twice, and a third time. I quickly tore off my mask as bloodied vomit exploded onto the table.

Keller bounced up quickly. Lopez rolled his eyes upward with a sigh and dropped his arms in disgust. A high-pitched sound resembling an electrical current hummed inside my head. Another burst of bloody vomit splashed onto the table and down my front. Then the concrete floor rushed up at me, and everything vanished without a sound.

Logan Landau

After a shower and the loan of an orange jumpsuit, I found myself behind bars, strapped to a bunk in the basement of the police station. They would be sending me to the nearby Sector Detention Center tomorrow, where they could hold me indefinitely under the sector's antiterrorism guidelines.

I lay on the hard bunk with my wrists manacled to the frame. I guessed it was what they did with crazies. A bottle of Blue-Checked water was on the floor beside my bunk. It was the government's potable water brand. Just a formality of little use to me, with my wrists tied down.

Dim gray light illuminated the cell from the ground-level window high up on the wall across the corridor. A tear burned like acid as it coursed through the gash on my cheek. One of the thugs who slugged me wore a gangsta ring, the latest hoodlum fad. It must have lacerated my cheek.

✦ ✦ ✦

Amy Ramsey

The black stretch limousine was on a dark side street outside the fortress-like police headquarters when my driver returned and rolled down the opaque window between us. Speaking in a heavy Hispanic accent, while focusing on my image in the rearview mirror, he said, "I'm sorry, Miss Ramsey, but prison authorities told me no one could see Mr. Landau, not even you. It's a government thing. The laws are strict in such matters."

I had watched the news bulletin featuring Logan's melee in the gutter. I held my face in my hands and wept. News reports said Logan was a prime suspect in the hacking of Buchart Industry's ADS. Genesis-leaning media described Logan as the dark ghost catch of the year. I didn't believe a word of it.

"Wait here," I told my driver. "I'll let you know when I'm ready to leave." The storm had moved out to sea. A cold, wet mist painted a pink halo around the corner streetlamp.

My driver rolled down his window. "Ms. Ramsey, please come back to the car. This area isn't safe. Please."

"I need a moment," I told him.

Two Genesis bodyguards immediately climbed out of the plain blue car behind my limo, but I put up my hand defiantly. There was a moment of indecision before they sat back down.

I walked across the street to a tall wire fence topped with coiled concertina wire. About thirty yards beyond it was a concrete wall. Behind the wall were cells, I assumed.

Backing away a couple of paces, I lifted my chin and shouted. "Don't you know I'm your friend?" My voice choked with emotion as I wiped a cold tear from my cheek with the back of my hand. "Don't you know I'll always love you?"

42

PRISON

Logan Landau

A white-haired corrections officer escorted me down a long gray corridor inside the archaic Sector Detention Center. He wore a tan shirt with gold sector logos on each shoulder. I was in an orange jumpsuit with my wrists and ankles manacled. Authorities matched my fingerprints to those on some sector files from the shipyard, so they had everything they needed.

Three tiers of cells inside a wire cage rose some forty feet above the gray cement floor to my left. A gray wall with evenly spaced, arched, barred windows ran the length of the corridor to my right. We walked together with eyes straight ahead, pretending not to hear the catcalls and jeers cascading from the tiers.

"Turn in here," the officer commanded gruffly. We

entered a ten-bed infirmary arranged dormitory style with five beds in a row on either side. A physically fit, athletic-looking officer with a short, military-style haircut sat behind a desk at the front of the room, engrossed in a reader. He stood and looked hard at me. A small dispensary behind a barred door was to his right. In his early thirties, the officer was tall and lean with piercing, judgmental eyes.

My escort handed over the keys to my shackles and prison ID card. "This is Landau. He's all yours," he said in a tired-sounding voice.

"Okay, I've got him." The infirmary officer entered my prison ID into his tablet and glanced at the results. Without a word, he took hold of my left arm, just under the armpit, and marched me to the third bed on the right, where he unlocked my shackles. I immediately discerned the officer's firm grip was a message that said he was in charge.

"Lie down," he ordered in an authoritarian tone. The tone was something I'd become used to with time. *Time*, I thought. *I wonder how much time I have to spend here.* I lay on the bed's blue wool blanket. During an earlier court appearance, my government-appointed attorney pleaded not guilty on my behalf.

"Your profile says I gotta put these restraints on you," the officer said, interrupting my thoughts. He flipped up the fabric restraints already fastened to the bed frame. I was relieved, as my wrists were sore from the metal ones.

He tied off the straps. "I'm Sergeant Ryan. You look pretty beat up. Anything broken I ought to know about?" I remained silent, my eyes darting around my new surroundings.

"Okay then. Doc will be in tomorrow and have a look at

you. Meanwhile, Jason here is in charge. He's the infirmary orderly." Ryan motioned to an inmate in his late twenties, mopping the floor at the foot of my bunk, dressed in a white T-shirt and jeans.

"Okay, listen up. Here's the spiel. The Sector Detention Center is more than one hundred fifty years old. It's been relegated to a processing facility for all the sector prisons and contains some fifteen hundred inmates," Ryan explained. "Those in work shirts and jeans, like Jason, serve short sentences for lesser nonviolent crimes. Like you, inmates in orange jumpsuits are awaiting trial for various offenses, even the most serious. Okay, that's the intro. Any questions?" I remained silent. "I thought so." Ryan left my bedside and went back to his desk.

An obese inmate in an orange jumpsuit, two beds down from me, was engrossed in a comic book and didn't even glance my way. I guessed he must be in his midtwenties.

Across the room was a strange-looking guy who looked to be in his late teens. He sported a goofy smirk and ears that fanned out like little wings. He was grinning at me in a way that made me uncomfortable. There were just the two inmates and me.

Three tall, barred windows lined the walls on either side, giving the infirmary plenty of light. The warm sunlight was like a soothing balm on my battered face. Officer Ryan returned to his desk, where I could hear him talking with Jason. I kept my eyes shut, not wanting them to know I was awake and listening.

"Hey, scroll the news. What's it say about our new guy? You know, our super-ghost," Jason whispered with a chuckle.

"According to Telstar, he's a prime suspect in the corridor thing," Ryan said loud enough to convey his indifference to whether I heard him or not. "Says here he was also planning an attack on the shipyard. He's a celebrity, all right. They found all kinds of incriminating software and terror-related stuff in his locker at the yard."

I heard Jason's voice once again. "Did you see the cool news clip last night? Dude, they're say'n he might be the one, you know, the ghost who's call'n the shots. Maybe they finally got lucky and caught the big fish. Know what I mean?"

Ryan scoffed. "Yeah, how many times have we heard that?"

Jason's tone was adamant, with a hint of anger. "Hey, a lot of guys in here lost people to them guys. Unless he's got serious backing, he ain't gonna last long in this place."

"Oh, look. Marston's in guarded condition at Sector General," Ryan went on with surprise while scrolling through the news.

"Sector Steel's Jack Marston? You know, from the yard?" Jason asked.

I shuddered. Jack Marston was John Ramsey's friend and my benefactor. He hired me sight unseen on Ramsey's recommendation.

"Yeah, a roadside bomb got him in his car the night of the blizzard. Big night."

"I hope the pig's busted up good," Jason quipped. "I worked at the yard for a while. I hated all them guys at the top. They're the ones who oughta be in here."

"Oh wait, there's more on our celebrity. He's got a terrorist hold on him, which means no contact with the outside world and no bail. Man, is he screwed. I'll bet they isolate him in solitary for his protection when he gets outta here. Hey, here's something else. Ramsey's back in the sector. He returned cuz of the Marston thing, or so he says."

"He should'a stayed on the moon. He's the first in a line of those porkers who need to get whacked," Jason grumbled.

I hope Mr. Ramsey doesn't come looking for me here in prison. If anyone could have access to me, it'd be him. He's got the connections to make it happen. The last thing I want is for Amy's father to see me incarcerated, especially beaten up as I am, but I can't think about that now. I need the whispers to stop so I can sleep.

Logan Landau

I was jolted awake at two in the morning by a rush of panic and noticed no one was at Ryan's desk. The orderly and the other two inmates were asleep. My jumpsuit was saturated, and my hair was wet with sweat. It was the worst panic attack ever. It frightened me out of whatever wits I had left. I had to get out of the restraints. I couldn't stand another minute on my back, unable to move. I shouted for help and thrashed back and forth. My metal-framed bed pounded against the gray-tiled floor, making a racket.

Jason sprang out of bed and immediately pushed the intercom button on the wall by his bunk. A squeal preceded a tired-sounding voice. "Command."

"That damn nut you guys brought in today has gone ballistic. Send some help."

Jason stood in his underwear at the foot of my bed with his arms folded on his chest. He was thin with bushy black hair and brown, deep-set eyes. "Dude, what the hell are you doing?" Thick black stubble covered his cheeks, and his hands trembled a little. He seemed to be a mix of young and old. "Why are you bouncing around?" He picked up my blanket from the floor. His manner hinted he'd confronted the bizarre before. "Dude, you screwed up big-time. See, here they come."

Three burly black correctional officers entered the infirmary with nightsticks and clear plastic shields. Without a word, they tied my legs down hard.

"That's right, tie 'm down good," Jason said. The officers ignored him and abruptly exited the room. Jason paused at the foot of my bed with a quizzical expression. "Dude, what's up with the anxiety? What? Were ya dream'n? That was bizarre, dude. You don't wanna carry on like that in this place. No-o-o-o, not in here. You have the doc give you meds to keep the demons away. He'll do it for ya, dude. Mellow you out good, Doc will."

He grinned. "Hey, you really gonna do the yard?" I looked away, not wanting to answer his questions. He followed my gaze to the obese guy reading comics earlier and whispered through a sadistic chuckle, "Know who that is? Dude, that's 'Hammer'n Harold.' They brought him in yesterday. The jackass beat his mother to death with a hammer after she'd just posted bail for him for some petty crap. Can you believe it?

"He don't realize what he's done yet, but you watch. It'll

dawn on him in three days. That's when, and he'll wig out big-time. Happens like clockwork with them guys.

"So, hey, when you dudes bringing down the yard?" I didn't respond. "Dude, that is so cool." I turned my head away. "Okay, have it your way, but don't be acting out no more, or they'll ship your ass to Hell House. Dude, no one comes back from that place."

43

A STRANGE PLACE

Logan Landau

In his mid to late fifties, Doc was a short, plump physician who wore thick, black-rimmed glasses and a tweed sport coat. He gnawed on an unlit cigar while he examined my cuts and bruises. Ryan and Jason stood at the foot of my bed.

"He probably has some broken ribs and a skull fracture," the doctor mumbled and looked up at Ryan. "With the charges against him, I don't suppose we can take him to City Hospital for an MRI."

Ryan wagged his head with a frown. "Not a chance."

Doc sighed and turned to me. "Okay, look, you want to get out of these restraints?" I nodded. "You don't wanna hurt yourself or anyone else, do you?" His voice was stern, but there was compassion in it too. I shook my head.

I was afraid to speak because I didn't want to get in the way of the truth. Old Rachael had told me long ago the truth needed time to work to the surface, like a sliver lodged under the skin. It'll always surface, no matter how many lies are stacked on top of. It just needs time to break through. When the truth emerged, I hoped authorities would realize my innocence and let me go home.

"Are you feeling nervous maybe?"

Doc was the first sympathetic person I had encountered, so I nodded. Doc reached in his pocket. "Okay, here, open." He placed a large capsule in my mouth. "Now swallow. I'm giving Officer Ryan this medication for you to take twice a day. It should help you relax and keep the panic attacks away."

"Thank you." *How odd*, I thought. *My first words in prison were "Thank you."*

Doc smirked at Ryan. "Okay, you can take these restraints off. What do we have next?"

Ryan led Doc to a new inmate across the room while Jason unfastened my restraints. They must have brought the new guy in after I finally dozed off. He was in the bunk beside the guy with the creepy grin and goofy ears. What immediately appeared peculiar about him was his mouth. It was so wide open his lower jaw seemed to almost press against his throat.

"Yeah," Ryan explained, "he came in like this last night. He's in for booze. He's been in and outta here for years. So we figured it's just the DTs again. He's shake'n pretty bad, and he sees the monkeys."

"For God's sake, how long have you been like this?" Doc asked. The man responded with unintelligible sounds but held up three shaking fingers. Doc glanced at me from over his shoulder. "Can't anybody talk around here?" He chuckled. "Your jaw's outta joint, for God's sake. Hell, it's not delirium tremors. How old are ya?"

The inmate held up four fingers.

"You're four?" Doc turned to Ryan. "What the hell is he doing here? We don't take kids, do we?" The inmate sighed with frustration and emphasized a zero with his other hand. "Oh, you're forty." Doc's stomach bounced with a chuckle.

The weird guy grinned at Officer Ryan and slowly descended beneath his blanket. Doc noticed. Ryan shook his head. "Second time this morning, Doc."

"The second time this morning?"

"That's right."

"Hmm. Find out what he eats, will ya?"

Doc reached down with both hands at the back of the new inmate's jaw and yanked hard. The guy screamed like a banshee when his teeth slammed back together.

"Oh wow. Thanks, Doc. Thanks a heap," he said in a quivering nasal voice while rubbing his cheeks with trembling hands. "Damn, that was painful. My tongue feels like a loaf of bread."

His Weirdness emerged slowly from under the covers until his silly grin was just above the blanket. Doc turned to him and pulled the cigar from his mouth for the first time. "You're going to Hell House, son." That was all he said to him before turning and walking with Ryan to the entryway.

A tall, effeminate Haitian inmate sauntered inside with an infirmary pass. Decorated with rouge and mascara, he spoke with a seductive smile and a breathy, feminine voice while blinking long eyelashes at the doctor.

"Well, if it isn't our handsome doctor." The inmate's blue denim work shirt was tied off just under his breastbone, exposing a bare midriff. He was tall and dark, with purple lips and nails.

Doc smirked. "Now, what are you doing here this early? You'll miss your beauty sleep. Wanna keep those wrinkles away, ya know."

"Oh, Doc, you take such good care of us girls."

"Yeah, well, don't make a floor show out of it. Officer Ryan will give you your medication. I've gotta run."

The center is such a strange place, I thought.

Jason stood at the foot of my bed with his mop in hand. "That's Jahna. They call her the Duchess. You don't mess with that bitch. She's one of the toughest dudes in here."

Ryan walked directly to my bedside. "Your lawyer's office called. He was taken ill. The court will have to appoint someone else. So I guess your meeting isn't going to happen today."

✦ ✦ ✦

Amy Ramsey

I exited the revolving doors of the Fletcher Building at noon and followed the asphalt path along the outskirts of World's End Park toward where my driver was waiting for me. With the ADS still down and the spate of local bombings, grounded vehicles weren't permitted access to most high-rise buildings. Discreetly placed cameras on lampposts along the walkway were spaced within view of one another, ensuring uninterrupted security between the Fletcher Complex and the parking facility.

Children were playing on the other side of the steep knoll to my left. Their laughter made me smile. The smell of a cooking fire in one of the public grills brought memories of picnics with Logan by the river. A child's kite fluttered overhead.

A man on a park bench by the walkway caught my attention. Wearing a stained white T-shirt under a soiled beige trench coat, he looked straight ahead through thick, wire-rimmed glasses while rocking rhythmically at the waist and giggling to himself. He was maskless, exposing pale cheeks, sweaty and unshaven. A black stocking cap covered his head to his ears. With the grass-covered hillside shielding his back, he cocked his head down and slightly to the side as if trying to avoid the cameras.

My brisk strides slowed. I glanced at the camera staring down at me. The guy was a creep, the kind you dread sitting next to on the subway. Just as I was about to reach into my coat pocket for my mace spray, there was a thunderous explosion on the other side of the hill, jolting me back on my heels. My face burned with a rush of fear.

The stranger instinctively ducked. "Oops," he said as he looked away, covering his mouth to hide his sinister giggle. When he turned back, he made eye contact with me. I was frozen motionless. Screams erupted behind the hill. "Oh, yes." He nodded as he nervously rocked back and forth at the waist. "There you go."

Gray smoke billowed skyward as a chemical smell floated in the cold air. The man's teeth were yellow-brown, and there was white scum at the corners of his mouth. He was rocking more violently now with vulgar grunts, as if he was deriving some degenerate pleasure from the experience. All the while, his magnified eyes kept staring at me and wouldn't let go.

Recollection of a news video from the summer triggered an internal alarm. *He must be the one who planted land mines on a popular beach last summer*, I thought. His bombs critically wounded several teens. *Now, he's in the park. You can't even set your foot down anymore.*

Suddenly, another explosion ripped the sky like pealing thunder. Mothers howled, and children screamed.

"Oh yes, there it is." He raised his brow as if from surprise and leaned forward with squealing laughter until he was out of breath. A strand of drool from his lower lip dripped onto his knee.

Security was approaching. I could hear their authoritarian shouts and squawking communications devices behind the hill. The bomber could too. The harsh slap of fear smacked his face.

He quickly donned a crumpled surgical mask, stood with his hands tucked into his coat pockets, and stared at me, mesmerized by his moment of importance. He alone would decide my fate. I took another step back.

Does he have a gun? Will he shoot me? No. He can't. If he does, they'll zero in on him. My life depended on what he did next. *The sick twist doesn't deserve the power.* Margo's image in the coffin flashed before my mind's eye.

"Please don't kill me," I involuntarily whispered.

He turned suddenly and hurried down the walkway with his face covered. I exhaled a quivering breath when he rounded the bend and disappeared. My knees began to give way. I went to steady myself on the bench but pulled back from the acrid smell of foul sweat and urine.

44

THE HOWLING

Logan Landau

A tired-appearing attorney with thinning yellow-white hair and sagging pockets under his eyes came and went uneventfully. Visiting me was a court-ordered formality. He relayed that the court wasn't convinced of my stability and recommended a psychiatric evaluation. I declined. Psych wards for criminals were notorious for making people nuts or at least declaring them, so to cover their diagnoses.

In any case, he said, it was probable that once the doc signed off on me as physically fit, the prison would isolate me for my protection. They called the place a detention center, but it was a prison, and I was hated there, given the media's portrayal of me.

The full moon hung like a luminous silver disk in the middle of the window by my bunk. The weird guy's bed was empty. As Doc had ordered, they manacled him in the early morning and shipped him to the laughing academy.

The sound of growling suddenly filled the room. I quickly turned to find Hammer'n Harold in his bunk on all fours, with bulging eyes fixed on the full moon. He lowered his butt and forced a wolflike howl as if he was vomiting the world's miseries. An icy chill raced up my spine, raising the hairs on my neck.

Jason woke with a start and burst into laughter. "Whoa. Did I tell ya? Huh? Did I tell ya it'd be three days? Listen to the fat ass howl, will ya?" Harold's cry was the most mournful I'd ever heard, animal or human. Jason bolted from his bunk. "Yo, dude. This place is off-center."

Harold was a twisting, sweating hulk entangled in blankets. "Mommy," he wailed over and over. "Mommy."

"Dude, chill," Jason demanded.

Old Rachael once told me our minds know what we've done, and they're hypnotically programmed to bring us the consequences. Harold's mind was taking him deeper into a hellish nightmare of his making. How do you rescue yourself from your mind? If you're honest with yourself, you know you can't. It's who you are.

✦ ✦ ✦

John Ramsey

I climbed the steps of Sector General Hospital, encircled by a swarm of reporters. It was where my longtime friend, Jack Marston, was fighting for his life. A bushy microphone at the end of a long pole struck my jaw. I shoved it aside. Marla Kaples stumbled up the stairs in front of me.

"Mr. Ramsey, is visiting Jack Marston your sole reason for returning to the sector?" she asked while extending a handheld microphone, forcing me to stop.

"Look, I don't wish to comment. Not now, please. I've come to see an old friend. That's all. I don't have anything further to say." I jammed my hands into my gray tweed overcoat pockets and continued to climb.

A tall male reporter in an open black leather coat and loosened tie circled in front of me with an arrogant smirk. "What about Moon Glow? Will you be submitting a bid to operate it?"

Stung by the reporter's brazen gotcha question, my face hardened to stone as I stormed through the horde.

"What about your robotic lover, Mr. Ramsey? Will you be bringing it to Earth?" the reporter shouted after me. Guards formed a barricade at the revolving doors. Jerry Weinstone approached from the lobby just as elevator doors slid open. We stepped inside. I put on my surgical mask and leaned back with an exhausted sigh as I watched the floor numbers ascend. I could still feel the strained relations between us. "Any word?" I asked.

"Not since we spoke on the phone. Jack's condition remains critical. They haven't found much of anything at the scene besides, you know, the obvious. At least three roadside devices explode somewhere in the sector every week. You know how it is. Law enforcement is overwhelmed. They don't pursue protest bombings so long as their death toll stays within acceptable levels."

I groaned. "Protest bombings, acceptable levels—what have we become?"

"There's an interesting sidebar though. Remember Amy's friend Logan Landau?"

"Of course. Why?"

"Well, he was arrested the same night."

"What?" I bellowed, then quickly lowered my voice as the elevator bobbed to a stop and the doors separated. I pulled up my mask as we stepped onto a working hospital floor and its overpowering antiseptic smell. "Why? What did he do?"

"He's being held on terrorist charges related to the corridor disaster. The government is withholding information regarding its investigations, but I learned they have incriminating evidence linking Logan to the cyberattack on the ADS."

"Logan?" I questioned incredulously before reducing my astonishment to a whisper. "They're saying Logan is a terrorist? Has everyone gone mad?"

"Word has it on the street that he was also planning an attack on the shipyard. Authorities are looking into a possible tie-in with the roadside bombing that injured Jack. When police arrested Logan, they said he overreacted, to put it mildly. They have him in the facility on Fourth Street 'til they sort it all out."

I ran my fingers through my thinning hair and shook my head in disgust. "That place is a hell hole, Jerry. He's probably scared to death. Why hasn't his attorney extricated him?"

"The government is holding him under the Antiterrorism

Act, and they've recommended psychiatric observation. They say he's exhibited bizarre behavior."

"So would I if I was in that place. I've known Logan since he was a kid, and so have you. Can't we do something to get him outta there?" I immediately thought of Shajon and my missed opportunity with him. I didn't want to miss another. "I don't care what it takes."

✦ ✦ ✦

John Ramsey

Jack lay unconscious during the entire time of my visit, so I didn't stay very long. He had grotesque burns on his face, neck, and hands. His physician told me Jack's car caught fire before first responders could free him from the wreckage.

I mixed a drink in my suite on the thirty-second floor of the Prescott building and studied the city through the tall parlor windows. It was late, so I decided to stay in town that night rather than drive up the mountain. A fire was burning in a downtown mall due to a car bomb. Another was raging out of control in the financial district. My internal voice warned that standing before the window was probably not a good idea.

I noticed General Hospital's dark outline where Jack lay dying. Then my gaze drifted south, as if magnetized, to City Medical Center's high-rise, where Margo's life ended, but another memory haunted the place too.

I recalled the day I walked Jessica home through the park after picnicking with her in the snow on White Ram's

Mountain before I had the mansion built. Jess was an SS medical doctor, so synchronizing our demanding schedules was no small feat.

While she performed with rational coolness under the most stressful conditions in the field, she reserved a more vulnerable personality for me. She'd be as open to me as I needed. Snow was piled waist-high along the sidewalk. Coal-black hair curled in against her neck, while her eyes were dark and exotic like Margo's. She raised her chin just a little, not disdainfully high but high enough to give her a sense of purpose, a trait reserved for Amy. Her camo SS fatigues were an outward expression of her dedicated lifestyle.

Bitter cold gnawed at my face while the sickle-shaped moon looked frozen in the sky. Ice-crusted snow crackled and squeaked beneath our leather boots when she paused to lean back against the trunk of a tall oak. She looked at me with seductive anticipation. I was shivering inside when I took hold of her lapels and brought her lips to mine. Suddenly, the night became soft and warm. Her sweet breath sighed against my face, savoring our first kiss.

Eleven years later, she was in an isolation room at the medical center. I stood helplessly on the other side of a thick, wire-glass window overlooking her bed. There were blue-black welts on her face, and her chest moved slowly to the rhythm of a respirator. Her mind had long since gone beyond the veil. Her hands lay open, wanting no more from the world. In just three agonizing days, the Tezca took her life. She never knew about Salah and Shajon. I never told her. What would've been the point?

Telstar's late-night newscast was on the television

screen behind me. I watched the broadcast from its reflection in the window. "Doctors treating Jack Marston have just announced the sixty-two-year-old chairman of Sector Steel, the sector's largest shipbuilding company, has died from injuries suffered in a roadside bombing two weeks ago today." I glared at the broadcaster's reflection. "Marston passed away while undergoing surgery."

45

MR. WALLACE

It was late evening when Edward Buchart sat alone in his office on the fifty-seventh floor of the Buchart Building. Mire was sending a high-level Genesis official to settle the corridor tragedy. Buchart flipped a switch in his desk drawer, turning on hidden audio/video recorders to appease his paranoia. He swiveled in his leather chair to gaze out the tall window at Amy's penthouse, a couple of high-rises away.

"She owes me," he reassured himself aloud for the recording. "She'll be obligated to put me in line for the Moon Glow project if I demand it of her, and tomorrow I will. After I square away the corridor debacle with Mire, I'll arrange to see our Ms. Ramsey and call in my chips."

His gaze drifted north toward the Rutledge Hotel and Mire's campaign offices. "I'm determined to stand firm on

Moon Glow when Mire's guy arrives. It's not negotiable. We had a deal."

The phone buzzed. He pivoted back around and pushed a button on the console. "Buchart."

"Mr. Buchart, this is Officer Renteria in security. I'm sorry to bother you at this late hour, sir, but there's a Mr. Wallace here to see you."

"Hold for a moment." He clicked a button on the phone for a moment of privacy with the ongoing recording. "Wallace? I've never heard of him," he said aloud. "I hope Mire isn't sending some underling to make such an important deal. Then again, perhaps it's a cover. They can't be overtly connected to me just now. Mire's playing it cool. I'll probably recognize this guy as soon as he walks in here," he concluded and returned to the call. "Okay, send him up."

He nervously rapped a pen against the rim of his desk while mumbling a rehearsal of what he would say. A knock on his office door jolted him. Buchart leaned forward on his forearms and squinted through shafts of light angling from ceiling fixtures. Draped in a black leather overcoat, a tall, middle-aged man with a long, gaunt face entered Buchart's inner office and walked through shadows to stand before his desk. The emissary's eyes were dark, his expression stoic. He wore a five o'clock shadow and long black hair slicked back straight.

Buchart squinted through a scowl. "Wait. I don't know you. Why did Mire ..."

The visitor reached into his coat pocket, withdrew a revolver, and slowly fastened a silencer onto the barrel. Buchart gasped and lurched back. The stranger placed the gun on the desk, reached into his pocket again, pulled out a small grade school photo of James, and flipped it next to the weapon. The emissary's deep voice was foreboding. "Your associates in the New Order would like you to do the right thing."

"They want me to kill myself. If I don't, they'll murder James and me as well. That's what you're telling me. I'm going to die here tonight. They think my death will end the corridor investigation. That's what they want." The recording showed Buchart taking rapid, jittery breaths and wrenching the tie from his neck. Beads of sweat were sprouting on his forehead. He was dumbfounded, unable to summon words that would save him.

"If you're unable to comply, I'm authorized to do it for you."

Elder Buchart looked up at the grim messenger in disbelief, his eyes pleading for a way out, but the emissary pivoted his head slowly from side to side, only once, signaling there was no reprieve, and backed out of the light. "I'll wait in your outer office until you've finished what you must do."

✦ ✦ ✦

James Buchart

I was sitting outdoors beside my mother beneath an unblemished sky. It was an uncharacteristically warm day for the season. We were on white lawn chairs just outside the stately stone mausoleum where they would lay my father to rest. Following brief services, in which I provided the closing tribute, six Harrenhaus members, dressed in blue and red uniforms reserved for special events, took Dad's gold-plated casket from the back of a black limousine. In march-step, they solemnly carried his casket into the dark shadows of his crypt and placed it on the marble altar before filing back outside. Two stayed behind to close and lock the tall iron doors before giving me the key with condolences and leaving the grounds with everyone else.

The Harrenhaus was a two-hundred-year-old, castle-like stone fortress built by a wealthy industrialist with a pension for privacy. The place had become an exclusive, private club in the countryside where Dad's fellow robber barons congregated and the cigar smoke was heavy.

Tezca prevented most people who knew Dad from attending. Of course, our board members were there, but Dad's business acquaintances and Harrenhaus friends were conspicuously absent due to the virus.

"I'm glad you're here, Mom." She wore a black dress with a shawl draped over her shoulders to ward off the morning chill. She was striking for her age. Her gray-streaked hair was held back by a turquoise clamp in the shape of a butterfly, matching the turquoise pendant that hung from her neck.

She chuckled. "Oh, I wouldn't have missed it for the world. I know he's your father, but it made my day to see him lying in that box with his mouth shut and knowing it's not a dream."

"You hated him that much?"

"I adored the son we made together and our wealth, but that's as far as it went."

"But he created one of the most successful corporations

in the world and left you well-off. Doesn't he deserve your respect for that?"

"Oh, hogwash. It was your great-grandfather, Bertrand Buchart, whose vision created the company. He was the one who took risks and weathered the hard times to build the Buchart brand. Your illustrious father and grandfather before him were only caretakers who had unearned success served to them on a silver platter. Your father cheated and lied his way through. You see, James? It's like I always told you. How you got your wealth isn't what matters in the end. People will envy you simply for having it."

"But he improved the company under his watch. Earnings are over the top."

"Oh, the company's bottom line increased, but he wasn't responsible. He had an eye for rare talent. I'll give him that. He put a cadre of leaders together that did his job for him. He just took the credit. It's how he's always operated. He was a fake who used people until he wrung them out, then threw them away, as he did me."

I immediately thought of Jerry Weinstone. Wasn't he Ramsey's go-to guy? "But isn't that what good managers of people do?" I asked her.

"Not really. You don't manage people. A good leader maps the way to success and inspires good people to find their way to it. Get what I mean?"

"I think so. I'll have to think about it."

"What happened to your friend Amy Ramsey? She's in the news quite often these days," she questioned from the corner of her mouth.

"We broke it off."

"I'm sorry to hear that. I liked Amy. She has a head on

her shoulders and an extraordinary career in front of her."
Mother paused to look hard at me. "I understand you're in
deep water over what happened in the commuter corridor."

"Yeah, but Dad put me in touch with people who can
help us."

"His hoodlum associates?" she asked callously.

Leery of what her response would be, I didn't answer.
"What happened in the corridor is eating me alive. I've
become a political outcast in the New Order." I glanced at
her so she could read the fear in my eyes.

"You're in pretty deep, aren't you? Something like that
has a way of getting out of control."

"Yeah, I know. What do you think I should do? I mean,
people died. How do you fix something like that?"

"What are your attorneys telling you to do?"

"They tell me to ride it out. You know, let the news cycle
pass before mounting a defense."

"Was there negligence involved on your part?"

"That's what they're saying,"

She exhaled a heavy sigh. "Well, I'd advise you not to
take one of your father's shortcuts by involving criminal
enterprises. I know that would be his first knee-jerk reaction.
Don't allow it."

"I already have."

"Oh my God, James. What did you agree to do?" she
questioned.

I'll never forget her worried, soul-searching stare. She
knew I wasn't fit for the position of president. She knew it
all along. It was as if she had expected something terrible
to come from it, and now it had. I watched a bee land on a
dandelion flower near my foot. *Damn, what can I do? I'm in*

a nightmare, and I can't wake up. I'd be better off if I shot myself in the face as Dad did. "I don't want to talk about it," I answered her.

"I can't imagine how you're coping. It's a heavy weight you're carrying. I'm sorry, James. I wish I could help you."

I realized then that I had lost her.

46

THE INNER WAR

James Buchart

My driver motored onto an overpass and stopped behind a long line of traffic backed up for miles. With PLAVs down, there were no less-traveled alternate routes anymore.

I gazed out the rear passenger window at a sweeping view of the city from the overpass when the infamous Sector Detention Center took center stage.

Logan is in that hell hole, I thought, *and I put him there.* I studied my reflection in the window. The cocky smirk I practiced in front of a mirror was gone. Guilt had found its way into me and tamped it down. I noticed I didn't laugh or smile much anymore, and new worry lines had etched into my face. *I think I've finally crossed over to the dark side.* The corridor disaster followed by my father's suicide had me continuously retreating deeper into myself.

I didn't feel well. I had thrown up again that morning, and I wasn't sleeping. I was a wreck. I couldn't remember when I slept through the night. As soon as I closed my eyes, judgments rushed at me. So I took another pill and poured another drink before the next dark thought found me. The episodes flashed on and off when I was alone, reminding me what I'd become and why I was hated, even by myself. *Yeah, I'm a bad seed. I know, but how did I get that way?* It was a question I continually asked myself. *Was it a choice I made in another life? If so, I can't recall the alternatives.*

✦ ✦ ✦

James Buchart

The other night, I took my girlfriend, Ohyah, to dinner at an exclusive club in a plush hotel across town, a place frequented by a mix of nouveau riche and techies. She was a young recording star with a following that even rivaled Amy's. I didn't even know her real name, and I didn't care. She was wickedly beautiful, rich, and willing. That was all that mattered to me.

Her tousled auburn hair was in disarray, the way her fans wanted her. Tomorrow it might be coal black or platinum blonde—whatever struck her fancy. Her tight emerald evening dress was suggestively revealing, but her stark, mysterious eyes were what drew you.

People snickered about her reputation for drug use and sexual exploits, but I didn't care. I knew the times she spent with me were for the media that followed us wherever we went. She craved controversy for no other reason than it brought her into conversations. She wanted someone on her arm who was controversial, from big business, and wore a suit. In other words, she wanted a high-profile rental no one expected. She loved shocking the Dudley Dorights of the world.

Yeah, I told myself, *she's way too young for me. So what? Why should I care what motivates her so long as she fulfills my fantasies? She'll probably die from an overdose or some gang-related crap in a year or two. She even laughs about it. I don't think she wants to outlive her fame.* I was as foreign to her as she was to me, so we learned from each other and used our drugs of choice to bridge the divide. Our relationship was shameless and without pretense.

"What else is there?" I remember Dad telling me once, which made me wonder what he was into when he was young. *Ugh, I don't want to know.*

We followed a tuxedoed maître d' to a secluded table close to the circular rotating stage, where a young woman in a glittering white gown was singing. An overhead spotlight beamed down on the angelic creature, causing sequins on her body-tight costume to wink as the platform slowly rotated so everyone had a view. There was never a bad seat in the house.

From the corner of my eye, I noticed a table of haughty thirty-something women who giggled to one another as we passed. They knew well who and what Ohyah was. My sordid reputation only fueled their gossip. I had to grin. They were doing what Ohyah wanted. Other audience members were gawking too, but for different reasons. As soon as we entered the hotel's restaurant, I noticed a rumbling of commotion.

Ohyah defiantly raised her chin as we passed the giggling gaggle. Criticism bounced from her like sunbeams from a mirror. It didn't sink in. She didn't let it. She was too confident, too good at what she did, and ready to flip her life on a whim.

The performer completed her number as Ohyah and I were seated at our table. With a laughing smile, the performer reached out with both arms to Ohyah. "Ohyah, welcome!" The spotlight rushed to Ohyah, enshrining her in light as the audience enthusiastically applauded.

You see, it's like Mom said. It doesn't matter how you get what you have. They'll applaud you just for having it. I noticed Ohyah's defensive countenance yield to youthful innocence, as if mesmerized by her fame. That's why her fans adored her. She had an unbridled naivety about her. I had to admit she aroused me.

After dinner, we walked through a private service entrance into the cavernous lobby. Even in the rain, I noticed Ohyah's fans were collecting by the hundreds outside the hotel's tall glass doors. She already missed the limelight. I could tell.

"I need to powder," she said and went to our suite. I sent a couple of my security people to escort her.

I was sure she was going there to take a hit. The drugs she took were harder than mine. But I let her do what she needed. I went to the bar, where I took a couple of mood enhancers with a cocktail. I noticed I was taking a double dose of enhancers with my cocktails these days.

I couldn't help but feel desire's coy tug. I imagined being in our suite, wrapped in Ohyah's soft, warm embrace, her dazzling green eyes staring into mine. I could see it. The city's dull, metallic light through the rain-streaked window painted us with a silver hue. It was a dreamlike setting in which I felt alive again.

Why does pleasure morph into our destruction? I thought of how a drug addict would overdose in pursuit of a feeling, obese gluttons would gorge on the food that was killing them for one more taste, and risk lovers would sacrifice all for the thrill of defeating their fears. We all shared in the inner war.

47

SIMON

Logan Landau

The moon came by to check on me last night, I thought. It sat aglow atop the prison wall. I thought of Mr. Ramsey and how he loved it up there. I was alone again when it moved past the tall, arched window across the hall. That was when walls pressed in close and D block's solitary confinement became unbearable.

Many nights had passed since they sent me there. I no longer knew how many. New synapses bypassed the damaged part of my brain injured in Umboten. My mind had trained itself to function with new routes to ideas and defaults. At least that's what I thought might be happening.

I was in one of those episodes when my defilements returned for reckoning. All good vanished during those dark hours of fitful turning and tossing in my bunk. My demons never slept. Every thought was an attack. Even the collective malignancies of the human condition visited me as debt holders demanding restitution. They did the same to Margo.

Last night, my skin cringed like a thousand insects were scurrying over me. I frantically scratched my arms, legs, and chest, leaving long red marks resembling hives. I turned over on my bunk and held Amy's image in my mind for as long as possible to keep the demons away. I was worried. Isolation and sleep deprivation were fertile grounds for delusions.

"Hey, what's with all the ruckus down there?" A deep male voice jolted me. It came from the cell directly above mine. Frantic whispers in my head hushed, turned off by the flip of an internal switch. "Don't you know what time it is?" the voice questioned.

It was the deep voice of a much older man, perhaps a black man. "When did they bring you in here? I must have been asleep."

"A while ago," he answered.

I wondered how I could imagine the voice coming from one of the cells above mine. Then I recalled how sounds seemed removed from me after the explosion in Umboten, like they were traveling through a long metal pipe.

"Well, what's going on down there?"

"I, ah … I was having a nightmare. I get them sometimes."

"H-mm. What happens in these nightmares of yours?"

He sounded concerned. I cricked my neck to look up between the bars to the cell above mine, but all I could see was the underside of the catwalk. "You know," I answered.

"They come with fearful thoughts. By the way, I can't see you from here. The catwalk is in the way."

There was a distant snicker. "Good. You won't be disappointed. Now, these dreams of yours, do they carry over to when you're awake?"

Where's he going with this? "Yes, yes, they do. The mood they leave behind stays with me for hours, sometimes days."

"I was that way too when they locked me away. I could still hear that infernal electronic buzz of the cell door when it locked me in. I'll never forget it, even after all these years."

"How many years?"

"Thirty-four. The court sent me here when I was twenty-six."

"So you're sixty. I can't imagine being in this cage for so long. You must be quite resilient," I told him.

"Well, when you don't have options, you do what you must. But back to your nightmares, Logan. I'm sorry you have them."

How does he know my name? His kindness seeped through the concrete and steel, falling over me like a soothing mist. My shoulders dropped as the tension left them.

"Who are you? Why did they send you to D block?"

"You can call me Simon. I'm here cuz I used to kill people when I was young and stupid. My being in D block is a mistake. I was supposed to be in lockdown for two weeks for some trouble in the yard, but not here in D block with you. You're supposed to be isolated from human contact. My being here is a mistake. Oh, I heard about you. You're the ghost that's run'n the show. You sure raised serious hell out there. If what they say about you is true, I suspect you won't be leave'n this place, not alive anyway."

"I'm not who they say I am."

He laughed. "Where have I heard that before? I've been in the system for a long time but never heard anyone locked down as hard as you. Someone high up in the pecking order has it in for you. You can be sure of that. They'll probably move me outta here as soon as they realize their blunder. They don't like witnesses. That's when you'll want to be careful." He paused for a moment. "Look, I might be able to help you. As I said, I don't think I'll be in D block for long, but if they ever send you into the population, I have a lot of friends out there who'll look out for you if I tell them to. Know what I mean?"

"What would I have to do in return?"

"This isn't one of those kinda deals. I'm offering my help because you remind me of what it was like when I first came here. We don't always get a chance to do anything good in this place, so I thought I'd give it a shot."

✦ ✦ ✦

Amy Ramsey

I was with Winters in my Southern Sector hotel suite, reviewing VIP seating arrangements for the evening's Genesis gala. I wagged my head with a disgruntled look. "Damn, I hope this rain doesn't screw everything up. It's pouring out there. Listen to it come down."

Winters ran his fingers along the cummerbund of his black tuxedo. *I must admit. He looks dashing.*

"Don't worry, Amy. By this time tomorrow, you'll have Antium in the bag. The Southern Sector will be yours. Then you can sit back and watch the demagogues compete for headlines."

"I hope you're right. We sure have a lot riding on these chapters. By the way, where's the senator? I've tried his suite twice in the last hour. He needs the bios of the VIPs at his table."

"Please, try to relax, okay? You're going to worry yourself into a frazzle. One thing at a time. First, let's finish the seating chart and get it downstairs to the staff." He looked at his watch. "Wow, it's later than I thought. Our guests will arrive in a few hours."

He hastily unrolled the ballroom schematic across the coffee table. "We should put von Avery next to Governor Barrington at the head table. She's big bucks. He can work with her. What do you think?"

There was a commotion outside. "Someone's shouting in the parking lot. Who would be out there ranting in the pouring rain?" I went to the window and opened the curtains. "Oh no, I don't believe it. Come here and look. It's him."

Winters quickly came to the window and gasped. "It's Mire!"

"He's not even wearing an overcoat," I growled. "He's in his tux, for heaven's sake, and in the—"

He cut me off. "He's yelling, but he's alone out there. What the hell's going on?"

I whipped my storm coat from the closet, grabbed a towel from the bathroom, and draped it over my head.

"Here, I'll go with you."

"No," I told him. "Bring the seating chart down to the staff and tell them to get started. Supervise until I get there. Don't leak a word of this to anyone. Let me see what's going on, and I'll contact you. Make sure you have your phone."

I took the elevator to the ground floor, opened the back door to the parking lot, and shouted over the deluge. "Senator, come in out of the rain. This way, Senator."

Mire turned with a start, appearing bewildered.

"It's me, Amy. This way, Senator. Hurry."

The beam of light from a streetlamp was his spotlight. Beyond the column of light, an imagined audience reached infinity.

"You've waited a long time for me, and now I'm here before you," he began, bellowing random fragments of his World's End speech. Wet hair lay plastered to his skull, his face dripping. "Oh yes, there's nothing new. The only difference is it's our turn. It's new to us!"

Mire was known to use the new mood enhancer medication the government rushed through approvals to calm the masses while keeping us productive. I'd seen a bottle of them in his suite. The drug had adverse effects on some people.

I gave up trying to avoid getting wet and ran into the parking lot, where I took hold of the senator's arm. "Senator, you must come inside out of the rain."

"I know you want Moon Glow back for your father. It's why you're here. Senator Gorcic wants it too, along with everyone else. They all want that." He squinted skyward, blinking against the pelting downpour. "Oh, we have to go quickly. It's pouring, and I'm afraid I've gotten wet."

"It's okay, Senator. Just follow me."

He hurried behind me, holding my hand like a bewildered child. I checked the hallway before rushing him into the elevator. He watched the floor numbers ticking away above the doors with a placid grin and began reciting numbers from his recent speech at the Sector Economic Forum. His demeanor was like a schoolboy pleasing his teacher with what he'd memorized.

When the elevator doors separated, I checked the hallway. It was clear. "Come on, Senator." I led him to his suite, where he dropped into a soft chair while I set to work untying his shoes. His hands shook, but perhaps it was from the cold, or so I hoped.

"I'm sorry, Amy," he said unemotionally, with an odd, computer-like cadence.

It appeared to me that he had suddenly collected himself. The new mood enhancers created temporary episodes of delusion followed by detached behavior in some people. The government wanted peaceful automatons but didn't anticipate the range of psychoses that came along for the ride.

"I had to get out of this room. I couldn't endure another sequestered minute. Do you understand? I can't be confined any longer."

Logan immediately came to mind. "I understand, Senator."

Mire's monotone voice was trancelike. "I know how bizarre it must have seemed, but I'm okay now. I need to rest for a while and take a hot shower."

"Sure, Senator."

"Oh, and you better have them send over another tux. I'm afraid this one's a little wet."

48

AMY'S BOOMERANG

John Ramsey

Amy called last week and asked to meet with me this afternoon. I waited on the settee behind the mansion, dressed in jeans and a maroon sweater under a beige jacket. Dark storm clouds were rumbling in from the sea, blanketing the city. Only the city's distant skyscrapers poked through.

I enjoyed impressing Margo when she was young by taking her to memorable places and events in the city. The metropolis seemed sad for having lost one of its most enthusiastic admirers.

I didn't talk much about Margo in Amy's presence, for fear of giving Amy the impression Margo's death made her special. I kept my thoughts in my heart and opened them occasionally when I was alone. I also had to avoid issues involving Cheryl. Amy never mentioned her.

In my hidden thoughts, I'd often find myself in the passenger seat of Margo's sleek white sports car, racing down the highway with Margo at the wheel.

It happened just before sleep or when the moments were right, like right then. It was always at night. I'd nervously watch the digital speedometer's numbers rapidly ascend and could even hear the wind screaming past my passenger window. White lane dividers would zip beneath the car, one after another, faster and faster. Then I glanced down at her foot, steadily depressing the accelerator. I looked at her eyes. They were glassy and closing. Her head jerked back when her eyes jolted open. I was helpless to intervene. Like a ghost, I was a voiceless bystander.

A tunnel with massive concrete pillars was fast approaching. Margo slumped forward against the steering wheel, and her head turned to face me. She forced her eyes half-open to look at me for the last time. "Goodbye, Daddy. I love you." Suddenly, all would go dark.

✦ ✦ ✦

John Ramsey

Amy approached through the corridor of apple trees. A light mist fell from a slate-gray sky, camouflaging my moistened eyes. Amy's green wool jacket was open to a gold sweater. She'd become so beautiful. Her raised chin and the way she carried herself reminded me of Jess.

She breathed in the crisp mountain air and smiled. "Hi,

Dad. It's so good to be home. The air always smells so clean up here."

I wrapped her in a firm embrace. "I'm happy you're home."

She leaned back in my arms. "I need to talk to you, but it has to stay between us, okay?"

"Of course, Amy. Whatever it is will stay up here on the mountain, like always." Because I assumed her visit was about Genesis's need for PLAVs to be back in the sky, I told her, "We're running tests on the ADS, working out a few kinks left by the hackers, and installing a more secure firewall. It won't be long before commuters are in the sky again."

"That's great, Dad, but it's not why I need to talk with you. There's something else. How about walking with me down to the river?"

"What you want to talk about isn't the adverse publicity surrounding my recent visit to Moon Glow, is it?"

"No. I think we've gone beyond that since your televised lunar funeral, right?"

"Okay, then, let's go."

She slipped her arm through mine and smiled. Wet grass painted a glistening sheen on her black boots. But it wasn't long before her exuberance fell away. "I think I may have done something terrible, Dad."

I raised an eyebrow. "Really? Now what could that be?"

"My Vanguard Chapters are taking a turn I never expected. Among other things, they've become a haven for dark ghosts."

I sent her a concerned glance from the corner of my eye.

"Oh, not the violent crazies you read about," she said,

quickly trying to lessen the blow, "but those who inspire them have surely come over. I know they're there by the corruption going on. There isn't a chapter unaffected. The problem has metastasized."

I nodded. "I know."

She looked up sharply. *Dad's known all along but never mentioned it.* She tucked the thought away to think about later. "I was so vain. I didn't care who gave me the opportunity. I just wanted the chance to win, to measure up to your standards. Most of all, I wanted you to be proud of me." Her eyes filled, and her voice quivered as a red blotch brightened on her cheek.

She groaned with frustration and shoved her cold hands into her pockets. "Genesis was the vehicle I needed. It had the money to market my strategy, but more importantly, it had the pretense of legitimacy criminals needed to do their nefarious business. It was just a game I had to play to win, but now it's out of control." Her voice suddenly choked off while tiny indentations appeared on her chin. She squinted against the mist when she sheepishly looked up at me again.

"I wanted defiant leaders, geniuses, and sincere activists, not criminals. The imposters have plundered businesses and corrupted Genesis to achieve their selfish ends. I permitted it to happen, Dad. I ruined everything. I'm scared. It's as though I opened Pandora's box." A tear slipped from the corner of her eye and raced down her cheek onto her frowning lips.

My voice remained calm. "Genesis was corrupted long before you arrived on the scene, sweetheart." A quick, stern glance told her she should've never become involved with

Mire and the Bucharts. She knew better. "Confession can be a powerful tool when followed by renunciation," I told her before looking away.

That was my cue to renounce Genesis before it was too late.

We walked the rest of the way down the mountain in silence. Tufts of wild grass were turning brown, ready to sleep. At the edge of the field bordering the river, she hugged my arm and rested her head against my shoulder.

Sadness rode on her voice. "I've heard kids don't swim here anymore. Look how it's overgrown." Reeds had spread out from the bank. The rock dam was just a jagged ruin, barely rippling the current. "What's happened to the kids from the river?" she thought aloud.

"I'm one of the kids from the river too. I used to swim here as a boy and later with your mother before you were born. The kids will return. The river will always be here waiting for them."

49

FATAL DISCLOSURE

Amy Ramsey

"Thank you, Amy," Akar, my assistant, said as he left my side for another concourse to make his flight. "I'll work on what we discussed first thing in the morning."

I nodded back to him. It was late. I wore a white scarf that crossed my face before draping over my shoulder. News articles I had read on the plane left me unsettled. Protests over social issues were a cover for political thugs seeking protection money from industries that bowed to their demands.

Antium's Vanguard Chapter was nothing more than a criminal mob that looted and burned their way through the city's main thoroughfare, destroying businesses and injuring scores of police. Chapters replaced the name

Genesis with Vanguard to distance themselves from the past. Everything had to be dismantled and reconstructed.

New Order of political gangsters were extorting businesses to either pay for protection or suffer the consequences at the hands of rioters and anarchists they organized. Some vanguard leaders were becoming wealthy robber barons overnight. My plan, which I sold to Mire, was running away from me. *It's like I'm riding that old horse again*.

I recalled the day Old Rachael arranged for me to have a horse ride in the countryside near home. I was only nine or ten at the time. The horse bolted when it stepped on a coiled length of discarded fence wire, the sound of which was like the hissing of a snake. I remember holding tight to the saddle horn, ducking branches while struggling to stay centered on the bouncing saddle. I thought of falling off and taking my knocks before the horse picked up even more speed in the open field outside the woods, but I managed to hold on until the horse tired.

My worries were interrupted when Governor Medquist unexpectedly appeared at my side. A scowl pinched between his eyes. "Amy, I have to talk to you. How about something in the VIP lounge?"

"Hello, Governor. Wow, this is a chance meeting. Or is it?" My long strides remained purposely uninterrupted, as if my need to move along meant more than what the governor had to say. Maybe he'd take the hint and leave me alone.

"I came in on an earlier flight and thought I'd wait here to speak with you. It's that important." He stumbled along at my side, trying to keep up while weaving through the stream of passengers with his overnight case in tow.

"Look, I'm tired, Governor. Can't it wait 'til morning?"

"It can't wait. It might already be too late."

It's all I need now, more trouble. I noticed a droplet of sweat trickled down the governor's temple. *Maybe he knows more than I do about what's going on. Perhaps I should listen to what he has to say.* "Oh, all right. Perhaps I need to unwind a little after that roller coaster I came in on. I'll sure be glad when PLAVs are up and running again."

We sat by a window in the VIP lounge, overlooking an empty runway. I let my scarf hang loosely around my neck. A small electronic candle glowed in a blue glass cup between us, while blue runway lights extended in parallel lines outside our window to the bay. A waiter took our order.

"Amy, these Vanguard Chapters of yours are going sour." I immediately noticed his anxiety mounting when he forced an awkward swallow in the middle of his sentence.

When our waiter returned with our drinks, I discreetly placed a white mood enhancer pill on my tongue and swallowed. Tranquility almost instantly warmed my abdomen and spilled down my limbs. My shoulders dropped, and the knot in the back of my neck loosened. Even my head felt lighter. I briefly closed my eyes, savoring the moment. *What relief,* I thought.

My eyes flicked open to a new mood. I smirked. "How does Mire feel about recent developments?"

Medquist grimaced with frustration at my apparent indifference. "He's taken with them, of course. Chapter memberships are swelling, and industries are buckling. It's all coming true, but what's marching behind the banners should concern you."

"What are you talking about?" I knew full well what he was about to tell me.

"These New Order hoodlums are roaming the streets like young lions. They'll pounce on anyone opposing them."

I defensively rolled my eyes and sighed but didn't have an answer.

"They're crossing over the rules of the game. Have you noticed how few Genesis campaign posters they display? It's all New Order Vanguard stuff with local heroes. Oh yeah, it's Mire's spirit throughout, but your New Order chapters are marching to a beat of their own. You have no idea which way or when the monster will turn."

Yup, just like dark ghosts, I thought. Maybe my plan was growing beyond what I imagined for it. The governor was right. My project had matured into a life of its own. I gazed out the window at the runway lights and replied in a conciliatory tone conjured by the drug I swallowed. "To tell you the truth, Governor, I've been feeling a little uneasy too. I'll see what I can do in the morning. For starters, we need to put a lid on those anarchists in Antium before we have any more confrontations. Too much autonomy isn't good. We need a stronger national structure to deal with it."

I immediately recalled advising Mire against a robust national structure when I first outlined my plan. I tossed the thought onto the stack of anomalies I had to reconsider. "It's just growing pains, Governor. I wouldn't get too excited." I downed my cocktail to give my false confidence a pause to collect itself.

His brow wrinkled with curiosity. "You've talked with Mire recently, haven't you?"

"Yes, why?"

He sighed when the waiter brought me another cocktail and waited until the waiter left before continuing in a whisper. "Has Mire been asking about your travel schedules, where you're staying, anything like that?"

"No, not that I recall." I shrugged. "Why do you ask?" There was a warning in the look he gave me. "What do you know, Governor?" My question had the ring of a demand.

"Mire has had secret meetings lately with some highly questionable characters. You know, 'the catalysts,' as he calls them. He met with some real notorious Venezuelans just a few days ago."

"He didn't tell me about that." My shoulders slumped forward in disgust. He had agreed to consult with me on everything involving the campaign.

"I checked on another of his late-night visitors through a friend. It turns out one of them was Benito Saret. Remember him? He's that conscious devil behind those cyberattacks in the South Sector. Whatever came from those attacks is Genesis cash now."

"What?" I shrieked and looked around to see if I had drawn attention, but the lounge was mostly empty.

"There've been others I'm still running checks on." He dragged his hands down his face and clasped them on the table. "Mire's suspicious of me. He's becoming increasingly paranoid. I think it's the drugs—you know, the enhancers."

My face flushed from a twinge of embarrassment, given that I had just taken an enhancer a few minutes before.

"It was all I could do to escape my security to meet your flight. My security is on Mire's payroll too. I knew Mire was becoming bizarre, but there's more to it, Amy. Something else is running him now. Maybe it was him all along, but we didn't notice or didn't want to notice." He wrenched his hands together nervously. "I also believe you may be in danger."

"I can't believe what I'm hearing." I leaned back against my chair and closed my eyes to gather myself. "What are you saying?"

"You're an idealist, Amy. They know you'd never go for what they're planning behind closed doors. You have an enormous following, and that worries them. Eventually, Genesis will have to deal with you. Mire knows that. I've heard him whisper it."

"Do you mean they'd do something violent?"

"They may want to avoid a scandal by taking their usual shortcut, as they did with Marston."

"Jack?"

"Yeah. Dark ghosts are everywhere, Amy. They've become your neighbors. They stand alone, unaffiliated right or left, unless they fake an affiliation to lead the government astray. They're hiding in plain sight. They say we'll all be dark ghosts someday."

"What are you going to do now?"

"I've left the campaign. Mire will find my resignation on his desk in the morning. I'm going back up north where I belong. There're forces at work here I don't understand. You'll get out too if you know what's good for you."

My face burned, and my voice quivered. "If what you said is true, I'll need you."

"No. I'm out. It was only a matter of time anyway. I mean, that was your plan, wasn't it?"

I remembered Old Rachael's promise that the truth would always surface.

"I came to warn you because I see my early beginnings in you. My life is consumed by what I've made of it. You still have innocence under that tough veneer of yours."

He was about to take a drink when he peered over the rim of his glass and froze. "Don't turn around, but one of our infamous New Order goons just entered the lounge and sat against the far wall. I've seen him around Mire before. Rumor has it he's one of the thugs involved in the Marston thing."

A chill raced up my spine. "The bombing?"

Droplets of sweat reappeared on his brow, and his face was ashen when he stood. "Look, I'm going now and won't be seeing you again. When you leave, have a porter walk you to your car." He glanced at the stone-faced gangster across the room again. "Do me one last favor, though, will you?"

"What's that?"

"Tell your father I always admired him even though I could never show it. Will you do that for me?"

I nodded. "Of course. I'll tell him." My father's advice regarding the power of confession came to mind. "Governor, I once counseled Mire to cut you loose. I feel terrible about that now. I want you to know how ashamed I am. I was wrong about you, and I want another chance."

"I've known about that for a long time. Don't feel alone. I've done the same thing to others in past campaigns, but I'm grateful you mentioned it." His eyes darted nervously across the room again. "I have to go." He left quickly and filed into the human stream on the concourse.

Suddenly, I was alone with the fear he had left behind.

✦ ✦ ✦

Amy Ramsey

"Good evening, Miss Ramsey." The doorman in a red coat and tall black hat grinned as he opened the door to my high-rise.

"Hello, Johnson," I said, then took the elevator to my penthouse a little before midnight. I turned on Telstar Radio's Soft Sounds broadcast, dropped my coat on the arm of the couch, and immediately picked up the telephone to call Dad. He'd know what I should do. I tried from the limo but only awakened his voicemail. A lonesome melody fell like mist from ceiling speakers. The ring reverted to voicemail again.

I stormed into the bathroom and splashed cold water on my hot red cheeks. The eerie melody was interrupted by harsh electronic sounds, signaling a news bulletin. It was a terrifying sound everyone feared, given its history as a harbinger of dreadful news. Though it made me shudder, I couldn't ignore it. I turned off the tap and stood motionless, bent over the sink with my face dripping.

"This is a news bulletin from Telstar's Radio Network. Former North Sector governor, Richard Medquist, was found dead at Boston's Logan Airport less than an hour ago."

An electrifying shock bolted down my body, trembling my limbs.

"Airport police preliminary findings indicate the former governor's death was due to heart failure. Stay tuned to Telstar's Radio Network for more details. Repeating Telstar's Radio Network news bulletin, Boston police discovered former North Sector governor, Richard Medquist, died from a heart attack at Boston's Logan Airport. Now, back to our regularly scheduled Soft Sounds program."

I gripped the counter to keep my hands from shaking. Heat spilled into my face, while queasiness boiled in the pit of my stomach. "Heart failure, my foot," I grumbled as I went into the living room for the phone and dialed again.

"Hello," a foggy voice growled from the receiver. I sighed with relief at finally making the connection.

"Dad, Governor Medquist was just found dead at the airport." My voice cracked against jumbled emotions stuck in my throat like a stone.

"I'm sorry to hear that, Amy." His tone was soft and consoling. "Was it the virus?"

I swallowed hard and flopped down on the couch. Tiny indentations appeared on my chin, signaling I was about to cry. My lips wrenched down and quivered at the corners. "He met me tonight at the airport, where he told me about crimes involving Mire and Genesis."

I wept openly. "It's not what I wanted, Dad." I wiped my eyes with the back of my hand and sniffled. "As I told you on the mountain, it's my fault. I let those criminal elements into Genesis without even cursory vetting. I opened the door for them," I lamented with a throaty groan. "They murdered him, a man I once maligned in secret."

I placed the back of my hand against my brow and closed my eyes. "The governor said something dangerous might involve me too, Daddy. He was investigating it independently, and now he's ... oh, that poor man. They killed him just like they did Jack Marston."

"He mentioned Jack?"

"Yes."

"Okay, let your friend Winters handle it for now and come home. I'm in the Southern Sector. I'll fire up the jet and meet you on the mountain in six hours."

"Okay, but there's something else. One of the last things the governor said to me was that he always admired you even though he couldn't express it politically. He wanted me to be sure to tell you."

"I remember the early days before that mob got to him. He was a brilliant man with ideals. Well, he's free of it all now. He won't have to imitate what he used to be anymore."

50

WINNERS AND LOSERS

John Ramsey

I was having dinner at the airport with Jerry following Governor Medquist's funeral, at which Mire had been a conspicuous no-show. It was the first time Jerry and I had broken bread together since I returned from Moon Glow. We both knew our relationship wasn't what it used to be. I wondered if it ever would be.

"Logan is getting out, you know," Jerry said calmly, watching with delight from the corner of his eye as I perked up straight with surprise and dropped my soup spoon into my chowder.

Jerry had always relished casually reporting news he knew was important to me—parceling each savory morsel with seeming disinterest and occasional yawns was like toying with a hooked fish. I wished he had been so forthright when he first learned of Cheryl's demise.

"Getting out, you say?" I leaned back against my chair. "Wonderful. I'm delighted. What happened?"

"The independent investigators we hired came upon a union steward from the shipyard involved in a bizarre plot to incriminate Logan. His plea deal required him to confess how he and others from the yard planted evidence tying Logan to the terrorist attack."

"Wow, I guess their plan unraveled. Mire's people were smart to give the steward up before government investigators dug deeper into Genesis. I guess the steward will fall victim to one of those mysterious heart attacks like the governor. The good news is Logan will soon be out of that awful place. Good work, Jerry. I'm pleased, but I wonder what else that union steward confessed in exchange for whatever concessions they gave him."

"It appears he gave up the chain of command that our investigators unraveled to the ultimate fall guy, someone important enough to close the investigation around and protect Genesis, their pressure release valve."

"H-mm. Now, who could that be?"

"Young Buchart," Jerry announced with a smirk.

"Well, well, whataya know?"

"He'll be indicted for crimes associated with the corridor disaster."

"I remember him as a kid. From time to time, you must recall seeing James at the mansion with Brian, Margo, Amy, and Logan," I commented.

"I do," he replied.

"James looked like a kid who had just pulled the wings off a butterfly. He always seemed to be hiding something, a sneaky little bugger. Mother said once, after catching him in a lie, he had no remorse for lying but only for being caught. I guess he's stayed true to form." I paused and looked up from my chowder. "Why Logan, though? Why did they target him? He hasn't anything to do with the ADS project."

"According to our sources, Logan was a personal issue. As you know from the many tabloid articles and talk shows, Amy has always fascinated young Buchart. He wanted Logan out of the way so he could pursue her. You knew about her relationship with James. There was a time when you couldn't have passed a newsstand or turned on the television without something about it blaring out at you."

I tore off a piece of bread. "Yes, I was aware of it. Amy either fell for James's deception or used him to get what she wanted. I have a feeling it was the latter. In any case, she'll be delighted when she hears Logan is free. She's left Genesis and Mire's campaign, you know," I added with calculated indifference, mirroring Jerry's tactic. It was a game we used to play.

Jerry's posture suddenly straightened. "No, I didn't know. I'm astonished. How are they ever going to cover it over? She's Genesis's personality. Genesis without Amy is unimaginable."

"You're right. Genesis can get rough, so I hired extra security around the mountain. I want to discuss her involvement as a Prescott spokesperson when we return."

"Wow, that'd be a coup."

"I know. The kids from the river, as Amy would say, you never know what to expect."

✦ ✦ ✦

Logan Landau

I was momentarily overcome with dizziness while walking through the prison's dank gray corridor from the outbound processing center. With my leather welder's jacket slung over my shoulder, I momentarily paused and leaned against the cool concrete wall.

I felt unplugged just then, like I was going to pass out. I wiped the cold sweat from my brow on the sleeve of my blue denim shirt. My queasiness must have been from the shock of what happened earlier when Murphy came to my cell. "Let's go, Logan. The judge says we gotta let you out today. You're a free man."

I knew the truth would find its way to the surface, like Old Rachael said, if I stayed out of the way. A hollow feeling emptied my chest as weakness spilled down my legs. *It's over, finally over*, I thought. My eyes filled.

I thought back to when Murphy unlocked my cell and shook my hand. "I'm going to miss you, Logan, but I'm glad you're leaving this place."

"I'm going to miss you too, Murph." He wasn't a prison officer anymore. He had become a familiar human being with a hidden kindness that reached out to me.

"Thanks for giving me the supplies I needed to write. I don't know what I would have done to pass the time without them." In a brief visit to the processing center, an officer returned the few valuables I had when I was arrested. I passed through a barred gate into a long gray hallway.

My joy was short-lived when a tall, brawny shipfitter approached from the far end of the hall. His leather boots pounded bold, angry strides until he stood before me with his yellow hard hat under his arm. His gruff tone was all too familiar.

"Look, they told me to come down here to tell you you're still considered an employee of the yard with back pay due. So here." He reluctantly handed me a sizable check he took from his vest pocket with a look of disdain. "They might still consider you an employee, but I wouldn't be seen in the yard soon if I were you." His eyes squinted with contempt before he turned abruptly and walked back down the hall. Genesis must have been worried about me, or they wouldn't have gone to the trouble of sending a Union steward to the prison with a check.

Near the last door leading outside, I was distracted by harsh fluorescent lights from the "special" reception area. It was where elite criminals, political types, gangster bosses, and attorneys registered or posted bail. Most prisoners, like me, came from police stations and overworked courts, chained together like animals in buses and vans.

I stopped suddenly and grabbed hold of the bars separating the reception area from the last few meters of the prison hallway leading to the outside world. James was on the other side in a disheveled gray suit and beige topcoat, standing between a pair of tall older gentlemen in black overcoats.

What's he doing here? He looked scared and confused. They were talking to him, but he wasn't listening. He was staring at the floor, pensively rubbing his chin. I read about the corridor disaster and his father's suicide. He looked overwhelmed, emaciated, pale, and drawn, while his suit appeared baggy from his considerable weight loss.

"James, it's me, Logan. What are you doing here? What's happening?"

He looked up sharply. I'll never forget his eyes. They were like lasers beaming bitter hatred. Why? I never liked James, no one did, but we were kids together. We had a bond—or at least I thought so.

James's eyes cooled, and he wagged his head in disbelief for coincidently having crossed my path. He stood silently with his hands stuffed into his overcoat pockets, as if studying patterns in the tile floor while his lawyers lectured him. His eyes bulged when he looked up at me again. His face wrenched with rage, and he growled like an animal through clenched teeth. "You think you've won? Well, think again!" he shouted. "I won the prize after all. Chew on that. Get him out of here," he demanded of his attorneys.

One of the attorneys attending to James walked briskly to the bars with an irritated sigh. He was tall with a barrel chest and a neatly trimmed black goatee. "I'm chief counsel to Mr. Buchart. He doesn't wish to answer any questions now. You can call his office in the morning."

"I'm his friend. We grew up together."

A uniformed prison officer came to the attorney's side. "You've processed out, so move along."

I ignored him and called out to James over the attorney's shoulder, but he ignored me. He seemed stunned. *Something dreadful is coming due. I think he's in big trouble*. Two more men in gray overcoats entered the room.

More attorneys. There was an entourage in there.

"You heard me," the officer demanded. "Now move along."

With my head bowed, I unceremoniously exited the prison alone. It was a moment I'd never forget.

✦ ✦ ✦

Logan Landau

Old Rachael was relieved when I finally telephoned. "I knew the truth would surface, and you'd find your way out of that awful place. I just knew it," she said spiritedly with a voice more gravely than I remembered. "I heard you even returned to work at the shipyard. That's quite courageous, considering what happened to you there. Getting back to a routine is important, but what took you so long to get word to us?"

"I'm sorry. I had a mundane puzzle to assemble, like finding a place to live, restoring my employment at the yard, updating communications, and dealing with government agencies, like the SS, to mention a few."

Her voice lowered with concern. "Amy needs to see you, Logan. She knows about your release, but her father asked us not to contact you for security reasons. Since Amy left Genesis, we've had to take special precautions."

"She left Genesis?" I asked in amazement. "Is she in danger?"

"Given her former position and its dark secrets, it's

certainly possible. But she's come home to Prescott, and we're all so grateful for that."

"Sorry to be so oblivious to current events, but being held under the Terrorist Act, I wasn't allowed sensitive news-related material. I didn't know about her new position at Prescott. Mr. Ramsey must be happy."

"I've not seen him so excited since his PLAVs took to the skies," she replied. "Media trucks have collected down the mountain, waiting for Amy to make a statement, not to mention what's flying overhead."

"I thought of Amy every night to keep the demons away."

"I can only imagine what you went through in that dreadful place, and to be isolated as you were." Old Rachael's voice cracked and squeaked with emotion. "But it may also have been a blessing in disguise, given it kept you isolated from exposure to the virus. A new, more virulent strain has taken so many lives recently."

"I'm sorry. I didn't learn about that until after my release. I've since read about how Amy's become a world-renowned celebrity like her dad. Our lives have evolved so differently."

"I wish you wouldn't view Amy with such distance." She sniffled. "Ever since you were kids, she's always loved you," she whimpered, causing her voice to crack again.

I paused for her to gather herself. "It's different now. I'm not the person I used to be."

"I understand," she said with a gentle voice. She'd always been respectful by allowing what mattered to have its way. "Well, I'm here for you if you need to talk."

"I can think of no one I'd trust more."

51

FORGIVENESS

John Ramsey

With the long, brick, three-story building slated for demolition, I walked the oil-stained concrete floor of the original Prescott factory. It was where I teamed with people much brighter than me to develop Programmed Low-Altitude Vehicles and their Automated Destination Systems. I continued into interstellar enterprises from there, bringing together new cadres of dedicated people.

Dressed casually in jeans, a blue checkered shirt with an open collar, and a dark blue blazer, I thought I'd stop by to say goodbye to the place. Machine parts lay strewn about like bones on a killing floor. The smell of oil, welding smoke, and melting plastic thickened the air.

Just ahead, thirty or more workers in dark blue Prescott uniforms were dismantling the leviathan-like carcass of a gigantic machine that reached the arched ceiling. Their hammers, drills, and cutting tools blended into a single rasping sound reverberating through the hanger-like space.

When the workers caught sight of me, something astonishing happened. They paused and stood reverently still, their tools falling silent. Then, following the lead of two among them, they respectfully removed their yellow hard hats and held them over their hearts as I passed. They took my humility by surprise. I felt somewhat embarrassed by their tribute but nodded my appreciation with a hint of a smile. If it hadn't been for workers like them, so loyal and skilled, Prescott and all the good it had done would never have happened.

✦ ✦ ✦

Logan Landau

It was a cold, early evening with darkening gray skies when I exited the shipyard in my leather welder's jacket. I volunteered to do the formality of closing circuits and valves the night shift didn't use and check for any flammable hazards lying around, so I was among the last to leave when the night crew arrived. Riley, Barstow, and the gang of thugs who pummeled me no longer worked there. I heard they were at the detention center awaiting trial. James's attorneys prevailed on the court to have him hospitalized in the sector asylum for observation and treatment.

I recalled seeing Telstar's news clip of James at the asylum. It was among the most-watched news stories of the year. Only Cheryl's lunar funeral rated higher. The short interview occurred in a dimly lit room on the asylum grounds. James emerged from the shadows in a wheelchair, wrapped in a blue blanket to his neck and wearing black leather gloves. He had become a bedraggled, emaciated-looking man with a pale, drawn face stretched over bony features, a death mask barely resembling his former self. His sparse, tousled hair had already turned white, and there were days of unshaven stubble on his sunken cheeks.

I didn't think James's lawyers should have granted Telstar the interview, as it bordered on exploitation, even though one of James's attorneys sat next to him at the interview table. "I dehumanized people into players in a game, replicating how I thought life worked," James said, growling words through his throat. "The game was never real, but it gave me a rush like nothing else could. It turned evil into good and good into evil. I swear, after a while, I didn't know the difference. Winning the game was everything. I thought it was life itself." His helpless expression seemed to say, "Can you imagine what I've become?"

"What about your relationship with Amy Ramsey?" the female voice of an out-of-view interviewer asked. "Have you been in contact with her since you entered the hospital?"

His bowed head bobbed on his neck as he slumped forward. "Oh," he moaned. When he looked up again from his lowered brow, I noticed his eyes had become like Mire's. Something happened to people when their soul abandoned them. An evil presence took its place, like vagrants in a derelict building.

"I relied upon wealth and position in a vain attempt to entice Amy into worshiping me, but she never did. No matter what shallow purpose we shared, my degenerate nature closed her heart to me. I knew it was happening but didn't know any other way to be."

James wore a vacant look. His eyes seemed to stare into oblivion when his head fell back to face the heavens he had offended. Though he was among us, his soul remained sequestered in a dark, alien world where dawn never broke.

It occurred to me there was no celestial court where our accusers and defenders decided our punishment or reward in an afterlife of torture or bliss. We created our defenders and accusers as the gods and demons of our minds. Whether we experienced heaven or hell, it was our self-display that we realized.

No one can help James, I thought as I watched the telecast. Demons his mind concocted would release him when they were satisfied and karmic balance was restored. There was no escaping the process. James groaned and began to cry, ending the brief cameo appearance. I remember being depressed for days after seeing it.

Gray skies had yielded to darkness when I walked up the cobbled way and saw a dark figure of a woman standing on the rise by the parking lot. A red scarf crossed her face before draping over her shoulder. Her beige storm coat was wet at the shoulders. She pulled her scarf down when I approached and forced a quivering smile. It was Amy!

Tears flashed in her eyes when she rushed through our estrangement into my embrace, as she did by the river when we were young. "Oh, Logan, you're safe, and I can finally hold you. So much has happened since we left the river. Tell me everything. I want to hold your story like I'm holding you now."

The gentle waves that danced with us when we were

young had all gone downstream. I wondered if it was possible to begin again, weighed down by the different people we'd become. It could be a new life for us, each liberated by the other. When I kissed her, she couldn't help but blurt out tearful emotions over the errant choices that separated us. *Memories are stabbing at her*, I thought. "Give your regrets to me," I whispered against her wet, salty cheek. "I'll take them to the river and set them free with mine on a crisp fall leaf to sail downstream, around the bend, and out of sight forever."

52

ATTACK OF THE TEZCA

John Ramsey

I veered off the factory floor and entered my old executive offices. Rather than calling the corporation Ramsey Industries, I named it in honor of Dr. Samuel Prescott, the ridiculed futurist who gave me a new perspective when I was a boy. I still remember his stories about tomorrow and what it would bring. What I don't know is anything about my stuttering. Dr. Prescott erased all references to it.

Inside, the air was stale and damp, the furnishings dust covered, broken, and disarrayed. There was a steady drip from a rusted intersection of pipe overhead, the red carpet stained and threadbare. Venturing farther down a dank, musty-smelling hallway, I came to what was once a bustling research laboratory. Everything there was always a work in progress.

We had hauled away the electronic equipment long ago that once filled the room with beeps, flashing lights, and excitement. Only scarred black marble counters and a few plastic chairs remained behind. Looking back on my path, it had been a wandering patchwork of trial and error. In those early days, I had no idea how impermanent everything was.

My recollection suddenly vanished when a spike of pain struck my left temple. I winced and shielded my eyes from a hot sunbeam spearing through the thick, wire-glass window to my left. I began to waver from dizziness.

My thoughts were running out of control. I recalled the night I spoke to Amy about my health concerns. Just a week ago, she was back home on the mountain. I tied off the fabric belt of my powder-blue bathrobe before visiting her room on the far wing of the mansion from mine and knocked on her door.

"Come in," she said. She set her book down, leaned back against her reading pillow, and pulled the blankets over her pink, satin nightgown. "Hi, Dad."

"What are you up to?" I asked.

"Oh, I'm just lying here reading 'til I doze off."

A soft red and gold carpet by her bed lay on the dark wood floor. She had the walls painted a pale Beijing red with distressed accents where stucco appeared weathered away, exposing the original rough stone masonry. The room was warm and dark but for a gold art deco reading lamp by her bed. She appeared dwarfed by her bed's sculpted wooden headboard and fluted columns. She looked at me, beaming her unique smile, her deep blue eyes aglow. I noticed the book opened on her lap.

"What are you reading, sweetheart?"

"Oh, just some speculative stuff."

"Interesting?"

"Not really. Just a lot of informed opinions." She shrugged.

"I came to your room tonight because I need to ask an important favor."

Her mood quickly mirrored mine. She leaned back expectantly. "You know you can ask me anything, Dad."

"You're aware everything we have, Prescott Industries, our properties, and investments, will be yours to do with as you wish when I go the way of the earth."

"Dad, what are you saying?" She immediately sat up and gently took hold of my shoulder. "You don't have a health issue you've not told me about, do you?"

"No, I'm just getting old, and life hasn't been easy. I notice progressive changes happening to me I can't control."

She leaned back on an elbow with a look of concern. "Like what?"

"Buddhists refer to my symptoms as the 'far away signs of death,' like when one's vision dims, hearing seems distant, and one's mind becomes distracted and wanders away."

"But you're so strong and healthy."

"Time has its way with me, nonetheless. I knew these days would be fast approaching. That was why I asked you to record important moments in your life that I could incorporate into my story. In the end, we are all just stories."

"I didn't realize you felt as you did, but yes, I wrote about some of my personal experiences. Loaded as they were with emotions, I found them difficult to reveal."

"Thank you for your honesty," I said, taking her hand. She nodded to me with her mischievous childhood grin that I loved so much. "Of course, Margo died before she could leave her memories behind for us. I had asked Logan and James to share what they could too, given they were like family when you were young."

"James?" she questioned incredulously.

"Yes. We all came together for a purpose that is sacred and beyond question. The kids from the river are a family, whether good, bad, or indifferent. You'll find what they wrote in the cloud, for which you have my password.

"May I prevail upon you to protect our recollections should something happen to me? Nothing else matters to me anymore besides Old Rachael, Prescott, and you. I trust you completely."

"Of course, I'll do as you wish, but please don't talk about dying," she said. She sat up and leaned her head against my shoulder. "I've made so many mistakes, Daddy," she moaned. "But through it all, you've always been my rock. I don't know what I'd do without you."

I'm frightening her. Her brow pinched, and her lips wrinkled as tiny telltale indentations appeared on her chin.

"Very well. We'll speak of it no more," I told her, kissing her forehead with my hand softly against her cheek. "Good night, my love." I turned off the light. Darkness rushed into the room.

✦ ✦ ✦

John Ramsey

The sounds of power tools brought me back to the factory. *What did I eat this morning? I can't remember. Maybe whatever I had was tainted.* I steadied myself against the wall and noticed a white plastic chair across the cluttered room by the door. *I better sit down for a couple of minutes.*

Stumbling through the debris, I couldn't help but notice how disconnected I was from my limbs. My footsteps were erratic, jerky, and hard to place. I had to concentrate on each step while maintaining a modicum of balance with my arms outstretched. I was breathless when I came to the chair and sat down hard, nearly spilling over the side onto the floor. My balance was deserting me. Noise in the factory intensified into a rasping sound that filled my head with painful throbs.

✦ ✦ ✦

Logan Landau

Since my release from prison, Old Rachael let me fill in the events of her son's life by allowing me access to his recordings. She also prevailed upon one of his physicians, Doctor Entian, a young neurosurgeon with curly black hair and an amiable smile, to kindly fill me in on what most likely happened to her son on that tragic day. As he did, I couldn't help but notice Doctor Entian's reverence for Mr. Ramsey.

We were having coffee in the Sector Hospital cafeteria. Doctor Entian sat across from me in his white smock with a stethoscope tucked in the breast pocket. He was young with an infectious exuberance for his work. I was still in work clothes, having just come from the shipyard. Doctor Entian explained "that a trauma caused by the Tezca virus severely compromised the left hemisphere of John's brain. When connected," he said, "the left and right hemispheres of the brain cooperate. But they can perceive apparent reality differently when separated by disease or trauma."

"Was that when confusion overtook him?" I asked.

"Probably," Dr. Entian said. "Mostly, the right hemisphere creates a vibrant montage of memories from John's past. Creative and impulsive, it's where his imagination was born and from where it took flight. It's free, without cravings or aversions, qualifiers or quantifiers, the source of his euphoric experiences."

"Would you say it's where the PLAVs and ADS were born?"

"Born, yes, but not developed. The development of John's vision needed the support of the left hemisphere, where ideas meet reality and moments separate into logical sequences based on his past experiences. It's where words string together into sentences. It's also where one's history resides. With neurons in his brain withering, John probably experienced brief sporadic moments of clarity, like breaks in storm clouds through which clarity angled through like sunbeams."

Because I was not well versed in medical terminology, Doctor Entian made Mr. Ramsey's situation understandable by painting vivid pictures to which I could relate. I could tell he was a good man.

"Imagine John on the floor of his old office, unable to move, and his ever-present thoughts likely replaced by silent pictorial bursts and flashes of color he didn't understand. His consciousness hinted he was present somewhere, but he probably didn't know where. You see, what he called his phantom self, the person who ruled his experiences, was the first to surrender because it required so much energy to sustain."

"You mean who he thought he was?" I asked to make sure I was on the same page.

"Yes, that's correct. With the death of who he thought he was, John became a docile captive, like a moth in a spider's web, so Tezca could enslave his cells to create more of itself."

Doctor Entian sipped his thick Turkish coffee and grinned at me.

"Mr. Ramsey's last recording confused me," I told him. "He said, 'The golden knob.' A few seconds later, he slurred what sounded like 'The way out.'"

"I recall a door with a shiny brass knob in the room where they found him," the doctor explained. "He most likely noticed it, forced himself up, and tried to reach for it but collapsed. It's how they found him."

53

THE DEEP SLEEP

Logan Landau

I entered the private medical facility in the foyer of the Ramsey mansion after my shift at the shipyard. Amy had asked me to watch over her father while she was out of town on Prescott business. She was due to return the next day. I already missed her.

A glass cubicle stood in the center of the enormous room in which Mr. Ramsey lay motionless on a hospital bed beneath starched white sheets pulled up to his chin. Doctor Entian and his assistant wore protective white bio-suits with bulky breathing apparatuses. They studied the bank of monitors above Mr. Ramsey's bed and recorded notes on their readers.

High in the foyer's dome, a stained glass skylight beamed a column of silver moonlight on the "Last Great

Man," like a heavenly pathway. *It's a sign*, I thought. Flowers stacked high against white marble walls emitted competing floral scents, reminding me of Margo's funeral.

According to Doctor Entian, when they admitted Mr. Ramsey to Sector Hospital, they thought he had suffered a stroke at first, only to find it was the deadliest strain of the Tezca virus that attacked the brain and the meninges of the spinal cord. If only they had found him sooner. He lay there all day until the end of their shift, when a Prescott worker discovered him, Doctor Entian explained.

✦ ✦ ✦

Logan Landau

The good doctor speculated, "For John, clarity's sudden brilliance must have resembled a shaft of sunlight through dark, boiling clouds, causing his brain to stir."

It was late at night and raining. Thunder rumbled in the distance. I read Mr. Ramsey's book, *Conversations with an Ishtok Monk*, while sitting on a soft chair beside the cubical. A gooseneck lamp reached over my shoulder.

I had visited Mr. Ramsey several times at Sector Hospital with Amy before she had the private facility constructed for him in the foyer.

According to Doctor Entian, Mr. Ramsey's brief sparks of awareness were like memory flares shot into the dead of night, like distress signals from a sinking ship. The flares quickly burned out and melted into the darkness of the strange dimension where he found himself.

"John may have panicked and tried to shout but didn't

know how," Doctor Entian said. "He probably thought he was angrily thrashing in bed and screaming for help, but in the world of appearances, he was deathly still and silent."

A monitor beeped as his blood pressure spiked. An injection given by Doctor Entian calmed the terrifying bolt of energy and slowed Mr. Ramsey's breathing.

I thought because dreams weren't chronologically continuous from one to another, Mr. Ramsey wasn't aware of the last time the storm clouds parted and clarity broke through. It could've been millenniums ago, in another lifetime, or just moments before his previous thought. It could even be occurring in the future. It was impossible to know. The storm of forgetfulness washed everything sensible away.

Inside the glass room, Doctor Entian looked down at Mr. Ramsey and felt his corroded artery out of habit. *Perhaps his dying neurons will release a kind memory of when he was a boy cradled in the river, gliding over the golden sunlit bottom on a warm summer day*, I thought.

In his book, Mr. Ramsey suggested that the river, the forest, and the lives that entered them were expressions of a life force disguised by its many manifestations.

I looked over at Mr. Ramsey. I couldn't imagine being so isolated as the only living thing. Talk about solitary confinement.

I read further. "There is nothing other than the One. It's all that has ever been. There is no other," Mr. Ramsey wrote. I stared at him through the glass wall. I couldn't begin to fathom the loneliness of being the only living thing. It would amount to total isolation, without hope of intervention, because there would be nothing to intervene. *There's no greater prison than the self*, I thought.

He wrote, "The manifestation of appearances imagined by the One overcame its abject solitude. Everything that exists became the phantom self of the One I loved dearly as a boy."

I never thought of nature being an imagined distraction from the loneliness of the One, but it was how Mr. Ramsey saw it.

✦ ✦ ✦

Logan Landau

While it was only my unqualified speculation, Mr. Ramsey's consciousness would probably remain dormant until another break in the storm and clarity reappeared. Maybe it would happen tomorrow or even centuries from now. Perhaps such clarity would again be confined to another brief life in the reality of appearances, the only existence our senses understood. I thought of Cheryl. *Where is she?* I wondered.

Dark clouds began to boil, mix, and rumble together again, choking off the flickering brilliance Mr. Ramsey experienced. It occurred to me he had to have sensed thoughtless hibernation returning, the deep sleep. The whine of electronic monitors marked the moment. Jolted by the alarm, Doctor Entian immediately turned to the row of monitors. But Mr. Ramsey had already gone downstream, around the bend, and out of sight forever.

Printed in the United States
by Baker & Taylor Publisher Services

Printed in the United States
by Baker & Taylor Publisher Services